Death by
Chocolate

Death by Chocolate

THE SERIAL POISONING OF VICTORIAN BRIGHTON

SOPHIE JACKSON

FONTHILL

Fonthill Media Limited
Fonthill Media LLC
www.fonthillmedia.com
office@fonthillmedia.com

First published 2012

British Library Cataloguing in Publication Data:
A catalogue record for this book is available from the British Library

ISBN 978-1-78155-104-2 (hardback)
ISBN 978-1-78155-216-2 (paperback)
ISBN 978-1-78155-217-9 (e-book)

Typeset in 10.5pt on 13pt Sabon LT Std
Printed and bound in England

Contents

Acknowledgements

A number of sources have been invaluable for piecing together this story. In particular, Berkshire Record Office were exceedingly helpful in providing copies of records regarding Christiana Edmunds and the Regency Society (www.regencysociety.org) were kind enough to provide images from Brighton of that period from the James Gray Collection.

Other important sources have been the digitised archives of various papers including *The Times* and the *New York Times*, which have provided an insight into the thoughts and views of the people directly involved in this case.

David Simkin (www.photohistory-sussex.co.uk) has also provided images from his own personal collection and an invaluable map to show where Christiana lived in relation to the Beard family.

Introduction

Prior to the famous case of Jack the Ripper, serial crime and serial killers were a completely alien idea to the Victorians. Crime, however bleak, had a logic to it. People were driven by motives of lust, greed and revenge. To imagine a person who would kill randomly, target strangers and show a complete disregard for the consequences was not only shocking, but terrifying. There were, of course, serial killers in the past, but it was harder for them to operate until the Industrial Revolution created vast cities and towns where anonymity and a constant influx of new faces favoured such individuals.

When Brighton experienced its first serial killer, it not only caused a national scandal, but an international one as well. It raised questions about the police system and the mental state of a person who could commit such crimes. In an age when insanity was finally being recognised as a medical condition and sufferers at last treated with a degree of compassion, the biggest controversy of all was whether a murderer should be allowed to walk free if they could be proved mad.

The poisoned chocolates case of 1871 awoke the public to a new dimension of crime. It provoked debate about food standards, the availability of poisons (already a controversial topic), but more significantly, it caused Victorians to reassess their ideas of femininity and insanity. The Brighton case has often been overshadowed by its sensational and odd nature. It is too easy to joke about poisoned chocolates and this has reduced the importance of the crime along with the fact that, aside from the unfortunate Sidney Barker, no one perished in the poisoning spree. But the case was dramatic in its time. Not only because it highlighted a new form of madness, one that was subtle and difficult to distinguish, but that it also asked people to be compassionate even to murderers. For the heroes and villains of this case, their lives were never the same. Some were ruined while others used events to propel themselves to fame and success.

Since the awful incidents of 1871, the case of the poisoned chocolates killer has become something of an icon of Victorian crime. The story was reused, relabelled and retold over and over in novels and, later, television. Early twentieth-century crime writers were particularly inspired by the case and more than one reused the idea in their work. The facts of the case slowly became muddled, the truth vanished behind fiction and the story took on a superficial and ridiculous appearance. Only now, with greater access to records, a better understanding of mental illness and criminal forensics can the legend of 'The Chocolate Cream Killer' be re-examined and the reality of the events of 1871 be presented. Many of the findings are new, but the heart of the case remains the same. Was this an act of madness or the actions of a clever and cold-blooded killer?

CHAPTER ONE

The Accidental Murder

Four-year-old Sidney Barker writhed in agony, tormented by violent convulsions that hooked his body into all manner of hideous contortions. His back arched in another horrific spasm, almost throwing him from the arms of his distraught mother, Leticia. Only half-an-hour before he had been a happy, playful child, enjoying his holiday in Brighton with his parents and uncles. Now he was clearly dying.

'Call for a doctor!' Leticia begged her brother, Charles Miller. He started to his feet, then fell back sharply as though all strength had gone from his body. Charles had begun to feel queer too. 'I feel as if all my body is without joints.'[1] He cried out, struggling to stand yet again. Despite his own illness, he managed to send a message to the nearest medical man and surgeon Mr Rugg came rushing to the scene. It was twenty minutes since Sidney had first begun to cry and had been swept up in his mother's arms, only to start his violent fitting. Leticia was beside herself. Mr Rugg barely had the chance to examine the boy – the convulsions making his job almost impossible – when Sidney suddenly went still. A moment passed. Dr Rugg stood back from his patient knowing, that at least for the child, the worst was over. Sidney was dead.

For the family, the suffering continued. Charles Miller was obviously deeply unwell. Another medical man, Mr Tuke, was called to see him. 'I felt at first a coppery taste in my throat, then my eyes became dim, my legs became rigid,' Charles explained to Tuke. 'As I attempted to move from my chair I fell backwards.'[2] Mr Tuke was not able to offer much in the way of aid, except to ensure that his patient remained as comfortable as possible. He had the nasty suspicion in his mind that he was witnessing the effects of poison. Mr Rugg was thinking along the same lines and had planned to perform a post-mortem on Sidney the next morning. Something very odd was going on.

Left alone in their lodging house, Leticia was torn by grief for her only son and fear that her younger brother might succumb too. Charles tried to appear as calm as he could, his other brother Ernest was looking on anxiously and trying to do his best to comfort Leticia. As evening came, they heard the door of their lodging house open and close. Albert Barker, Sidney's father, appeared. He took in the scene with an expression of confusion; the joyful house he had left that morning had suddenly become sombre and grim. Leticia did not have the words to explain, so Charles spoke: 'Sidney just started crying. Leticia took him up and asked what was the matter with him. He did not reply but his limbs became stiff and he died within 20 minutes.'[3] Albert was stunned. There was no logic to what he was witnessing and while he knew children did die, the sudden affliction that had swept Sidney away beggared belief.

Sidney's body was to be taken away for an official post-mortem in the morning. Leticia had one last night to spend with her little boy before he vanished forever. The Barkers and Millers spent a lonely night wrapped in grief, privately mourning a life cut abruptly short for no obvious reason.

When the Millers visited Brighton in 1871, it was a relatively new resort. Its popularity had arisen in the previous century thanks to Dr Richard Russell of Lewes publishing his claims that seawater was good for the health. In those early days, it had been the exclusive holiday destination of the wealthy, but by the 1870s, the railways had opened it up to all classes of the public. It was even possible to have a day trip from London on the train.

Albert had a fondness for the resort with its strange amalgamation of Georgian architecture and tourist novelties. There was a grand pier for promenading and, of course, the famous Royal Pavilion that stood like an Indian palace overlooking the sea. Brighton had accepted its role as a tourist hotspot with open arms. Lodging houses sprang up everywhere: from cheap rooms for the working-class masses to the palatial hotels that welcomed the richer echelons of Victorian society. Most visitors were drawn by one thing – the notion that Brighton could cure all that ailed them. The town had been a triumph of early advertising which proclaimed not only that the water had medicinal properties, but that the very air of the resort was good for the health. Being just a short train ride from London boosted the appeal of Brighton, meaning anyone could pop down for a restorative visit. Doctors recommended a little Brighton air for their chronic patients, many of whom were suffering from the smog of industrial London. The clear, unpolluted skies of the coast could indeed provide a welcome relief to clogged lungs and even the working classes would try to make an annual trip to the health-giving town.

For the more adventurous there was the great expanse of ocean. Water therapy was surging in popularity and taking to the sea was seen as a definitive remedy for most modern ills. Of course, sea bathing came with all the Victorian trappings, from horse-drawn bathing huts to rented bathing suits for those too poor to afford their own. While children and men could splash in the waters naked without anyone raising a disapproving eye, women had to be draped head-to-foot in clothing that made a mockery of swimming. The slightest flash of skin could raise a scornful outcry among the more delicate Brighton residents.

This was the world Albert Barker had stepped into from his thriving silver and dressing case business, bringing his wife and young family to test the therapeutic properties of Brighton. The Barkers had only been married five years but already had two children: four-year-old Sidney and two-year-old Florence. Leticia was recovering from her last pregnancy and the change of scenery was a welcome respite. The children, however, were excited by the prospect of a holiday and to complete the family arrangements, uncles Charles and Ernest (Leticia's brothers) were included in the excursion. Charles Miller was only eighteen and learning the trade of coachbuilder from his father in Hammersmith, London. Ernest Miller was just seventeen and described by his parents as a scholar. All in all, they were a close family and Charles doted on little Sidney, which only made his death harder to bear. He blamed himself for the boy's demise.

On 13 June, the day after the Barker tragedy, Mr Rugg collected Sidney's corpse and returned to his surgery. He performed a rudimentary post-mortem to the best of his abilities. He could find nothing obvious to suggest a cause of death. The brain was 'congested'[4] but no more so than he would expect in a child that had died of violent convulsions. He was effectively stumped.

Had the case been left to Mr Rugg, he would have had to leave the cause of death unknown or perhaps use a vague Victorian term such as 'apoplexy' to offer some explanation, even if it was incorrect. Fortunately, he had reported Sidney's death to the coroner who had made it explicit that Rugg should remove the boy's stomach intact for further examination. Partly this was due to a new presence on the scene: Inspector Gibbs. Gibbs was a quiet, discreet figure in the Brighton precincts. Sharp-witted and a conscientious evidence gatherer who held a great deal of faith in the new forensic methods for solving crime, he was a formidable policeman. Sidney's death had raised alarm bells in Rugg and the suspicious nature of the boy's demise had filtered down to Gibbs who now stood present at the post-mortem. When Rugg removed the stomach, careful not to spill its contents, he placed it in a jar and handed it straight to Gibbs. The jar was sealed and Gibbs bid him good-day as he set out with his strange gift to the chemist Dr Letheby.

Professor Letheby was a well-regarded medical expert[5] known for his talents at criminal forensics. Born 1816 in Plymouth, he had been an adept medical student and had quickly shown a talent for chemistry. In 1846, he became the London Chair of chemistry and toxicology and was soon an avid campaigner for legislation against the adulteration of food and drugs: an illegal business practice that had caused many accidental poisonings[6]. In 1855, Letheby was elected to the post of the City of London's medical officer (he was already serving as its gas examiner), a post he would hold until 1874. He caused a spasm of controversy as it was said he was in the pay of the water companies and gave optimistic analyses of pumps during the Victorian Cholera scare.[7] But his real interests lay elsewhere, namely forensic chemistry and toxicology. He was a natural choice to send Sidney's stomach contents to for analysis. Clearly, Mr Rugg and Inspector Gibbs were severely worried by the death.

Letheby opened the child's stomach and inspected the contents. There was not much inside and his first reaction was that the organ appeared healthy. He could smell a faint odour of chocolate, but no food matter remained. Tests for a mineral poison (such as arsenic) proved negative, but a test for strychnine, another common poison, proved that Sidney's stomach contained a quarter of a gram. Though an adult might have survived such a dose, for a small child it was enough to kill. And besides, that was what *remained* of the strychnine, the body would have absorbed some of the poison before death, so the dose Sidney consumed must have been higher. Letheby was satisfied. Rugg's report on Sidney's symptoms had all the hallmarks of strychnine poisoning and he had not been disappointed by his discovery.

Strychnine was first successfully extracted from the St Ignatius bean in 1817. Other plants of the same family soon yielded the poison and it was being commercially extracted from the seeds of the Indian tree Strychnos nux-vomica throughout the nineteenth century and widely used in pest control. Named after the Strychnos genus of plants – of which there are 196 types many of which produce the poison – it was recognised as a toxic drug as far back as the seventeenth century, though at that period the entire seed or bean of a plant had to be used as the extraction process had not been developed. Like so many poisons it had a dual nature being also used as a medicine to cure cholera and fevers. Strychnine is an alkaloid characterised by its extremely bitter taste. In fact, it is the bitterest chemical known to man and can be detected at minute concentrations of just eight parts per million[8], which explains the complaint of many murder victims of a 'nasty' taste in their food or drink before they perish.

Strychnine acts on the motor nerves in the spinal cord, blocking neuroreceptors that prevent the over-stimulation of nerves. As a result, the body loses its ability to inhibit motor neurons from firing and they begin to react to the slightest amount of neurotransmitter causing spasms and convulsions. The mildest of stimulations will cause the nerves of an affected person to fire violently, which is why one treatment for a strychnine victim is to place them in a darkened room to limit their exposure to stimuli. Strychnine victims that are not treated display the characteristic painfully-arched back where the muscles around the spine, being stronger than those at the front of the body, contract violently and force the body to arch up, so only the base of the heels and skull remain touching the ground. Death is usually a result of the diaphragm contracting so ferociously that the patient is suffocated. The most distressing element of the poisoning is that the victim remains conscious throughout the ordeal. For those who survive being poisoned, the devastating effects of the drug on the body can leave them with permanent kidney and nerve damage. There is no antidote, just therapies to minimise the symptoms and keep the patient alive until the body can work the poison out of its system.

The question on everyone's mind was how Sidney had been poisoned. Usually, suspicions would fall on a parent, poison being an all too familiar method of infanticide, but as Charles had also been taken ill, it seemed more likely the Barkers had been the victims of an accidental poisoning. Letheby knew all about such cases and food was the likeliest source (though by no means the only one).

Charles Miller also had his suspicions. On that fateful day, he had wandered up West Street from his lodging house to a smart-looking confectioner's shop called Maynards. The shop in West Street was well-known among the inhabitants of Brighton. Built up from a single store by its namesake owner, Mr Maynard, it had subsequently come to dominate three buildings side-by-side and sold a host of sweets and chocolates, both to the public and wholesale. Charles popped in and bought some of the best chocolates on display, French creams, and carried them home in a paper bag printed with the Maynards' name. It was around 8 a.m. in the morning on the 12 June.

Back at the lodging house, he gave some of the creams to his nephew who liked them and quickly ate them up. The day continued as normal with Charles enjoying the chance to relax from his work. In the afternoon, he fancied some chocolate himself and returned to the bag to take four or five creams. Sidney asked for one and was given a solitary chocolate. He swallowed it swiftly then looked unhappy. He complained that the chocolate tasted 'nasty' and he did not like it at all. Within ten minutes, both he and his uncle were showing the symptoms that would lead Rugg, Gibbs and Letheby to think strychnine was at work.

After Sidney's death and with everyone trying to reason out the cause, Charles' mind returned to the chocolates. Both he and Sidney had eaten some and been made ill. All other food and drink the family had consumed that day had been shared among them and no one else was sick. It had to be something only he and Sidney had eaten. Charles was feeling shaky and strange. His body seemed out of his control and he wondered if his own death was imminent. The only solace was to try and pinpoint the cause. He turned to his brother Ernest for help. 'Here, try these chocolates and see what you think,' he said to his brother, offering the bag. Ernest cautiously bit into one. It had an unpleasant coppery taste and he spat it out instantly. 'Try another,' Charles urged. Ernest complied with the same result. He spat out the second chocolate. 'They're bad aren't they? I knew it. Throw them away Ernest.'

After the bag of chocolates was safely disposed of the brothers sat for some time lost in their thoughts. Leticia was distraught and desperate for answers. Rugg had returned to discuss performing the post-mortem and told the family he had informed the coroner and the police that the death looked suspiciously like a poisoning. Once he was gone, Charles began to regret his decision to throw out the chocolates. 'I rather think I was over hasty just now, Ernest,' he told his brother. 'I think it was those chocolates that done in Sidney and I should have saved the bag for the police.' Ernest considered this. 'If it is them, I could go buy some more from the same place to prove it. Can't just be a handful that was bad. Perhaps the whole batch was poisoned?' Charles nodded. 'Yes, go buy some more.' It was early evening but Maynards kept long hours and Ernest hurried out for another bag. When he came back, he handed it to Charles who looked at it grimly. On 15 June, he handed it over to Inspector Gibbs who was beginning his inquiries on the case. Gibbs labelled it as '1' for evidence purposes and, to ensure a fair analysis, went and bought his own packet of creams from Maynards carefully labelling it '2'. These, along with Sidney's stomach, made their way to Professor Letheby.

Letheby was an expert at chemical analysis and knew all its pitfalls and perils. He regularly produced in-depth articles for the papers refuting claims by the public that poison tests were fallible. 'So many inconsistencies and insecurities have lately appeared in the public papers respecting the discovery of strychnia in the dead body ... to do away with all doubt and fallacy ... I may state that the putting of a little strychnia and sulphuric acid on a piece of platinum foil, then connecting the foil with the positive pole of a single cell of Grove's or Smee's battery and touching the acid with the negative pole, terminating in a piece of platinum wire, the violent colour so characteristic of strychnia is instantly produced ... so delicate is the galvanic test that it will discover the presence of the 10,000th of a grain of strychnia ... and besides this, its very nature is such as to do away with all possible sources of fallacy.'[9]

Presumably it was this test Letheby used on the contents of the chocolates sent to him by Gibbs because of its 'infallibility', not that he wasn't confident of his skills as a chemist. 'I think it right to say that there is not any material with which [strychnine] can be mixed in the animal body or process of putrefaction that can in any way interfere with its extraction and recognition.' As he stood up at Sidney's inquest he had no doubt of his findings. 'I examined parcel 'No. 1' of the drops of chocolate creams and I found strychnia among them. They were broken and mixed drops as if they had been handled. There was no strychnia in parcel 'No. 2' nor any other poison.'[10] It was as simple as that. Sidney and Charles had both been affected by strychnine concealed in chocolates. The only question remaining was how the poison had managed to get into food.

John Goddard Maynard was deeply troubled as he stood up at the inquest to try and explain how his chocolates could have poisoned someone. He had been in the confectionary business over twenty years and, now in his fifties, was training his son to take over the thriving company he had created. He considered himself a 'confectionary wholesaler', but would quite happily sell to the general public. To provide for both aspects of his trade, he had acquired two extra buildings over the years and now owned 39, 40 and 41 West Street. Though all the shops were connected, it was generally considered that those on the left were for wholesale customers, not that Maynard would turn away an ordinary customer who had wandered in the wrong shop, just as Charles Miller had done on 12 June.

Maynard found the general management of the business kept him mostly away from the shop floor and relied on a team of assistants (usually girls) to man his counters, along with his daughters Charlotte and Edith. So he had not witnessed the fateful transaction, nor had anything like this ever happened before. As he stood before the magistrates and the assembled audience, he realised he had none of the answers they wanted. What was more his business hung in the balance, dependant on the outcome of that day.

'The French creams are bought from the factory of Mr Ware in London,' Maynard stated plainly when asked where the chocolates came from. 'I don't make them or alter them.' Maynard hoped this would get him off the hook, but he was still under suspicion of allowing the chocolates to be tampered with. Perhaps one of his employees had a grudge or was inclined to mischief? His assistants did not help his case greatly. Anne Meadows stood before the crowd and explained how the chocolates were handled in the shop. 'We keep the French creams in a case. There isn't much call for them in June and the case doesn't get filled often. 12 June was a Monday and I think the case had last been filled on Saturday the 10 June.' She told the hearing, 'I remember Mr Miller coming in about eight o'clock on Monday. He bought a shilling worth of French creams. They're considered the best we have in the shop and cost 4d an ounce.'

There was little more she could add, but to the audience it was with a note of anxiety that they imagined the chocolates sitting in their cases for days at a time, open to any sort of tampering or contamination. Even so, there was no evidence to suggest Mr Maynard or any of his staff had committed the adulteration. Mr Ware was next to defend himself before the worried crowd. He had been in Liverpool at the time of the murder and rushed to Brighton. In desperation, he explained how well run his factory was, how it passed all the standards and how his staff were all well-trained and responsible. Other French creams made at the same time as Maynard's bad batch had gone across the country and caused no harm. He made it plain that nothing done at his factory could have caused the poisoning, but he left the stand feeling he was tainted with suspicion. Along with Mr Maynard, he waited anxiously for the verdict.

It was not long in coming. Inspector Gibbs had gone over the matter with the magistrates and given his own private thoughts. After a lengthy discussion, Sidney Barker's death was ruled accidental. No suggestion of how the poison entered the chocolates was given and the troubled residents of Brighton who had come to listen left feeling as worried as they had when they arrived. Would anyone ever be able to account for how the French creams had become fatally poisoned?

Albert and Leticia Barker, with their baby Florence, returned to London. Charles and Ernest followed. There was no option but to return to their normal lives. The death of a child was not an uncommon occurrence and Leticia was far from unusual as a mother to lose a young son, but the method of his death seemed so random and fickle that it left bitterness in its wake. Albert went back to his silversmithing. He was a talented artisan with a knack for designs that were out-of-the-ordinary and his small business was just beginning to turn into something bigger. Still, his mind was not on his work as he tried to concentrate on his newest designs and the arrival of a letter by a hand he did not recognise caused even more distraction.

'Sir, having seen the results of the investigation of the inquest of Thursday last, I feel great surprise that no blame is attached to anyone. I have felt great interest in the case and fully sympathise in your sad loss. Great dissatisfaction is felt at the result by most of the inhabitants and we all feel it rests with yourself now to take proceedings against Mr Maynard. As a parent myself I could not rest satisfied nor would one in a hundred. I trust you will come forward for your own sake and the public good. You shall have all the assistance possible. I feel sure the young lady [a witness at the inquest] will willingly come forward as I know from good authority she was very dissatisfied with Mr Maynard's conduct; [she] of course supposed he would have taken the same step she did and have [the chocolates] analysed. I can only say that Mr Maynard, after being duly warned his chocolates were injurious and had made three persons ill, ought to have them analysed or destroy them. The public mind is not satisfied and feel great blame is attached to him for selling to your family chocolates from the same stock he had been warned against. He spoke of investigating and what was he investigating? Merely looking over and tasting a few chocolates with his shop woman. Why, the young lady was not satisfied with that, even; and as to writing to his French agent, it appears he never did. I hope no monetary considerations will prevent you taking proceedings. The Brighton inhabitants are all up in arms at the laxity of proceedings in the want of justice and will assist you in every way, and, with the facts tried before unbiased and unprejudiced men, I think Mr Maynard will not escape scot free. My feeling of disgust is felt by most of the influential and respectable inhabitants of this town. I am, Sir, an Old Inhabitant and Seeker of Justice.'[11]

Albert was mildly astonished by the letter and a touch offended. The writer implied he was neglecting his duty as a father and public citizen. Still, he had no intention of pursuing the matter now the inquest had ruled, so he ignored his indignation and put the letter aside with his other correspondence. Anyway he doubted Leticia could take the strain of another investigation and all he wanted to do was try to put Sidney's death behind him and cope with his grief. However, it seemed the publically-minded residents of Brighton had other ideas.

Shortly after the first letter another came, this one signed with the initials 'G. C. B.', it reiterated the points of the first but asked Albert directly: 'Why should Mr Maynard be screened?' There was also once again mention of the 'young lady' who had been a witness at the inquest. She had claimed she had also been made ill by chocolates bought from Maynards. Albert vaguely recalled she had been a Miss Edmunds. The second letter troubled him: it seemed some people believed he was in the wrong for not pursuing the matter. To set the record straight he wrote a letter to the *Daily News* stating that he was not even sure who he should pursue a case against. Unfortunately, this merely prompted a third letter to come claiming to be from a 'London Tradesman now in Brighton'. This one made it clear that if the writer had experienced a similar loss he would not hesitate to pursue the matter against the 'seller of the chocolates'.

Albert was tired of the proceedings and filed the letters together. It was only then, when he looked at them as a group, that he noticed how similar in composition and style they were. It caused him a moment of curiosity, but he saw nothing suspicious about it and presumed someone in Brighton had become rather troubled over his case. He closed the letters in a drawer and hoped his silence would prevent further correspondence.

CHAPTER TWO

The Poisoned Parcel

Elizabeth Boys entered her house at 59 Grand Parade, Brighton, in the early evening. It had been a long day for her visiting Tunbridge Wells and she was glad to be home. Elizabeth was the second wife of Jacob Boys, a retired solicitor now well into his seventies. The Boys were a familiar Brighton family with roots in the town stretching back to the eighteenth century. Elizabeth considered herself lucky to have married such a wealthy and well-respected individual. He had already been retired when they married in 1861, not quite a year after the death of the former Mrs Boys, Harriett. Elizabeth had been thirty-six at the time and inclined to believe she would never marry. The engagement with Mr Boys had been fortuitous and had resulted in two daughters – Emily and Gertrude – the youngest being born when Elizabeth had passed her fortieth year.

She could now consider herself a lady of leisure, a far cry from the days when she and her sister assisted their father in running a hotel in London, albeit a high-class one. Her sister, Mary Ann Barrack, had joined her at Brighton and helped with the children. Elizabeth's health had deteriorated since the birth of Gertrude and she required constant care. Jacob had the disposable income to provide her with her own private nurse and negate the need for Mary Ann to look after her sister.[12] Jacob was a considerate and indulgent husband to the wife who had provided him with his only children and he was happy to meet her every need. He had even taken the move of shifting his household from No. 60 Grand Parade to No. 59, so Elizabeth did not have to tread the rooms where her predecessor had once walked.

It was 10 August and faint evening light drifted in through the windows as Elizabeth retreated into the dining room, her gloves and hat dispensed to the waiting parlour maid Emma Helsey. Jacob was not around and the children were in bed. Elizabeth was contemplating whether to have a last cup of tea before retiring when she noticed a parcel sitting on the sideboard. It was a long thin box wrapped in brown paper. 'Emma, who has delivered this?' 'It came by the railway van about half past six, madam.' Emma explained. Elizabeth examined the box that was addressed to her in an unfamiliar hand. Opening it she discovered it contained several pieces of cake and a note: 'I send you some cakes for your two little girls – those directed to you are my first efforts; I hope to see you soon. Your old friend G. M.'[13] Elizabeth could not place the name of her well wisher, but she was too tired to trouble over it much. 'Oh, I can't be eating cake now.' She grumbled and took the box into the garden room, handing the brown paper to Emma for disposal. She gave up on the thought of tea and drifted to her bed with her nurse in attendance.

Around eleven o'clock the following morning, Elizabeth remembered the box. 'Amelia?' she called for her nurse. 'I do not want those cakes, they will do my constitution no good. Please take them and share them with the servants.' 'Yes madam, what about the children, madam?' 'Oh, they can have a little too, but not much as they will spoil their appetites.' Amelia took the box and her mistress settled and, with her mistress not requiring her attentions for the moment, she went to the housekeeper's room where she found Emma Helsey. 'Would you like some cake? Where are the girls? Emily! Gertrude!' Amelia found a plate and emptied the box of its contents. There were two pieces of gingerbread, two cheesecakes, two macaroons, two plum cakes and two tartlets. The tartlets were wrapped in a small slip of paper stating they were for Mrs Boys alone. Knowing her mistress was not inclined for cake, Amelia slipped off the paper and set the tartlets with the rest. Emma's eyes went wide at the sight. She rarely got cake unless the cook had made some for the household.

Amelia broke a tartlet in half and gave a portion to Emma. By now, the children had appeared and she offered them one of the plum cakes. Emily tasted a small portion of the cake. 'I don't like it,' she said instantly and refused to have more. Emma offered her a piece from her half of the tartlet. Gertrude liked the plum cake. She eat a couple of mouthfuls and then put it down. 'I don't feel well,' she said, her hands rubbing her stomach. She visibly began to tremble to the women's astonishment and before Amelia could do anything she was violently sick. 'Come, you best go to bed.' Amelia coaxed the child who was now crying at feeling so ill. 'My throat burns,' Gertrude murmured as she was led away. Emma set to cleaning up the mess with little Emily still to hand. A few moments passed then Emily started to shake. 'I don't feel very well Emma,' she complained. Emma looked up and she did not like to tell the girl that she was feeling odd herself. She had begun to feel very sick and there was a burning pain in her throat. Her legs ached and felt as if they wanted to draw up into her body. 'You best go with your sister,' Emma told the girl and Emily left the room. Slowly, Emma placed her hand on the housekeeper's table and steadied herself. She was beginning to feel quite giddy. She finished cleaning up the vomit as best she could and hesitantly went into the kitchen. She found Amelia sitting at the kitchen table looking extremely pale. She was trembling all over, just like the girls. 'I feel right giddy,' she said to Emma, 'and so sick.' 'So do I,' Emma replied. Matilda Hope, the cook, turned to the women. 'What is wrong with you two?' she asked. 'Does your throat burn like it's on fire?' Emma said to the nurse. Amelia nodded. 'I think it was those cakes. Both girls are sick too.' Matilda studied the women curiously. 'Well, someone better inform Mrs Boys, and Amelia, you ought to get to bed. You look half-dead girl.' Amelia could say nothing as she awkwardly stood and headed out of the kitchen. She barely made it to her private room when the sickness became too much and she had to vomit. Emma was not so badly taken and managed to make her way to Mrs Boys who was still where Amelia had left her. 'My Emma, you look sick to your soul,' Elizabeth said, startled by the sight of her trembling maid. 'Where is Amelia?' 'Madam, those cakes you were sent. They have made us all quite queer. Amelia, myself, and the girls too.' Elizabeth was suddenly beside herself. She made her way to the housekeeper's room and took up the plate of cakes. They looked perfectly normal, but she was not about to risk more of the household. 'Matilda, destroy these,' she instructed the cook, carefully removing one of the remaining tartlets labelled for her before she did so. She did not explain to Matilda what was in her mind as she took the tartlet to a safe place and locked it away.

By nightfall, Emily and Gertrude seemed to be recovering, much to the relief of their mother. Emma had managed to continue most of her duties throughout the day despite the weird sensations wracking her body. By ten o'clock that evening, she was beginning to feel better. It was Amelia Mills who was causing the greatest concern. Amelia had not stopped vomiting since she had started. She trembled in her bed, her throat and stomach on fire. There was little left inside her to expel, but still she violently retched. Emma reported to her mistress the continuing illness of the nurse and Elizabeth thought it best that a medical man be called for. Mr Blaker was duly summoned. Around quarter to eleven that night, Blaker found Amelia in her bed wracked with symptoms that he immediately felt suggested poisoning. The burning sensation in her throat and stomach and the constant vomiting indicated arsenic was at work.

Arsenic is one of the most familiar and deadliest of poisons. A stock tool for murder mystery writers, it gained notoriety due to its easy availability, difficulty to trace and ability to cause death suddenly or slowly. Throughout the Victorian period, there was an 'arsenic hysteria' as more and more stories were reported of deaths by the dangerous mineral. Some of these were accidental. Arsenic had many industrial uses and could be found in paints, wallpapers, dyes and, alarmingly, food products and medicines. Gradual arsenic poisoning could mimic one of the many wasting diseases or long-term sicknesses which killed people while a sudden death was often misdiagnosed as the result of cholera. During cholera outbreaks, the media liked to provoke public panic by questioning how many poisoners would not take the opportunity to dispose of their victims at such a time?

By the 1870s, regulations had been tightened concerning the sale of poisons and chemists and pharmacists were supposed to keep a 'poisons book' that listed the sales of such substances as arsenic. These were far from infallible and did little to stop a determined murderer obtaining a fatal dose, and besides, arsenic was such a common household item that few would look suspiciously at someone buying it. Arsenic was used to poison rats and mice; to seep grain in and prevent rot; to dip sheep; to line fly papers; to colour wallpapers and dyes green; to improve the condition of horses; to act as a beauty treatment to whiten the skin; and to even form part of restorative medicines. Arsenic, quite simply, was everywhere.

Arsenic has the nasty potential of disrupting the biochemistry of every tissue and organ in the body, in particular it attacks the enzymes in mitochondria, stopping energy production, preventing cell repair and, eventually, starving the cell. The first reaction to taking arsenic is for the body to try and expel it via diarrhoea and vomiting. Unfortunately, the fine particles of white arsenic – the commonest form of the poison – are able to adhere to the lining of the stomach, thus no amount of violent retching can expel them. The body continues to vomit, resulting in damage to the lining of the gut and severe dehydration. Intense thirst, burning sensation in the mouth and throat and acute stomach pains are all part of the arsenic package. Depending on the dosage and subsequent treatment, a victim can die within twenty and thirty-six hours, first falling into a coma.

Some murderers preferred the slow approach, especially after the 1850s when tests made death by acute arsenic poisoning easier to detect. Gradual, repeated doses of arsenic slowly deteriorate the body as the poison accumulates faster than the body can process and void it. Digestive complaints were typically the only symptom and, as this was rather a common problem in Victorian England due to inadequate or overly rich diets, it was often misdiagnosed by doctors. Ironically, there was a popular myth that dosing yourself with arsenic would improve your health. It began with an article on the 'Styrian Arsenic Eaters' who were said to accustom their body to arsenic by taking small doses that they increased with time. The Styrian defence became a popular tool in trials of arsenical murders

– the victim was claimed to be an 'arsenic-eater' who had accidentally overdosed. In the modern world, arsenic is still a big problem and there are unconscious arsenic eaters in some of the poorest regions. In Bangladesh, the vast majority of the population are drinking water contaminated with natural arsenic, though it is not an acute dose. Over the course of decades, it develops into a wealth of conditions including skin problems and breathing difficulties. As arsenic is a carcinogen long-term exposure can result in a range of cancers.

Mr Blaker had little time to contemplate the strange case at No. 59 when he was called out again, this time to No. 64 Grand Parade where another servant had been taken grievously ill. Nathaniel Payne Blaker recognised the house as that belonging to Dr Beard, an eminent private physician who, he had heard, was tipped to become the medical inspector for the new vaccinations board. Blaker realised there must be something amiss within the Beard household for him to be called. Even if Dr Beard was on one of his regular visits to London, he would not be pleased that another medical man had been called in if a case could wait. It must be something urgent.

In the world of Victorian medicine, there was a huge gulf between Beard and Blaker, not just in training but in social status. Physicians were university-educated men, licensed and entitled to call themselves doctors. They were a Victorian phenomenon that had rapidly grown from 1800 when only 179 physicians were licensed to 1847 when there were 683. Beard had trained at Trinity College in Cambridge and could rank himself among the upper echelons of Brighton society. As a university man he was deemed the most knowledgeable among the various medical ranks, though he was not permitted by his licence to perform surgical operations, and it was only in the last few years that he had been allowed to dispense drugs like an apothecary. In contrast, Mr Blaker, while a medical man, could not call himself doctor and moved in less exalted circles. Classed as a surgeon, he was effectively a skilled craftsman who had served an apprenticeship rather than attained a degree. Surgeons carried an air of suspicion about them because they were not educated like the physicians and their training could be variable. Quacks and medical conmen would happily label themselves 'surgeons' causing disrepute for their genuine counterparts. On the other hand, they were also the only medical class permitted to perform operations and many were also apothecaries and could dispense drugs.

As Mr Blaker stood before No. 64, he knew he had been either called to set a broken bone or dispense medicine, but whatever it was, it was urgent enough to not wait for Dr Beard to return. The Beard household was in a mild uproar. A servant had been taken severely ill and when Blaker saw her he was troubled by the similarities between her condition and that of

Amelia Mills. His suspicions that a poison was at work demanded further action. The patient had vomited several times and the result had yet to be cleared away. Blaker asked for two jars and took care to put a sample of vomit in each. The first jar contained vomit from one of the victim's first evacuations, the second jar contained some from later on. He labelled them carefully and set them aside. He also discovered a handkerchief the servant had used to wipe her mouth and he removed it for analysis. Back downstairs, he approached Mrs Beard. 'I fear it is arsenic poisoning,' he told her simply. 'I have taken some samples for analysis to confirm it.' Mrs Beard was grim, but there was something about her demeanour that suggested she was not entirely surprised. 'Were you aware that your neighbours, the Boys, are experiencing something similar in their household?' Blaker said cautiously. 'I don't suppose you have received a package of cakes?' Mrs Beard hesitated for a moment. 'Actually I have. I didn't eat them, but gave them to my servants.' Mr Blaker nodded. 'Mrs Boys received a parcel from the railway van at half-past-six in the evening. She has given me a piece of a tartlet she feared was poisoned and I also received a piece of cake from her cook which she had saved from disposal with the rest. I am going to take them to a chemist for analysis.' 'You think someone deliberately sent us poisoned food?' Mrs Beard asked anxiously. 'I cannot say. It would not be the first time arsenic has accidentally found its way into cakes. It could simply be a contaminated batch of flour that your well-wisher has used.'

Blaker sounded convincing but Mrs Beard was not fooled for she, like a number of residents of Brighton, were becoming deeply suspicious of the poison that was seeping into their households. Mr Blaker took his leave of No. 64 with his evidence and instructions for the unfortunate servant to drink a little water. As he wandered back out into the Brighton night it crossed his mind to wonder how many more households would fall sick that evening.

CHAPTER THREE

Poor Mr Maynard

John Goddard Maynard was a worried man as he went about his business. It was two months since the bizarre case of little Sidney Barker and he had made sure to destroy all his remaining stock of French creams. However, it was noticeable the sales of his chocolates were down and people were wary. He had had lengthy meetings with Mr Ware, his supplier, during which the latter had again and again denied that contamination could have occurred at his factory. He was effectively saying that someone at Maynards had poisoned the chocolates.

Maynard had been over his business from top to bottom to try and work out the source of the problem. He had studied his storage areas and made sure boxes and bags were kept secure. He checked with his staff and surreptitiously watched their handling practices. He went through the few raw ingredients he kept on the premises to see if any were laced with strychnine and had somehow come into contact with the French creams. He had found nothing.

Mr Maynard spoke with Mr Ware, still trying to fathom how his business had come under this curse. 'It must be from the factory,' he repeated. 'I have been in business for thirty-two years,' Mr Ware said crossly, 'making French chocolate and only French chocolate.[14] My factory practices are sound.' 'Then how could it happen?' Maynard said plaintively. 'It could be easily done, you know. English creams get hard in the centre, but French creams are soft when warmed by a hand, and anything may be pricked in and the puncture glazed over with the finger.'[15] 'One of my staff could have done it then.' Maynard shook his head sadly. 'Could still do it, in fact.' 'The question remains my dear Maynard, why?' For that Maynard had no answer. 'I should have listened to that woman.' 'Which woman?' Ware asked. 'The one who was at the inquest.' Maynard thought for a moment.

'Miss Edmunds, I believe, she comes in quite often to buy sweets. She came in one day and told one of my assistants that she had received bad French creams from us and they had made a friend ill.' 'Was this before or after the death of the Barker boy?' Ware asked keenly. Maynard could not remember, shaking his head. 'It could have been any time,' he said. 'She did not come to the shop but to my private door. She was not familiar to me as a customer. She said a lady had been nearly poisoned by a chocolate cream bought by her at my shop. She said a gentleman had said he would have the creams analysed without saying what gentleman. I told her I wished he would and to communicate the result to me. I never did receive any result of an analysis. I went back into the shop and tasted some of the French creams, but nothing seemed amiss.'[16] 'Well, there wouldn't be,' Mr Ware said stoutly. 'I have been supplying you for a number of years without incident. In spring, I sent out half-a-ton of French creams around the country, including those that came to you and no others were reported bad. I also supply most of the large houses here in Brighton. There is nothing wrong with my chocolates.'

Maynard was determined to discover the origins of the fatal chocolates. Returning to his shop floor he planned to quietly interrogate his staff. He spoke to Anne Meadows, one of his older girls who was due to leave and move to Lincolnshire. Taking her to one side he asked if she could remember anything concerning the case of French creams around the time of Sidney Barker's death. Anne considered for a moment.

'I remember that boy Adam May coming to the shop about the beginning of June for sixpennyworth (sic) of the best chocolate creams. I gave him an ounce-and-a-half in paper and he returned shortly after to have the ounce and a half exchanged for a packet of Cadbury's Creams.[17] I exchanged them and after giving the boy a packet of Cadbury's Creams, placed those I had taken from him in the case for four-penny creams.' Anne indicated the case. 'The case had not been filled up between Saturday and Monday, Miss Page having filled them up on the tenth. On Monday the twelfth, I served Mr Miller with a shilling's worth of the creams from the case where I had put the chocolate creams which Adam May brought back.'[18]

Maynard nodded and could not fault Anne's behaviour. He, too, would have been inclined to replace the chocolates in the case. They were too expensive to waste just because the boy had bought the wrong ones. 'He bought them for someone else?' he suggested. 'You would have to ask Kate,' Anne answered. 'She knows more about this than I do.' Maynard went to find twenty-four-year-old Kate Page, currently his oldest female assistant and one he placed a good deal of trust in. 'Kate, do you remember anything odd about the sales of French creams in the last few weeks?' Kate looked up from her work. 'If you recall, sir, I was suspicious about the number of boys who kept coming in to buy chocolates and then returning them shortly after. It wasn't usual practice especially after the incident.' Maynard nodded. Kate had mentioned her concerns and he had suggested she have the boys followed to see if any clue could be found as to who was buying and returning so many chocolates. 'Did you learn anything?' he asked. 'I served a boy at the end of May, I think his name is Brooks, with four-penny creams. Before he left the shop, I told John Parker, who was working with me, to follow him and see who he was giving them to. I had asked him to do that a couple of times before. I've also asked Charles Schooly to follow a couple of boys on errands to buy chocolates.'[19]

Maynard knew the lads to be reliable and was glad at Kate's choices. 'What did they find?' 'On both occasions they saw the boys give the chocolates to a lady,' Kate explained. 'I did not think that suspicious, some ladies won't come in a shop like this themselves. Sometimes when the chocolates were returned one or two were broken. But that is quite usual and I put them in the broken chocolate drawer and returned the rest to the case.' It was indeed quite usual. Maynard found himself at a dead end yet again.

'Have you seen the *Brighton Herald* tonight?' Mrs Maynard asked her husband who was becoming more and more preoccupied by the problems with his chocolates. The *Brighton Herald* was the oldest paper in Brighton, first printed in 1806 and establishing itself as the town's leading provincial paper. Its greatest claim to fame was that it was the first paper to print news of the escape of Napoleon in 1815 from Elba. But for Maynard, the instant attraction of the paper on that night was the odd advert printed inside which his wife was pointing out.

'Brighton residents are hereby informed that some evil-disposed person has lately sent to different families in Brighton parcels of fruit, cakes and sweets, which have been found to contain poison. A notice has been issued by the police that whoever would give such information to the chief constable as should lead to the apprehension and conviction of the offender would be paid a reward.'[20]

A spark of hope hit Maynard. If there was a poisoner at large in Brighton, then his chocolates and staff would be free of the suspicion of causing the death of little Sidney Barker. 'Who has received these parcels?' 'I have heard Mr Curtis at the *Brighton Gazette* received one,' Mrs Maynard explained. 'But he did not eat any of the contents, but two workmen did and were made severely ill. And Mr Tatham the surgeon and magistrate received one too. I have also heard that lady, Miss Edmunds, came forward to say someone had sent her a parcel.' Maynard mulled on this news. 'She was the one who first said my chocolates were bad.' 'Yes, and she was at the inquest for the little boy who died.' 'Could this be a plot against Miss

Edmunds?' Maynard mused aloud. 'She certainly seems to be at the centre of it all.' 'I can see no reason someone would want to kill Miss Edmunds,' Mrs Maynard replied. 'She is quite respectable, even if her family has fallen on hard times. Though… she is a little… odd.'

Maynard could not deny that there was something a touch peculiar about the dear woman. She was quite clearly getting on in years and should have accepted her misfortune to be a spinster, but her vanity kept her dressing her hair and face as though she was much younger. She also insisted on being considered a lady, despite her widowed mother having to earn their keep as a landlady. He still found it hard to imagine anyone could have enough against her to try and poison her. 'Then there are the others who received the parcels. Who would want to kill them?; he said. 'As a magistrate, Mr Tatham is always at risk of incurring the dislike of some nefarious individual,' Mrs Maynard shrugged, 'and Mr Curtis prints a good deal of gossip in his paper. Someone may have taken offence.' 'Someone must take offence quite easily to poison all these people!' John Goddard snorted. 'And what of Sidney Barker?' Mrs Maynard reached out for her husband's arm. 'I think we must view that as an unfortunate accident. The chocolates could not have been meant for him. It wasn't your fault you know.' Maynard needed something more convincing than platitudes about an accident. He would blame himself and so would all of Brighton until it was proved there was a poisoner at large. Perhaps these parcels would go some way towards that, but there was still no suspect with an obvious motive. The future of Maynards hung in the balance.

The strange advert in the *Brighton Herald* caught the attention of a number of local residents. Harriett Cole, the wife of a grocer in Church Street, took particular interest in the notice. A few months earlier, she had experienced a similar occurrence that had been worrying at the time, but had slipped her mind since. The notice brought it back to her. Mrs Cole spent most of her days working in her husband's shop. One cold afternoon in March, she had come across a bag of mixed sweets left on the shop counter. They bore the name of Maynards. Since customers quite often mislaid items in the shop, she kept them to one side to see if someone would collect them. No one ever did and she eventually shared the sweets with her daughter and some of the children who came into the grocery.

About a week before the inquest on Sidney Barker, another bag had appeared, this time, however, it appeared to have been dropped in a zinc pail. The bag contained lemon bulls-eyes and chocolates and again was labelled as originating from Maynards. Mrs Cole had wondered who had left it. A few moments before the discovery, one of her usual customers, Miss Edmunds, had been buying some sundry items, but she was not a great one for chocolates as far as Mrs Cole could recall.

Remembering how the last bag and been left and never claimed, Mrs Cole decided there would be no harm in eating the sweets. She rarely got such luxuries, always too busy in the shop and with so many other expenses to worry about, buying sweets was not a priority. She was also quite fond of bulls-eyes. She could not resist eating one from the bag, enjoying the sharp lemon taste and its sweetness. When her daughter joined her, she offered her a bulls-eye and took another for herself. The two women felt rather indulgent to be eating sweets while working. 'Can I try a chocolate?' asked Miss Cole. Mrs Cole saw no harm and agreed. The girl bit into a chocolate and then spat out the portion she had tried. 'It isn't very nice,' she grimaced. 'You have to get a taste for eating chocolate,' Mrs Cole remarked. 'It is quite different from drinking chocolate which you can sweeten.' 'I think I prefer not to develop a taste.' Miss Cole laughed and they carried on with work.

What had seemed such a good idea at the time and so innocent began to trouble Mrs Cole as she lay in bed that night. What if the rightful owner of the sweets did come back and ask for them? It would look very bad indeed if they discovered they were half gone. Mrs Cole started to feel quite guilty about the matter – had she not effectively stolen the sweets? Mrs Cole concluded to dispose of the bag and if anyone came in and asked about it she would claim she had never seen them. After all, anyone could have spotted the bag in the zinc pail. But finding someone to take the chocolates was not so simple. It could not be an adult who might be suspicious and it would look odd for her to be handing out sweets to customers. No, it had to be one of the children who would run errands for their parents to her shop.

Mrs Cole finally found her stooge to pass the stolen chocolates to when ten-year-old Henry Walker came in.[21] Walker's family were not very well off and would appreciate the sweets. Mrs Cole handed the bag to him. As she expected, Henry was too pleased with the gift to ask much about it, besides children rarely thought suspiciously like adults did. He rushed off with his prize, though Mrs Cole could not help but still feel a twinge of guilt at her conduct.

At the Walker household, Henry proudly presented the bag to his mother. Mrs Walker was delighted with the surprise and took one of the chocolate creams. Biting into it she noted its bitter taste. 'I find eating chocolate not to my liking,' she said to herself and put aside the remainder of the cream and continued with her chores, but it was only a matter of ten minutes before something peculiar began to happen. It started with a strange sensation in her head. She felt as though her eyes were popping out of their sockets.[22] She fetched a glass of water and attempted to drink some, but her hand and arm shook so much she could not bring the glass to her mouth. Mrs Walker was now trembling all over and was terrified.

Managing to climb the stairs, she collapsed into a chair. Henry realised something was wrong and followed her anxiously. She was beginning to convulse violently. 'I am taken for sudden death!' she groaned.

Henry was petrified, but could not leave his mother where she was. Somehow he helped her trembling body into her own bed where she continued to be wracked by vile contortions while remaining sensible to her surroundings. Little did Mrs Walker know that she was probably the first victim of Brighton's serial poisoner. Her body was suffering the effects of strychnine, the chocolate she had nibbled must have been heavily laced to induce such a strong reaction with the small amount she had eaten. However, the Walkers did not have the funds to send for a doctor, so unlike Sidney Baker and Charles Miller, there was no medical man to see their suffering. Mrs Walker remained in her bed for three or four days. The convulsions eventually eased, but her body remained weak as her kidneys slowly processed and filtered out the poison.

Henry had to watch his mother fighting the strychnine, at times quite convinced she would die. Eventually, he had to go to Mrs Cole's shop to buy some supplies and once there he mentioned his mother's illness. Henry had no reason to connect the gift of chocolate with his mother's sickness, but Mrs Cole had heard of the death of Sidney Barker and was to attend the inquest. She now had a troubled feeling that her guilt had caused an innocent women to eat poisoned chocolates. But where had they come from?

Later, she ventured to the inquest where Miss Edmunds got on the stand and testified she too had received bad chocolates from Maynards. The testimony triggered a memory in Mrs Cole. Had not Miss Edmunds been in the shop moments before she found the bag? Desperate for an answer, she stopped Miss Edmunds on the way out. 'Miss Edmunds, I hope you don't mind me asking, but did you happen to leave behind a bag of Maynards' chocolates in my shop the other day?' Miss Edmunds smiled. 'Oh no,' she said. 'I don't eat chocolates. I only like dry sweets.' She moved on leaving Mrs Cole feeling quite flustered, having just heard her testify about buying chocolates from Maynards.

As rumours spread about the notices in the *Brighton Herald*, an increasing number of residents began to wonder about their own sudden illnesses after eating chocolates. In March, thirteen-year-old Henry Halliwell discovered a bag of Maynards chocolates in his father's stationers shop. After no one claimed them, a customer suggested to him that he might as well eat them. When he did, he suffered symptoms of strychnine poison and was ill for almost a week. When another bag mysteriously appeared it was destroyed in the household fire. Matters became even more worrying when local children experienced sickness after accepting sweets from a nice stranger.

Though none died, all were severely ill. One little girl even brought an entire bag of Maynards chocolates home to her mother, explaining they were a gift from a stranger. Even so, people were cautious about their suspicions. Serial killers were virtually unknown in Victorian Britain. The famous case of Jack the Ripper that would spotlight such murderers did not occur until over a decade after the Brighton killings.

Multiple poisonings had been known, but in all cases a logical motive had been apparent. Dr William Palmer was one example. Born in Staffordshire in 1824, as a young man he quickly developed a love for expensive living and easy money. His father had perished when he was twelve, leaving his mother a substantial legacy. It is possible this provided inspiration for Palmer's later crime: he was certainly not a man who liked to work for his income. Apprenticed to an apothecary, he was dismissed for stealing. In 1846, he managed to train as a doctor, but this only enabled him to not only commit but conceal his crimes. His first victim was said by his contemporaries to be George Abley who he challenged to a drinking contest one evening. Abley died in his bed shortly after, having had to be carried home from the tavern where they had staged the contest. Though popular belief after Palmer's trial held that Abley had been poisoned as the doctor had taken a liking to his wife, it is far more likely that this was a case of alcohol poisoning. Palmer's later crimes proved that he only killed for financial motives.

His first true victim was his mother-in-law, Ann Thornton, who had been left money by a colonel she had been mistress to. She died in 1849, only two weeks after coming to live with her daughter and her son-in-law. It was known she had lent money to Palmer who was a spendthrift and interested in gambling on horse racing. She was probably killed for the inheritance Palmer believed his wife would get from her mother. Clearly, Ann Thornton had been overemphasising the wealth left her by the colonel, however, as Palmer discovered when his wife inherited a disappointingly small sum.

The deaths began to mount up. Leonard Bladen loaned Palmer £600 to cover the debts he was rapidly accruing, but died at the doctor's house in dreadful agony in May 1850. Mrs Palmer was surprised to find Bladen had hardly any money on him, despite a big win at the races recently and his betting books were missing making it impossible to prove his loan to Palmer. As the doctor present at the death, Palmer was well placed to influence the coroner's verdict on Bladen's sudden departure from life. His death certificate blamed an abscess on Bladen's pelvis caused by a hip injury for his agonising demise.

Bladen's death was followed by the mortalities of four of Palmer's five children, each dying before they were a year old, some only within days of their birth. Infant death was so common, especially in new babies, that the losses did not arouse great suspicions, though it was now known the good doctor was in dreadful debt and desperate to have no more mouths to feed. Palmer was forging his mother's signature to pay off creditors and in 1854, he took life insurance of £13,000 out on his wife. She was dead soon after during a cholera epidemic, though a suspicious mind might reflect on how easy it was for arsenic to be mistaken for the fatal illness.

Palmer's life was now spiralling out of control with his debtors closing in and threatening to speak to his mother. In 1855, this signed the death warrant for his brother Walter who was a well-known drunk. Palmer took out a £14,000 life insurance policy on him and by August he was dead. The insurance company, however, were unhappy with the situation and sent out inspectors to investigate. The case swung against Palmer when it was discovered he was trying to take out a life insurance policy on a farmer who had once worked for him. The company refused to pay out for Walter.

Palmer was now desperate for money. He had befriended a sickly young man named John Cook who had inherited £12,000 and was proving himself rather lucky at the horse races. Cook first fell sick on 15 November after sharing a drink with Palmer after the races. He complained of burning in his throat and accused Palmer of drugging him, but by 17 November, he had recovered both his health and trust to have a coffee with the doctor. He was soon sick again and was taken into his 'caring' friend's household to recover. His demise was now assured. A dreadful concoction of soup laced with arsenic, strychnine and ammonia carried off poor Cook who spent his final hours in agony and screaming that he was suffocating (the soup also made a chambermaid sick when she tasted it).

Palmer got a fellow aged doctor to sign Cook's death certificate as 'death by apoplexy', but on this occasion he had gone too far. Cook's stepfather called for an inquest and despite Palmer's efforts to interfere with the autopsy of Cook – including shoving the medical student performing the procedure, carrying off the stomach contents and trying to bribe the coroner – the inquest jury believed him guilty of murdering Cook. In June 1856, he was hanged for the crime.

Palmer stunned Victorian Britain due to his callousness and the power he had as a doctor over his victims. Yet people still found it hard to contemplate a person going on an extended killing spree. Even Cook, who at first had blamed Palmer, eventually decided it was too far-fetched an idea to be possible. It would be laughable to suggest there had never been a serial killer before the advent of the Victorian period, but the idea had not penetrated the popular mind. Palmer, despite his multiple crimes, was seen as merely a greedy man and his story fed into the prevalent 'arsenic hysteria' of the 1850s. Palmer kept his crimes within his family and friends: strangers were safe from him. That soothed the public consciousness and made them feel safe. The notion of a person killing strangers apparently at random was far more frightening a prospect and one people did not want to contemplate.

The term 'serial killer' appeared in the 1970s and has been attributed to both FBI profiler Robert Ressler and LAPD detective Pierce Brooks. In the 1960s, experts in the crime field had talked of 'serial murders' and 'serial murderers', yet it was not until the 1980s that the modern term came into popular usage. Since then it has become absorbed into the media, used liberally and often erroneously to define murder cases and popularised via films and novels. Serial killers are in fact quite rare, but popular imagination has them existing around every corner.

Serial killers are defined in modern terms as a person who has murdered three or more people over a period longer than a month (murders committed over a shorter period are attributed to mass murderers or spree killers). The FBI includes financial gain, attention seeking, thrill and anger as motives, but there is always an element of psychological gratification and usually there is a sexual element. Victims follow a pattern and will normally have something in common, either their gender, race, appearance or occupation and the murders will also follow a similar process each time. In 1870s Brighton, the main target group was children. The Boys and Beards parcels were labelled 'For your children' and the weapon of choice was always poisoned treats.

History is rather void of stories of serial killers and those that are remembered were usually notable figures. Hungarian aristocrat Elizabeth Bathory (1560-1614) allegedly tortured and killed over 650 girls stolen from local villages before her arrest in 1610 where she became known as the Blood Countess of Transylvania. Gilles de Rais (1404-1440), a Breton knight and comrade-in-arms to Joan of Arc, killed an unknown number of children, usually boys, after sexually assaulting them. Children vanished from local villages and in Machecoul, forty bodies alone were discovered in 1437. Some reports give his death total as 800 and contemporaries linked it to witchcraft and demon summoning. Such exaggeration is common with historical serial killers and tends to make it difficult to assess their crimes.

Some suggest the legends of werewolves and vampires stem from medieval serial killers, but it seems this kind of criminal was more a product of the eighteenth century onwards when the changing world offered greater opportunities for such crimes. Early serial killers, unless powerful figures such as Bathory and de Rais, would have struggled to find victims and mask them from the community. The population was not only more spread out, but also close-knit and early policing relied on this fact. When cities and towns began to swell in population with strangers, it became easier for a serial killer to work anonymously. There was no longer a close community watching over him, so he could operate with less concern of being caught.

The advent of the newspaper also contributed. Unusual crimes could now be reported across the country within days. In one way this harmed the serial killer as it generated undue publicity, but it also encouraged him/her to select strangers over family or to keep his killings as low-key and mistakable for natural causes as possible. Throughout the nineteenth century, newspapers were blamed for generating public hysterias, often blowing crimes or problems immensely out of proportion. Also in the Victorian period, doctors began to take an interest in the mental health, or lack of, in their patients. Investigations into the causes of insanity and other psychological problems fascinated the academic worlds and also the bored upper classes who were desperate for mental distraction. This spurred the creation of phrenology and other quack arts, but also developed a genuine study into behavioural aberrations.

In 1886, psychiatrist Richard von Krafft-Ebing wrote *Psychopathia Sexualis*, a clinical forensic study of human sexual behaviour, in which he recorded the case of a Frenchman in the 1870s who had derived sexual pleasure from murder and confessed to killing six people. It is perhaps the earliest scientific analysis of a serial killer.

CHAPTER FOUR

Inspector Gibbs becomes Curious

Brighton was a difficult place to be a policeman. The town's evolution had not been entirely natural. It had jumped from a fading fishing town to a holiday resort almost overnight due to the magic worked by Dr Russell and his claims of the healing properties of sea water. The result was regular, yet temporary, population swells of fashionable outsiders seeking to restore their health before vanishing back to where they had come from. They spurred the development of boarding houses to accommodate them, eventually leading to fabulous hotels (which were a Victorian French idea) and a wealth of business that revolved around tourism. But this also sparked great swathes of crime. Prostitution was rife in Brighton and girls were lured into the lifestyle by the promise of wealthy visiting patrons. In 1860, it was '...well known to the police that there were at least seven public houses and ten beer-shops which were notorious resorts for thieves and prostitutes of the lowest grade' and '...twenty more are described as suspected houses [of ill repute]'.[23]

The Judicial Statistics for 1859 recorded 325 known prostitutes in the town, though there was good reason to believe the real figure was double that. Twenty-five of them were under the age of sixteen. No account was made of the other notorious women who would travel down from London during the Brighton season to steal some of the local girls' trade. The figures were alarmingly high for a location that did not boast a population much over 100,000.[24] There were said to be ninety-seven brothels, but numerous other places such as public houses featured prostitution on the side. A lack of rooms for assignations meant that many occurred on the beach in front of King's Road and around the Royal Pavilion – the fine home of the man who had brought sex to Brighton.

'The colonnade of the Theatre Royal after eleven o'clock presented a very animated appearance being then used principally as a promenade of the women of the town.'[25] Church Street and Edward Street were deemed 'infested' by the problem and in one of the lanes leading off Church Street, an entire block of houses was said to be '...garrisoned by females of the most depraved and abandoned class'. The situation was not helped when the militia were stationed near the town. In Jane Austen's *Pride and Prejudice*, Lydia Bennet was ecstatic at the prospect of visiting Brighton while the militia were in town. 'In Lydia's imagination a visit to Brighton comprised every possibility of earthly happiness. She saw with the creative eye of fancy, the streets of that gay bathing-place covered with officers. She saw herself the object of attention to tens and scores of them at present unknown. She saw all the glories of the camp – its tents stretched forth in beauteous uniformity of lines, crowded with the young and gay, and dazzling with scarlet; and to complete the view, she saw herself seated beneath a tent, tenderly flirting with at least six officers at once.'[26] Lydia was soon to find the temptations of Brighton too great and she came close to becoming a fallen woman, running off with the notorious Wickham. A hasty marriage was her only saving grace.

But for many 'Lydias' in the time Austen was writing and the decades after, there was no safety net to save them once they had fallen in with the militia. The *Gazette* of 17 October 1796 remarked in a surprisingly sympathetic tone that there were now 300 girls with the militia and the fact that these '...good-natured but unfortunate creatures could be supported by the wages of prostitution cast a melancholy reflection on the increasing depravity of the age'.[27] Alongside the prostitutes worked the gangs, often involved with betting rings at the horse races. They made a nuisance of themselves extorting protection money from beach front traders and cafes. Certain music halls and pubs were their headquarters. A policeman working in these districts had to be prepared for trouble.

Money and sex had quickly become the bywords for Brighton. The arrival of Prince George (later George IV) had seemed at the time a boom for Brighton's revival as a resort, but his carefree and decadent private life started to taint the town he had laid claim to. Locals resented the Pavilion he raised as an eyesore, the folly of a man with too much time and wealth on his hands. The arrival of Mrs Fitzherbert, the King's mistress and unofficial wife, did not exactly improve the town's reputation. Too many people saw Brighton as the place to cast off the normal regulations of Victorian life and to indulge in illicit pleasures. Whether that was watching the ladies bathing from the cliff-top or gambling the family fortune away, Brighton became notorious as the place for loose morals and wastrel decadence.

Brighton had long ago put up a façade of elegance and respectability to mask the deep undercurrents of sex and crime that ran through it. People came to Brighton to become someone else and to move up in the world, even if just in name alone to pretend they were more respectable than they really were. Mrs Boys knew this only too well: she had been a hotel keeper's assistant. However fashionable and well-to-do the hotel, she was still effectively a 'tradesperson'. Yet she came to Brighton with her sister to become 'independent ladies'. She cast off her former life like a cloak and held her head high as she supped in hotels instead of working in them. All this paid off when she met retired solicitor Jacob Boys and married him. Brighton had the power to hide a person's past, but if it worked for Elizabeth Boys who else might be hiding their real selves behind the faux glamour of the seaside town?

Inspector Gibbs understood the world he worked in. Brighton was a hotbed for drunkenness and the violence it led to, helped by the large number of public houses established to serve the tourist population. In 1860, there were 479 liquor shops compared to 541 provision shops. A decade on the number could only have risen. But Gibbs could console himself that, aside from prostitution, most of the serious crime in the town was caused by strangers down from London. Thieves and gangs who worked the race courses were his biggest problem, but they fluctuated with the seasons and drifted off with their prey – the foolish and affluent – when they moved on. He could deal with everything else that came across his desk, until now. Crimes relating to sex and money he understood, but poisoning children? That was a new one for Brighton.

The first victim to come to his attention had been from London and Gibbs was hopeful that this was another case of imported crime, but more and more it seemed he was dealing with a home-grown problem. The gangs who walked on his turf would have no reason to poison local youngsters and as far as he could tell Mr Maynard had stayed clear of them with his shop in the respectable West Street. Besides, extortion crimes tended to be more obvious. This was far too subtle and was clearly not getting the message across if Maynard was supposed to be paying up. Prostitutes and the local beer shops were also off his list. He could not relate this to them at all. In fact, currently he could not relate it to anything as the victims seemed so random and unconnected. In his notes, he had the victims listed along with the dates to try and establish a pattern:

March:
Mrs Walker
Chocolates found in Mrs Cole's shop and given to Henry Walker, son of Mrs Walker

Henry Halliwell
13 years old
Maynard's chocolates found in his father's stationers shop

Benjamin Calthrope
13 years old
Given chocolates by a stranger

Henry Dickens
15 years old
Received chocolate from Calthrope

April (approx.):
Emily Baker
9 years old
Given bag of sweets by a stranger

June:
Sidney Barker
4 years old
Poisoned by Strychnine

Charles Miller
Uncle to above

August:
Mrs Boys
Box directed for herself and children
Married to Jacob Boys retired solicitor

Mrs Beard
Married to Dr Beard
Resided in Grand Parade as did above

Mr Garret
Chemist

Mr Curtis
Editor at the Brighton Gazette

Mr G. Tatham
Surgeon and magistrate

Miss Edmunds
Also present at Sidney Barker's inquest

If there was any logic to the crimes it seemed several children had been targeted, but was that perhaps just coincidence? There was at least some consolation that Dickens, Calthrope and Baker had all said it had been a woman who had given them the sweets, so that narrowed his search slightly. Though it troubled Inspector Gibbs deeply that a woman would want to poison random children. He did at least have two tangible leads to follow up. First, he must discover where the poison came from. Secondly, he would interview the main victims and see if they could provide an idea for a possible motive, though he still could not understand why anyone would want to deliberately set out to poison Brighton.

It seemed rather coincidental that a chemist had been one of the victims of the deadly parcels when Inspector Gibbs was looking for poison. Acting on a hunch he decided to have Mr Isaac Garret interviewed about any odd poison transactions. Mr Garret owned a smart chemist shop at No. 10 Queen's Road, Brighton, and was relieved to see the police were taking his receipt of a poisonous parcel seriously. Inspector Gibbs, now working under the assumption that a woman was his main suspect, wanted to know if Garret had served any ladies with strychnine or arsenic, both of which could be obtained via a chemist.

'There was one lady,' Mr Garret remembered. 'She has been a customer here about four years. I never knew her by name until last March. She always came in to buy quinine and iron for neuralgia. After buying her usual items last March, she asked if I would oblige her with a small quantity of strychnine as she and her husband found their garden much infested by cats which she wished to destroy. I objected to supply so strong a poison and she assured me there would be no danger as there were no children in the house and that the poison would only pass through her and her husband's hands.'

Gibbs' ears pricked up at news of the strange purchase and how carefully the woman had specified the drug would not come into contact with children. 'Did you supply the strychnine?' 'I told her that if I did supply her I should require a witness who knew her and whom I knew. She told me that the only person she knew in the neighbourhood was Mrs Stone, a milliner living nearby, and I told her Mrs Stone would be sufficient.' Mr Garret looked a touch abashed. 'On reflection, I am not sure Mrs Stone knew the woman any more than I did, but the lady had been a good customer for four years and I didn't want to refuse her.' Inspector Gibbs gave no comment. It was known that the poisons book, which was supposed to prevent the sale of dangerous drugs wholesale and reduce risk of accidental or deliberate deaths, was rather inefficient and did not seem to be combating the high numbers of murders by poison. 'So she fetched Mrs Stone?' 'Yes and Mrs Stone signed the "poison book" and I then supplied the lady with ten grains of strychnine entering the sale "March 28 1871, Mrs Wood, Hill-side, Kingston, 10gr. strychnine for destroying cats."' 'So she gave the name Mrs Wood?' Gibbs asked. 'That is what she signed the book as. I never knew her name before then.' 'Did she come back afterwards?' Gibbs wanted to be sure he really had a lead and not just a commonplace case of a woman wanting to clear her garden of cats. After all, many innocent people bought strychnine too.

'I saw her several times afterwards coming in to buy her usual dose of quinine and iron, but on 15 April, she asked for more strychnine as the cats were as numerous as ever. I told her I was very careful about the sale of such things and she again assured me there was no danger.' Mr Garret hesitated knowing it was not a very convincing argument for his ethics. 'I told her that if I supplied her with more strychnine I should require a witness as before. She went out and brought in Mrs Stone and signed the "poison book" as Mrs Wood before I supplied her with ten grains of the poison.' 'And that was the last of it?' 'No,' sighed Garret.

'On 11 May, Mrs Wood came again, and having bought quinine and iron as before, asked for a little more strychnine to kill an old and diseased dog. I supplied her this time without a witness and gave her ten grains as before.'[28] 'I thought you were very careful about the sale of such things, Mr Garret.' 'I had no cause to think she had done any harm with the stuff and she was a good customer.' Mr Garret felt ashamed about the transaction, even though he knew he was one of the more reliable chemists in Brighton and many of his rivals would not have been as careful as he had been. 'And that was the last occasion she bought strychnia?' 'The last time she came in person.' Mr Garret admitted, 'I received these letters but at the time I saw nothing wrong with them.' Mr Garret retrieved some letters he had been keeping for his records. The first he had received on 8 June and purported to come from Messrs. Glaisyer and Kemp, another chemist in the town. It read:

Messrs. Glaisyer and Kemp would be much obliged if Mr Garret could supply them with a little strychnia. They are in immediate want of half an ounce; or, if not able, a smaller quantity will do. Will Mr Garret send it in a bottle and sealed up? The bearer can be safely trusted with it – GLAISYER and KEMP, 11 and 12 North Street.

'Do chemists often request things from one another?' Gibbs asked. 'Sometimes, if we run short,' Garret nodded. 'And who was the bearer of this letter?' 'A boy. I never took his name.' Mr Garret did not like the inspector's look. 'I didn't just give them the poison, though. I took the precaution of sending back a note with the boy asking them to send a formal order and that I could only provide a drachm of strychnia. I received a letter back confirming the order and that a drachm would be sufficient. I put the drug in a bottle, which I corked and sealed and sent back with the boy.' 'I think I better see your poison book for Mrs Wood's transaction.' Mr Garret again had cause to look uncomfortable. 'That was another thing. Sometime after I sent the strychnia to Glaisyer and Kemp, a boy brought me this note.' He produced another short letter that read:

Ship-Street, July 1871 – Sir, I would be much obliged if you would allow me the loan of the book wherein you register the poisonous drugs you sell. It is merely in furtherance to an inquiry I am making as to the sale of certain poisons, and bears no reference to anything you have sold, or any irregularity in selling, but only to aid me in my investigation. You will tie up your book and send it at once by the bearer; it shall be returned to you soon, as you may need it. Yours Truly D. Black, Borough Coroner.

'You sent it?' Gibbs enquired. 'Well, yes. It seemed in order and with all these odd things that have been happening I thought perhaps the coroner was making some quiet investigations. I had the book back within the hour.' Mr Garret hesitated. 'Only when I looked at it later it seemed some pages had been torn out.'

Gibbs wanted to see this for himself and examined the poison book. Indeed, some leaves were missing, apparently hastily torn out. However, they did not include the page that listed the sale of strychnine to Mrs Wood and it almost seemed a random destruction – unless the poisoner was trying to throw suspicion elsewhere. 'Is there anything else?' the inspector asked confiscating the letters and damaged book. 'I had one last letter from Glaisyer and Kemp. It was actually this that made me take a closer look at my poison book.' He produced the final letter:

Messrs. Glaisyer[29] and Kemp will be much obliged if Mr Garrett could supply then with 2ozs. of arsenic or 3ozs, if he can. So please send back directly. Their signatures will be sufficient.

'Only I didn't think the signatures were sufficient and I was starting to have my doubts that a chemist could be so neglectful of their stock supplies. So I made direct contact with Glaisyer and Kemp and they said they had never sent any notes to me at all.' Mr Garrett looked slightly sick at the thought that he had been fooled into sending poison to a possible murderer. Gibbs was merely fascinated by the ingenuity of his killer. The cunning and forethought placed into the obtaining of poison and masking the murderer's trail was impressive. He was dealing with someone with more than a modicum of intelligence and education. He decided his next stop would be to the accommodating Mrs Stone.

The term 'milliner' brings to mind neat little shops of hats and fabrics where a Victorian lady could waste several hours being measured and assisted by equally neatly dressed female dressmakers before making a commission for a new gown. In fact, the Mrs Stones of the Victorian world were a much more humble and simple trading class. Millinery was one of the few 'respectable' trades a woman could operate in the Victorian period, a step up from performing piecework like her sister lace-makers or spinners. The female milliner often operated from her own home and walked a perilous line between profitability and bankruptcy. Early twentieth century fictional character Miss Esther remarked, 'In those days [1860s] the milliners' shops wasn't the big, elegant affairs they are now. Instead they were usually one room in a little cottage that was home to the milliner too.'[30]

While men might operate large stores, women effectively ran home businesses, expecting their clients to pay for raw materials if not to purchase and bring material themselves. Mrs Stone was such a businesswoman. Her shop was situated at No. 90 North Street, an area that had rapidly gone from a poor-lit and unpaved outlying area to an important thoroughfare in the 1790s. Her shop was right next door to '...a pleasant little building of fifteenth-century French Gothic design with a charming oriel window and finely-carved foliated capitals to the columns flanking the entrance door'.[31] It had recently opened to serve as a poor school for girls founded by Rev. Henry Michell Wagner in 1867. Opposite Mrs Stone was Wykeham Terrace, a place that had a reputation as a home for 'female penitents', usually prostitutes. This had been founded by Rev. George Wager, nephew to Henry, who was viewed suspiciously by Brighton residents for his 'addiction to idolatrous "Romish" practices'. Local rumour had it that beneath Wykeham Terrace ran secret tunnels to link it with another of George's female penitents' homes in Queen's Square as both buildings backed on to each other.

Mrs Stone lived among this strange concoction of charity and criminality. Her situation made her unfortunate enough to become embroiled in more than one high profile Victorian criminal case. In 1863, the infamous Constance Kent who was suspected of murdering her young half-brother spent time at Wagner's homes and came into contact with Rev. Arthur Wagner, son of Henry, who had taken over the running of the establishment after the death of George. Arthur wielded considerable control over his inmates and particularly Constance, finally managing to make her confess to the crime. The case was a sensation that was remembered for decades after (and recently has drawn modern attention after the publication of *The Suspicions of Mr Whicher*). If it was not bad enough that Mrs Stone worked opposite a home for recovering prostitutes that was connected with the grim murderess Constance Kent, she now had the grave misfortune of discovering she had assisted another female killer.

Mrs Stone had been placed in an awkward position when a heavily-veiled lady entered her shop one day to buy a Shetland veil. She explained the need for two veils due to her terrible problems with neuralgia. (A condition caused by nerve damage that results in a sharp pain running along a nerve. Neuralgia can affect the back of the throat, but most Victorian 'neuralgia' sufferers used the term to refer to sharp pains behind the eyes, back of the head and neck. The pain does not require a trigger, but a common belief was that cold air could cause an attack, so Mrs Wood wore veils supposedly to prevent cold affecting her.)

Mrs Stone had no reason to doubt this confession on the part of her customer, especially as she was purchasing one of her more expensive items – Shetland veils being formed of knitted lace and often bought as Christening presents to be kept in the family for generations. When the lady explained she was trying to purchase some poison from Mr Garrett's chemist so that her husband and herself could stuff birds (taxidermy being a popular Victorian hobby) and required a witness, Mrs Stone felt obliged to assist her.

She followed Mrs Wood to the chemist shop and stood beside her as she signed, though she did not read the entry. Such casual witnesses were a common flaw of the poison book system and neither Inspector Gibbs or Mr Garrett would have been surprised that Mrs Stone was wholly ignorant of the person she was helping. The poison book was a deterrent, at best, designed to make a would-be poisoner think twice and at least provide some clue to a perpetrator if a crime was committed. However, it was an inadequate system that entirely failed to manage the sales of dangerous drugs.

Sometime later, the mysterious veiled creature came to Mrs Stone's shop again and purchased another veil. Expressing how in debt she was for the last favour the milliner had done for her, she begged to ask if she would assist again. Mrs Stone could hardly deny such a good customer and so witnessed a second murderous transaction. It was only after Mrs Stone was paid a visit by the police that she realised what she had done. And although she was a link in the chain, she was of little help in identifying the killer. She only knew the veiled woman as Mrs Wood and as Inspector Gibbs was soon to learn, there was no such woman living in Kingston being troubled by a gang of cats.

CHAPTER FIVE

Could it be a Coincidence?

June had come and gone in Brighton, the height of the summer season with day-trippers down from London was in full swing. The town was undergoing yet another revival as the last decades of the nineteenth century played out. While Queen Victoria had not proved a fan of Brighton, other royal family members still delighted in the seaside and it was commonly said that almost every famous person of the era had visited Brighton at least once. No one wanted to put off these lucrative visitors, nor the day-trippers who had been arriving by train since the 1840s, by rumours of murder.

Since the death of poor Sidney Barker there had been an absence of mysterious bags of chocolates appearing over the town. New visitors had arrived and, without knowledge of the death of a child, bought Maynards sweets and suffered no ill-effects. The Brighton population was all too eager to believe that the police had been wrong, that in fact there was no dreadful murderer lurking about and that the poisoning of the French creams had been an accident. Even when the six odd parcels appeared in August and a notice was printed in the papers, it was all too easy to believe these were unconnected – after all, these parcels had been sent to specific people and the chocolates had been randomly 'lost'. Besides, it was well known that arsenic could get mixed into flour by all manner of means and the parcels may have been unintentionally poisoned. Anyway, the parcels were laced with arsenic while the chocolates were full of strychnine.

No, it was all too circumstantial for the cynical minds of those who relied on the thriving Brighton tourist industry and who desperately wanted the commotion to die down so the season could run as usual. No one wanted to believe that a poisoner was at large: it would be bad for business.

Victorian newspapers were full of graphic stories of accidental poisonings caused sometimes by chance and sometimes by deliberate 'food adulteration'. It was far from a new practice. Since the dawn of the market trader, the butcher, baker and brewer, there had been unscrupulous individuals determined to force more profit out of their produce by introducing cheaper ingredients. Milk was watered down, expensive flour topped up with plaster dust or chalk and all manner of tricks were employed to improve the appearance of inferior food.

There was nothing new about the problem when the *Morning Chronicle* reported in 1820: 'Nothing is talked of – nay, nothing thought of – nay, nor dreamt of but the horrible mixtures of deleterious ingredients which inhuman bakers, brewers, druggists, grocers, oil-men, wine merchants, publicans and others impose upon us as wholesome articles of food, drink and medicine for our daily consumption! ... Woe to the unfortunate resident of London and Westminster, for he is apparently condemned to eat and drink perdition to himself, however simple and unsophisticated may be his diet!'[32]

While some substitutions were harmless enough, if rather unpalatable, others were downright hazardous. 'In large towns the goodness of bread is judged by its colour, and even the cheaper sorts are required to be very white. Now, unless the best flour is used, bread cannot be made of such a colour without using Alum; which bleaches the flour ...The quantity of this salt employed is comparatively small; but it is not withstanding, sufficient to cause constipation in the weak, either the very young or very old and to aggravate it when already existing.'[33]

Alum is a term for both a specific and a group of chemical compounds, which was well-known for its 'whitening' properties and thus often legitimately used in cosmetics. Today, it is mainly used as a pickling agent for fruit and vegetables or in commercial baking powders. The problem of Alum in bread was so widespread that the Sale of Food and Drugs Act 1875 specifically banned it. But there were other products that could slip into bread.

In 1844, Liverpool was up in arms to discover powdered Gypsum, a very soft mineral found in alabaster, was smuggled to a local miller from Carlisle and mixed with flour. The police were alerted and the miller fined ten pounds. The local paper was furious, one angered reporter stated: 'Gypsum is solid rock; it is altogether indigestible; and the deterioration of health and the destruction of life itself, must be the consequence of using it mixed in food!'[34] Unfortunately for the irate journalist who had listed his tirade under the title 'Death in the Loaf', Gypsum is harmless and is used today in soya-based Asian foods. But the point of the matter was not only how common food adulteration was, but the hysteria it evoked in the general public.

Beer was notorious for being mixed with various chemicals to improve its quality, usually by the publican who had watered it down and needed to mask his alterations. One drug used to give the beer a good 'head' was nux vomica, as mentioned in chapter one, a form of strychnine. With so many incidents of industrial poisoning caused by the introduction of cheaper or improving ingredients, no wonder it was hard for Brighton to believe that the Maynards case was nothing but an accident and the real blame should not lie on a fictitious murderer but on Mr Ware who had supplied the French creams.

Accidental poisoning was a frequent occurrence in Victorian Britain where the laws governing the sale of deadly substances were pathetically lax. A large part of this was due to the attitude of the British as they rebelled at acts or regulations that restricted the sale of chemicals and would have brought the country in line with European nations such as France. The Houses of Parliament were in uproar each time such a bill was suggested – surely the British did not need to be governed with such tyranny? Surely we were sensible enough to trade in poison without restriction? Common sense, cried the MPs, was what the French and other Europeans lacked. Perhaps *they* could not be trusted to take care of their own poisons, but the British were much different. *We* knew how to take care of ourselves and did not need government dictating to us. Echoes of the 'Nanny State' debate that has opened up in modern times can be seen here. The British have not changed greatly, even if we have finally had to cave-in to Health and Safety regulations. Throughout the nineteenth century, the debate raged about whether poisons should be regulated at all. The regular scare stories that featured in the papers started to have an impact and even MPs began to think that, no matter how careful, a person could accidentally poison themselves.

Unfortunate Mr Brooks, a lace-maker, was one such victim that the papers reported. Brooks was accustomed to taking peppermint water distilled by his wife to help settle his stomach after a night of drinking. Mrs Brooks kept the peppermint water as a sure remedy for preventing cholera. One morning in 1848, Mr Brooks reached out for the bottle of water and drank his usual dose. His first reaction was that the water was exceptionally cold. Mr Brooks was then violently sick. Mrs Brooks came rushing to her husband and the first thing she saw was the bottle he had drunk from. It was not one of the bottles she used for her pepper mint water, but a black bottle with poison written on it. 'Surely you have not been drinking the stuff Mrs Morris left to kill the bugs!' Mrs Brooks cried.

Her husband could hardly answer and she sent immediately for Mr Griffithes the surgeon. Richard Griffithes was quickly informed of the poison and knowing that the usual bug killing concoction contained corrosive sublimate, set about treating his patient for poison. He made him take milk, water and egg white, and decided that the amount of purging

Mr Brooks had done negated the need for a stomach pump and promised to visit again that evening. When he returned Mr Brooks seemed to be improving. He was warmer and his only complaints were 'of purging and cramps in the limbs'.[35]

Satisfied his patient was on the mend, Griffithes attended him only occasionally. On Monday, Brooks complained of stomach ache and Griffithes applied leeches which eased the pain. Brooks did not mention the nose bleed he had had on Saturday as it seemed a minor issue. On Tuesday morning, Brooks was downstairs helping his wife in the little shop she ran. Griffithes was pleased to see he seemed much improved and the surgeon was convinced his patient had survived his unfortunate encounter with bug poison. However, on Wednesday evening, Brooks suffered another bad nose bleed. A kindly neighbour offered him a home remedy of antimonial wine. (The wine was placed in a cup made of antimony for twenty-four hours, long enough for it to absorb some of the toxic chemical and gain an emetic or laxative quality. The remedy was popular in the seventeenth and eighteenth centuries. Captain James Cook even had his own antimonial cup.) The wine made Brooks vomit as it was meant to, but this did nothing for the nose bleed.

The next morning Griffithes arrived to find his patient in a stupor, as if in an apoplectic fit. He managed to rouse him with a dose of smelling salts long enough for Brooks to complain of a terrible headache before he sank back into his stupor and died shortly after. Death was recorded as being '... in consequence of drinking a poison used for bugs, in mistake for peppermint water'.

A more shocking case of error occurred in Carlisle in 1849 when thirteen-month-old Elizabeth Chapman was prescribed a medicine containing 'Dover's powder', an opium-based concoction. The prescription was taken to the chemist shop run by Mr Sowerby and was mixed by one of his apprentices, George Sim. George misread the prescription and put eight grains of Dover's powder into the medicine instead of the one-eighth of a grain it should have been (perhaps doctors' handwriting was as appalling then as it is commonly said to be now). Elizabeth overdosed on the medicine, though the following inquest deemed it a complete accident and acquitted both George and the doctor who had written the prescription (though it does seem rather unfair the doctor was accused at all).[36]

In an age when people grew and made most of their own food, the accidental addition of poison could be a natural process. In Scotland in 1856, local provost John Maciver held a private dinner party. Five guests at the dinner, including Maciver, became ill, starting with a parched mouth followed by vomiting. Only Maciver and one other guest, Mr Macdonald, survived the incident that was caused by a servant sent by the cook to fetch horseradish but who picked poisonous Monkshood instead. The deadly Monkshood formed the basis of a 'horseradish sauce' to serve at the dinner with beef and thus the five men were made ill.

What of the poisoned parcels? Was that so simple to explain? Certainly there was precedent for accidental, multiple illnesses being caused by innocently baked cakes. In 1848, Mrs Jones prepared a tea of light cakes for her three children and two stepchildren and a guest, another Mrs Jones of Cerrigengan. Not long after eating the cakes all seven of them began to feel ill. Mrs Jones of Cerrigengan made her excuses and headed home in severe pain and vomiting, leaving the family suffering in the house. For several hours the family had no idea what was wrong with them. Eventually, Mrs Jones, who was taken the worst by the illness, asked a servant to go fetch a doctor. Unfortunately, the only medical man at home was Mr Lloyd who himself was sick and after hearing the symptoms of the patients dispatched some routine remedies via his assistant Mr Kent Jones. It was apparent to Kent Jones that the routine medicines were going to do nothing for the ailing family. He returned the next morning to see their progress and was not surprised when Mrs Jones passed away. The rest of the family were sick for several days, but eventually all five children and neighbouring Mrs Jones recovered.

The next obvious question was what had caused the rapid death of Mrs Jones. An inquest was held and it was discovered that Mrs Jones had a quantity of arsenic in her stomach. Suspicion now fell on the light cakes and after examination these were found to contain sufficient arsenic to have killed the whole family. A terrible trail of misfortune and error now became apparent. A fortnight before the deaths, husbandman William Morris had been sent by Mrs Jones to get a pennyworth of arsenic to kill rats. Though the druggist impressed upon him that arsenic was a dreadful poison, there was nothing on the plain package to indicate its deadly nature and Morris took the parcel home without paying it much thought. Mrs Jones put the package away in a cupboard, alarmingly near her cooking supplies – but then, that was far from uncommon and few people bothered to keep their poisons separate from their food.

On the fateful night of the light cakes, Jane Jones, Mrs Jones' stepdaughter, saw her stepmother go the cupboard and take out a packet of what she thought was carbonate of soda to put in the cakes. It seems Mrs Jones believed the packet also contained baking soda and as arsenic came in the form of a fine white powder, it was easy for the fatal mistake to be made. The result of the mix-up had been the death of Mrs Jones. She had died in the same bed as her two sick daughters lay. They saw her breathe her last and admitted to the inquest it made them wonder when their time would come. Neither expected to survive.[37]

Yet another case of innocent arsenic ingestion happened at a party hosted by Isaac Lynn. To help his party flow, he served homemade wine produced by his wife two years previously. All the men were very ill and suspicion fell on the wine. Lynn eventually died and his distraught widow told the inquest she had stored the wine in bottles purchased from a sale. She had cleaned them thoroughly with cinder dirt before using them and they seemed quite clean. The bottles were probably of dark glass or stoneware that made it difficult to see through them completely, so Mrs Lynn failed to notice the crusted white residue at the bottom. This proved to be arsenic. It seemed at some time previously the bottles had been used for storing a sheep dressing to prevent parasites affecting their fleeces. Arsenic was a major ingredient of such products. Mrs Lynn's efforts could not remove the last traces of arsenic from the bottle and she had unwittingly poisoned her husband and several friends. The coroner recorded the death as accidental, only adding one statement that perhaps this would serve as a warning to all those who bought second-hand wine bottles!

Accidental poisoning was so prevalent in the Victorian period that no year went by without several cases being reported in the papers. In 1870, just a year before the Brighton incidents, three people in Ireland were found dead after sharing a bottle of whisky that was supposed to have been accidentally contaminated by poison. Five-year-old Ellen Sparrow of Sudbury, Ipswich, fell ill with five other children, it was suspected they had eaten poisonous berries while playing. Ellen subsequently died. Mary Jane Jelbert of Truro, Cornwall, died after an accidental overdose of 'Tincture of Squills'. Her sister-in-law, who was hard of hearing, mistook the doctor's request that she have his 'Tincture of Squills' bottle refilled so he could make Mrs Jelbert's medicine, as actually meaning she should fill the bottle and take it home to poor Mary Jane. All three cases were widely reported by the press, but no doubt there were many more that failed to be recorded.

Arsenic was the bane of the Victorian age: it literally contaminated the population. Regulating its sale to private persons was merely the tip of a very large iceberg. Arsenic was widely used in industry and in certain situations such as the refining of metals and electroplating, the deadly and innocuous arsine gas was given off and killed many workers. Farm workers died when they came into contact with arsenical sheep dip or mixtures for soaking grain to prevent disease and pest problems. Chemists worked with the substance on a daily basis, often buying in arsenic by the barrel-load. They not only risked themselves but their customers by accidently giving out the powder as in the unfortunate peppermints case. An unwitting apprentice mistook arsenic for plaster of Paris, which the unscrupulous sweet-maker wanted to use to replace expensive sugar in his confectionary.

Within the home, people were in danger from accidental ingestion, not just from contamination of food but from other products. In the second half of the nineteenth century, Arsenical Green, a vibrant dye, came on the market to replace the natural green dyes that had previously been used. It found favour with designers such as William Morris for its rich tone and it quickly appeared in wallpaper, stained book covers and even in clothing. In higher-end products, the dye was securely sealed, but in cheaper reproductions the arsenic could flake off as a dust or the dye would leak onto exposed skin and slowly poison a person. Most hideous was the deliberate use of Arsenical Green to stain food products such as cake icing. It was such a common practice that even when a person was killed by dyed food their death was deemed accidental. Then, of course, there were the poor souls who had to make, pack or transport the product. Arsenic had to come from somewhere, usually a by-product of other industries, and the exposure levels of those working with it was horrendous.

Strychnine was less high-profile as it had fewer widespread uses, though as has been seen it appeared in products created by the unscrupulous. It tended to be more for industrial purposes and less commonly found about the home. Though, as Gibbs' murderess had informed Mrs Stone, it did have its role in Victorian life. Taxidermy had found popularity through the interest in natural sciences and some Victorians had taken to stuffing animals at home as a hobby. When Mrs Wood gave this reason for wanting to obtain strychnine, it would have seemed quite usual to Mrs Stone. No wonder then that the Brighton population, who only had a restricted knowledge of the facts of the case, were inclined to think the poisonings were purely accidental.

To Inspector Gibbs, this told him something more sinister. It seemed his killer had attempted to make the poisonings *appear* accidental, which meant he was dealing with a very clever and cunning person: someone who had taken note of the regular news reports of accidental poisoning and decided to use it to their advantage. He was not looking for a killer motivated by a sudden explosion of passion, but someone who was cold and calculating, prepared to bide their time and poison innocents to cover their real motive.

He had to find this intelligent murderess before she struck again, but to do that he needed to hone his evidence and find out who was the key to this crime.

CHAPTER SIX

The Chemist's Art

The heart of a poisoning case was always the evidence a reliable chemist could provide on the substance used, its quantity and how it entered the victim – speculation on whether the poisoning was accidental or deliberate could then commence. However, chemists were still a mixture of professionals and amateurs. While steps had been made to regulate the chemistry trade, effectively turning the apprentice apothecary into a trained pharmacist, there was still a long way to go before all chemists could be deemed reliable for the analysis of evidence.

The majority of Victorian police did not have access to specific labs or specialists. They had to rely on whatever 'experts' they could find in their local area or, if worst came to the worst, material had to be sent to a known expert in London. Experts in the field of poison could range from dispensers in the local hospital and high-street pharmacists to trained toxicologists. Also hampering the police was the general public's lack of confidence in them. Local police forces were still a relatively new phenomenon in the 1870s and older members of Brighton would remember a time when there was no such thing. Therefore, people were inclined to take matters into their own hands. So when Mrs Boys saved one of the poisoned cakes sent to her, she only gave half to Inspector Gibbs and took the remainder for private analysis. Such was the level of faith people placed in the local police force.

Before Gibbs had even received his own results, a number of other chemists had been testing portions of poisoned food on behalf of the parcel victims, making the list of experts that had to be called in the case both extensive and diverse. Gibbs relied on established London experts Professor Rodgers (toxicologist) and Professor Letheby (chemist) while the victims of the poisonings favoured Mr Glaisyer – the same Glaisyer whose name had been forged for accepting poisons and who was given a portion of a tartlet by Mrs Boys – and Mr W. H. Smith[38], hospital dispenser and pharmaceutical chemist who was handed a sample by surgeon Mr Blaker. All four would add their own testimony to the case, though their backgrounds and experience were remarkably different.

The biggest issue all these chemists faced was testing for poison in a reliable and foolproof manner. Prior to the revelations of chemistry in the nineteenth century, tests for poison had been woefully inadequate and unscientific. A large part of this was due to the misunderstanding of how chemicals affected the body. While it had been known for centuries that purging a person after taking poison was a possible saviour, very little else was certain as can be seen in the case of poor Mr Brooks whose doctor could offer him no better than digestive remedies.

The revolution in chemistry and toxicology had been slow in coming, though early pioneers had been endeavouring with their own experiments (some decidedly morbid). The 1850s saw the tide turning and by the 1870s, chemists now found themselves with an arsenal of methods for proving death by poison. But just like the new police force, this new science was greeted by the general public as dubious. Could this strange new science be counted on? Was a chemical reaction enough to sentence a person to death for murder?

Tests for poison prior to the chemistry revolution had been, to the Georgian and Victorian mind, satisfyingly visual and understandable. First steps would be to assess a victim's symptoms: did they exhibit the typical appearance of being affected by a certain poison? Interestingly, even the symptoms of poisoning had been misunderstood. There were many myths pervading about arsenic including that it provided a painless, quick death. Such a story made it a choice for would-be suicides who found their deaths neither guaranteed or pleasant.

Scientists realised that to be able to prove poison, first its effects on the body had to be understood. In 1813, Catalan Mathieu Orfila (1787-1853) published a landmark book on poisons, *Traites des Poisons*. This was the first time a study of the symptoms and mechanisms of poison, along with their detection and possible treatment, had been published. It was revolutionary and Orfila has been heralded as the father of modern toxicology. By the 1840s, he was known as an authority on arsenic, especially in the instance of murder and was influential in the famous Marie LaFarge case in proving she had poisoned her husband. Orfila had become an expert on arsenic due to his gruesome experiments on animals, particularly dogs, which enabled him to study the way the mineral affected the body. While his studies led to more and more poisoners being caught, the great suffering he inflicted on thousands of animals is appalling to modern readers (and probably would have caused some nineteenth century minds to reel). Yet his methods were quite standard. When another famous physician, Marshal Hall (1790-1857), wanted to learn about the effects of strychnine, he experimented on a range of animals, particularly frogs, who were highly susceptible to the toxin. He did, however, create strict guidelines for limiting suffering in his subjects.

Animals served another purpose as test subjects: they could become witnesses to a murder. Without chemical tests, early criminal trials had to rely on more basic methods, which usually involved feeding an animal (or animals) either a sample of suspected food or drink or causing them to ingest the stomach contents of a victim. The animal was then observed to see if it died and if its sufferings were akin to the poison suspected. While these trials were crude, they did have a certain appeal to the Victorian mind. They were obvious for a start. If an animal ate a dose of poisoned bread and then perished, what further proof could you need? The animal bodies could be produced to a court and virtually everyone understood how household poisons dealt with such creatures.

In 1856, the *Hampshire Advertiser* and *Salisbury Guardian* reported that the recent death of Mrs Dove in Leeds had been discovered to be caused by strychnia after two surgeons fed material from her stomach to two rabbits, two mice and a guinea pig. To provide a control, they also poisoned five other small animals with normal strychnia.[39] Of course, surgeons were not chemists and in less than twenty years it would not be expected that they would conduct experiments themselves. Instead, professional chemists were emerging who could use scientific tests to prove poison. Unfortunately for the general public, these tests were a specialist art and therefore difficult to understand, which instantly aroused suspicion.

'I cannot conceive an opinion more dangerous to public safety than that a fatal dose of poison can be so nicely adjusted as to escape discovery after death,'[40] wrote Mr J. Rodgers, lecturer on chymistry (sic) at St George's Medical School in 1856. He was responding to a recent letter by one of his former colleagues on the subject of testing for strychnine, which had indicated that in certain cases the poison could be missed. Rodgers was appalled: '...of all known poisons...there is not one more readily detected in the tissues than strychnine'. It was a common misconception among the public that small doses of poison could be overlooked and the new breed of chemists could be fooled. Rodgers feared, perhaps justifiably in the wake of the 1850s poison hysteria, that if his learned colleague expressed his own concerns over the difficulty of testing for strychnine, poisoners would be more tempted to use it.

The problem was that for many decades poison had been difficult to discover and a good defence lawyer could tear apart the testimony of a surgeon or apothecary who had performed a test. After all, Mrs Dove's case rested on whether animals who ate her stomach contents appeared to die from strychnine poisoning and it was not the most infallible of methods. Rodgers, as a forerunner in chemistry at a time when it was still a very new and controversial subject, was determined to prove that no murderer could escape his methods. The main difficulty he faced was the theory that if the deceased had been dead and buried for some time the poison would become undetectable. Rodgers was so outraged that people failed to appreciate the powers of detection chemistry held, he felt the need to detail the full process of a typical test for strychnine.

> The tissues of the body are rubbed with distilled water in a mortar to a pulp, and then digested after the addition of a little hydrochloric acid, in an evaporating basin; then strained and evaporated to a dryness over a water bath; digest the residue in spirit filter, and again evaporate to dryness; treat with distilled water, acidulated with a few drops of hydrochloric acid, and filter; add excess of ammonia, and agitate in a tube with chloroform; the strychnine in an impure condition is entirely separated with the chloroform. This chloroform solution is to be carefully separated by a pipette, and poured into a small dish, and evaporated to dryness; the residue is moistened with concentrated sulphuric acid, and heated over a water bath for half an hour; water is then added, and excess of ammonia – again agitated by chloroform, and the strychnine will be again separated with the chloroform, now in a state of sufficient purity for testing, which can be done by evaporating a few drops on a piece of white porcelain, adding a drop of strong sulphuric acid, a minute crystal of bichromate of potash being added in the usual way.

It can be presumed that such a test would have been used on the poisoned Maynards' chocolates and Sidney's stomach contents to separate the strychnine for testing. The significant aspect of Rodgers' test was that it worked even when a person had been dead for some time. He had also experimented with tissues from a dog they had poisoned twelve months earlier and found the strychnine was still present. But as much as Rodgers lauded his tests, they built a barrier that had never before existed between the public viewing a criminal case and the experts testifying. The ordinary layperson's knowledge of chemistry was limited and the test would have seemed complicated and protracted. It was also a delicate matter and could not be performed easily by the inexperienced.

The more sophisticated chemistry became the more doubts were raised as to the competency of those who conducted tests and verdicts which should have seemed secure trembled on the basis that people were wary of trusting on the word alone of one man. By the 1870s, while chemistry experts were more accepted, they were not felt to be relied upon. Dramatic mistakes in previous criminal cases had upset the balance – the infallible science of chemistry was highly fallible. No wonder then that Mrs Boys and Mr Blaker hedged their bets and sought the advice of local chemists they knew well and trusted. They did not feel they could rely solely on the police experts.

Arsenic was by far the older poison compared to strychnine and had been used in murders for centuries, perhaps since its earliest discovery during the Bronze Age when it was added to bronze to make the alloy harder. Arsenic was viewed as 'untraceable' especially when given in small doses over a long period. The body was found to process and expel most of the mineral over the course of time making it harder to discover. The earliest tests for arsenical poisoning – based on Orfila's and other studies of the pathology of the mineral – was to conduct an autopsy and look for telltale signs. Inflammation of the gut and stomach was the obvious indicator as was a thick yellow coating to the stomach wall caused by hydrogen sulphide gas produced by putrefaction transforming any remaining arsenic into arsenic trisulphide. Gritty arsenical residue could also be sometimes found adhering to the mucous stomach lining. Arsenic is also a great preservative as it is toxic to the micro-organisms that cause decomposition. Suspected poisoning victims were often dug up months (even occasionally years) after death and found to be perfectly preserved. This was viewed as a clear sign of arsenical death.

The great problem with all this was that arsenic was unpredictable. It affected some people extremely badly while others were only mildly ill and it did not always preserve the body leading to inconclusive evidence. By the early 1800s, it was seen that there was a great need for a scientific approach to examining the tissues of the dead for arsenic. By the 1750s, chemical reactions were understood as a means of identifying minerals: these were known as colour tests. There were several that could be used on arsenic and often they had to be done in conjunction as material mixed with the poison would give a false result. They would not, however, work when arsenic was mixed with organic matter such as vomit.

Other early tests for arsenic were decidedly haphazard. In one trial, a Dr Addington found sediment in gruel fed to a man who later died of apparent poisoning. His evidence included that it was milky white, had no taste, did not dissolve in water and when placed onto a red hot iron gave off the small of garlic – classic signs of arsenic. He had also conducted colour tests, but so much of his evidence was purely subjective and too easy to dismiss. There was desperate need for something better.

That 'something better' came from disgruntled chemist James Marsh (1794-1846). Marsh had been called to testify at the trial of a young man accused of murdering his grandfather by lacing her coffee with arsenic. Marsh used the various colour tests in his analysis of the mineral in the coffee and proved it was arsenic, but the grandson could not be proved to be the killer (he did, however, later confess to the crime). Marsh found the trial an eye-opener, especially as to the difficulty in proving arsenic conclusively when it was mixed with other substances. The debatable nature of the colour tests let many poisoners escape from the hangman's noose, even when other evidence was compelling. Marsh began to develop a new, reliable test.

In 1836, he announced the Marsh Test that was hailed as both highly sensitive and irrefutable. It remained the standard test for arsenic poisoning (sometimes backed up by the simpler but less sensitive Reinsch Test invented by a German physician in the latter half of the nineteenth century) until the 1970s. When the various chemists tested their respective samples of cake and fruit from the Brighton parcels for arsenic they would have been using the Marsh Test. The Marsh Test was ideal for the Brighton case as it could extract and detect arsenic from other matter such as food or vomit, but did not rely on the examination of a dead body which would have been problematic as, fortunately, no one had died. Marsh based his test on the knowledge that arsenic readily combined with hydrogen to form arsine gas. Sulphuric or hydrochloric acid was added to the test sample followed by zinc which reacted with the acid to create hydrogen. Any arsenic present bonded with the hydrogen to produce arsine, which would then bubble out of the solution. By passing the gas through a glass tube and out a fine nozzle over a flame, the arsine would ignite and form a black film on a piece of glass held close to the nozzle.

The test was highly sensitive. In one extraordinary case it found arsenic in the body of a person that had been dead for over twenty-two years. But it did have its flaws, not least the dangers of inhaling arsine gas if the apparatus for the test was not correctly set up. While at first the test was lauded as being able to be reproduced in any household by anyone with a smidgeon of chemical knowledge, it quickly became apparent that it required an experienced hand. Still, it paved the way for capturing more and more poisoners, and while the arsenic epidemic was slow to disappear, fewer and fewer deaths by deliberate poisoning were being missed. For the murderer in Brighton in 1871 this would prove fundamental.

CHAPTER SEVEN

Poison is a
Woman's Weapon

Inspector Gibbs now had enough evidence to prove that someone had deliberately tried to poison Brighton residents. The tests performed by Professor Rodgers and Professor Letheby showed that arsenic had been added to the cakes and fruit in the parcels *after* they had been baked. There was no longer a possibility that this was a terrible accident. Not that Gibbs had really believed it could be. The suspicious appearance of poisoned chocolates about the town was enough to convince him of that, but now he also had the type of evidence he could produce in court. All he needed was a suspect.

His search was narrowed down to a woman of reasonable wealth to be deemed a 'lady' by many of his witnesses. The Victorians did not use the word lightly: it implied the murderess gave an impression of being of a certain social class. But that still left a plethora of potential local killers, not to mention the many transient visitors that passed through Brighton. The thought that someone may have come to the town merely to poison was awful, but Gibbs doubted that theory. He suspected his killer was a resident with a grudge.

Female murderers generated a great deal of debate and disillusionment among the Victorians. The nineteenth century view of womanhood was one of purity, spirituality and goodliness. The modern view of Victorian machismo was that women were deemed as the weaker sex. There is truth in that statement, but there was also a flipside. There was a great wave of thinking that women were in some ways superior to men because they were purer in thought and mind, and intrinsically more innocent. Because of their purity and their inherent belief in the goodness of mankind, women would be unduly shocked by news of savageries and gruesome tragedies. As such, ran the thinking, they should be shielded from the worst.

What today is considered chauvinistic had its basis in the popular stereotype of the Victorian woman being angelic in both her thinking and actions. Of course, this was the literary and philosophical view and how many of the general population truly believed it is debatable. While no doubt some men held to this concept, many ordinary folk knew that women were no precious flowers who would faint away at the slightest horror. The working-class woman had no time to be an ideal of innocence. She dealt with hardship, death and gruesome accidents or illnesses without a thought. It was the newly forming middle classes, those who could shield their daughters from the world and restrain them to the drawing room, who believed in this ideal and were the most stunned when life taught them otherwise.

Female killers deeply shocked the middle class. It went against everything they believed of womankind, especially when victims were children or the crime included elements of adultery. The Manning murder trial particularly stunned the Victorian sensibilities in 1849 and opened a new controversy over the female state of mind. Maria Manning had had an affair with Patrick O'Connor, but when she tired of him she embroiled her husband in a plot to do away with him. The trial twisted Victorian concepts on its head. Maria came across as a strong, defiant woman, while her husband slipped in and out of her shadow. At one time it was even suggested he was of so delicate a constitution that he had fainted when his wife took the fatal shot at O'Connor.

The public was stunned. Maria was so extraordinary to the imagination that she was painted as a modern Lady Macbeth by *The Times* and other papers. Even her defence counsel after the trial confessed he believed Maria had been the instigator of the murderous plot. Maria came across in court as a confident but cold woman who had complete control over her husband and manipulated Mr Manning into finishing off O'Connor with a crowbar when the bullet did not kill him instantly. She stunned the public and made many of the male fraternity feel quite uncomfortable while also holding their fascination.

But it could not last. By the time of her execution, excuses were being made to explain the motives behind this abnormal female who contorted and destroyed the Victorian ideal. Murder could only be '...the action of a whore, witch, monster or mad woman'.[41] No normal woman could ever contemplate murder. This was a typical Victorian double standard. Men could be justified in killing someone or have their actions explained away due to passion. They were rarely insinuated to be mad or intrinsically evil.

Edinburgh detective James McLevy (operating between the 1830s and 1860s) described the character of a female criminal as '...the mind of these creatures is so peculiarly formed that they make none of nature's signs [of emotion], and are utterly beyond our knowledge. That something goes on within, deep and far away from even conjecture, we cannot doubt; but it is something that never has been known, and never will be, because they themselves have no words and no symbols to tell what it is.'[42]

McLevy largely dealt with the impoverished lower classes of Edinburgh who he had some sympathy for (and even referred to the criminal element as his 'bairns'), but his words, though describing a woman at the bottom of the social scale, reflected the pervading feeling that female criminals were cold-hearted and unfeeling in comparison to the imaginary, ideal parlour belle who oozed warmth and unmasked emotion. Unfortunately for the moralists, by the middle of the nineteenth century events were turning the quaint Victorian ideal on its head. Sensation had become the byword of the age and the development of both better newspapers and the sensationalist novel with their reliance on murder, adultery and divorce to sell them meant it was no longer possible to believe in innocence of any sort.

Critics regularly railed against the sight of hundreds of women turning up to criminal trials with their opera glasses and sandwiches. Courtrooms could be crushed by women and executions until they were stopped from being a public spectacle. These women could not be written off as from the lower classes whose morals were suspect. They were refined ladies from the higher classes who were 'bored' and took to watching trials as entertainment. Male contemporaries were shocked by the sight: where had female innocence gone?

The creation of divorce courts in 1858 tipped the balance further. Usually only an outlet for the wealthier classes, it meant washing private dirty laundry very publically. The nation was gripped when a new divorce case emerged – what secrets would be aired? Men usually tried to obtain divorce by proving adultery on their wife's part and this invariably led to juicy sex scandals. Women would try to prove cruelty and often both parties would attempt to do as much verbal harm to each other as possible. Once again women hung on every word and were very public in their appearance, but the newspapers also had a field day and pulled few punches when reporting every little detail.

By the 1860s, the male concept of womanhood was under attack, both from the scandals of the century and the very earliest female campaigners – intrinsically brave women who confronted taboo subjects such as contraception and child prostitution. Even so, murder by a woman was a difficult notion to handle. The old stereotypes died hard, perhaps explaining why in cases such as Madeleine Smith in Edinburgh accused of poisoning her lover, jurors (all male) preferred to rule not guilty if they were convinced that the defendant's naivety about life had affected her situation. Innocence was relative: a woman may have killed, but perhaps she did not mean to or was thrust into a terrible situation by a male seducer. That was one area where women came up trumps. In any illicit romance, the man was deemed to be the wily seducer who had corrupted an innocent girl. When a woman was neither young nor pretty or showed a worldliness that undermined her 'innocence' in life, juries, judges and reporters fell back on the old notion that only a woman who was mad or wicked could commit such a crime. This concept appeared time and again in Victorian trials.

The Bruisyard case of 1835 reflected the nineteenth century controversy of female killers. It has so many parallels with the attempted murders in Brighton it could almost have been the inspiration for the crime. It also contained all the typical elements of a Victorian scandal: sex, violence and, ultimately, insanity. Early on the morning of the 21 April, widower Jane Wells received a parcel purportedly from her father. These were the early days of the postal service when recipients paid for the items delivered to them, not the sender. Jane, who was illiterate and far from well-off, asked the postman to read out the name on the parcel just to be certain it was for her before she paid a penny. It stated plainly: Abraham Watson, Thorpe to Jane Wells, Farnham.

Inside the parcel was a large cake and several smaller ones. Jane gave a pair of small cakes to each of her children and ate another herself, but something made her suspicious of the larger cake. Jane was not used to receiving gifts and it puzzled her where her father had obtained the large cake from. She had also been the recipient of another strange parcel of two bottles of drink, which she had turned away because she did not know the sender. She might have been less concerned had she not recently become embroiled in a love affair with a neighbour that had enraged another woman in the village.

Troubled by the parcel, Jane made the tiring journey to Saxmundham on foot to try and source where the cakes had come from (her father living in nearby Thorpe would most likely have bought them from Saxmundham). Traipsing around what passed for shops in the town – usually no more than people's front rooms – she eventually stumbled upon Mrs Mills who sold identical small cakes to the ones in the parcel. Mills remembered the transaction of several small cakes. It had occurred on the previous morning and she described her customer as a middle-aged woman wearing a light-coloured gown and a black bonnet with white lining. Mills had put the cakes into an open parcel the woman was carrying and then gave her directions to the post office.

Jane felt sick at the thought. Not only was this clearly not her father, but the description tallied with the woman who had become Jane's rival in the affections of a local farmer. Jane delivered half the suspect cake to the house of local surgeon Mr King and told his apprentice that she wished it tested for poison. It seemed an odd request, but the woman was sincere and quite worried. The cake was locked in a cupboard for the surgeon to view later. Unfortunately, the apprentice was a typical absent-minded youth who failed to tell Mr King about the cake. A week later, Jane returned to the house and delivered the other half of the cake directly to the surgeon insisting it be tested. The first portion was still locked in his cupboard – it was only fortunate no one had made the error of believing it was a gift and eaten it for both halves of the cake were laced with arsenic.

The only suspect was a woman in her forties named Elizabeth Gooch of Bruisyard near Saxmundham. Gooch was the sort of woman to have a 'reputation' in the little village of Bruisyard. She was an unmarried mother and her daughter Mary, who was sixteen in 1885, was the wife of William Jacobs. Gooch was poor, uneducated and, to a Victorian mind, immoral. She existed mostly on outside labour though she would do laundry on the side. Her life was one of hardship, derision and deprivation. She therefore felt that her fortunes had finally changed when Bruisyard labourer James Maltster asked her to be his housekeeper.

Maltster was in his thirties and was described as a farm labourer – though the title implies a station below that which he seemed to live as he was able to employ workers such as Gooch. Perhaps he was a skilled workman who earned slightly higher pay than typical workers. Within the small village community of Bruisyard, he would have known Gooch for most of his life. She had worked at Bruisyard Hall Farm, both outside and in the laundry, for the last nine years and Maltster had worked there too.

As a widower with two young children, Maltster had found it imperative to employ a woman who could serve both as housekeeper and nursemaid. Gooch would not be the first woman to serve this role nor would it take long for her to discover that her new job came with certain 'conditions'. Maltster expected his live-in housekeepers to share his bed in all senses of the word. Maltster's character seems to have had little to redeem itself. He was a womaniser who encouraged liaisons with his employees and then abandoned them when he grew bored. He preyed on vulnerable women, Gooch being a prime example. She was far from a beauty, her face weatherworn from years toiling outside and the deprivations of her life. She was around forty-five, considerably older than Maltster and already someone known to have a 'reputation' in the village. She was an easy target to be coaxed into Maltster's house and bed.

Gooch moved in on Michaelmas Day, the traditional time for the beginning and end of rural employment. She would have anticipated remaining in the Maltster household for the next year, a welcome relief from her toil in the fields. But it was not to be. Maltster grew tired of his new housekeeper after three or four months – this seems to have been his pattern. He complained of their arguments and the bad language she used. Gooch complained she was always kept short of housekeeping money and Maltster was starving his children as a consequence. Since later evidence indicates Maltster had very little conscience when it came to his own offspring this was probably true.

At the same time, Maltster had begun a relationship with the widow Jane Wells and made no secret that he spent many evenings with Jane. Gooch might have seen this situation coming from her past knowledge of Maltster, but she appears to have been completely beguiled by him and was devastated to be so betrayed. Who knows exactly what she had imagined would become of their relationship, but it certainly seems she expected it to be long term. Instead, she was left home alone to watch over Maltster's unloved children. Jane knew of Gooch and the others that had shared themselves with Maltster. It seems at the very least she was under no illusion about the man. She never married him and the 'friendship' seems to have been quite casual on both sides.

But Gooch was inconsolable at the seeming loss of Maltster and the roof over her head. The difficult situation had deteriorated rapidly. It appears Maltster was not used to his conquests being determined to stay after he had 'ditched' them and he could not get rid of Gooch. The arguments grew worse and Maltster's temper became volatile enough that Gooch asked her daughter, Mary, to stay with her in the house. The question of why she did not just leave is answered easily enough in that she probably had nowhere to go. Even so, inviting her daughter to stay and sleep in Maltster's bed was pushing things too far. Maltster burst into the room in the early hours of one morning and wrenched the bed clothes from the women. In the darkness, he grabbed Mary and threatened to throw her down the stairs. If she was killed, he declared, he would gladly hang for it. Thankfully, he realised he was not holding his housekeeper and the matter blew over as quickly as it had begun.

Maltster had failed to take into account the desperate nature of his late lover. Gooch, despite it all, did not want to give him up. She marched to Farnham and confronted Jane, but the visit only resulted in another row with Maltster. He had finally had enough, but he could not kick out Gooch – she just would not go! Therefore, he decided to leave the home. There was a scuffle on the doorstep as Gooch tried to stop him and his former housekeeper was left crying in hysterics in the road as he walked off. It would be logical to assume he went to Jane's house, but she later swore in court he did not stay with her. Of course, she would not have cared to soil her reputation by admitting she had shared a house with a single man. It says very little for Maltster's character that he left his children behind and expected Gooch to continue caring for them.

It was now that Gooch's misery became vindictive and she sent poisoned drink and the arsenic-laced cake to Jane Wells. She was cunning enough to disguise the sending of the poisoned parcels as being from a relative (echoes of Brighton and the cakes sent by a 'friend'), but as she was illiterate she had to involve two fellow labourers in addressing the parcel. Eventually there was so much circumstantial evidence as well as witnesses to her actions that Gooch was hauled before the magistrates and sent for trial at Bury St Edmunds.   But how could a woman described by co-workers as honest and trustworthy stoop to such actions as attempted murder? It baffled Victorian minds and so they fell back on the only solution that could ease their troubled thoughts – Elizabeth Gooch had to be insane. Her family knew this was potentially the only way to get her some leniency. Courts could be exceptionally hard on women who had fallen from the Victorian ideal.

Mary told stories of her mother raving after Maltster walked out and insisting that two men would come to take her away, men who were both dead. Gooch fainted in a fit in court and Mr King, surgeon of Saxmundham, assured the judge that this was due to a real illness caused by the 'excitement' of the trial and that she was not normally an epileptic. Surprisingly, the jury felt a lot of sympathy for Gooch. They clearly did not care for the conniving Maltster and tried their hardest to spare her from punishment. They played on the idea of insanity. It was a loophole in the law – an insane person could not be found guilty and had to be acquitted. However, when the jury realised they would affectively be setting Gooch free by judging her insane, they could not quite do it. In the end, they found her guilty but recommended mercy.

There was little of that in 1835. Gooch was sentenced to death by hanging. The judge, however, obeyed the jury and tried to be 'merciful' by commuting her sentence to transportation for life. This was little more than a drawn-out death sentence. Gooch, love lost and insane as she was, was placed on a ship bound for Australia never to see her daughter again. Who knows what became of her?

Nearly forty years later, the Brighton crimes would follow almost the exact same pattern, but their outcome would be quite different, reflecting a change in both the attitudes of the Victorians and the legal system.

Right: This map from 1865 illustrates Christiana Edmunds' immediate neighbourhood. West Street, where Maynard's stood, is shown coming off East Cliff and joining with North Street. Gloucester Place where Christiana lived is further up, almost in a direct line to the Pavilion and immediately opposite Grand Parade where Dr Beard lived. (*Courtesy of David Simkin, Sussex Photo History*)

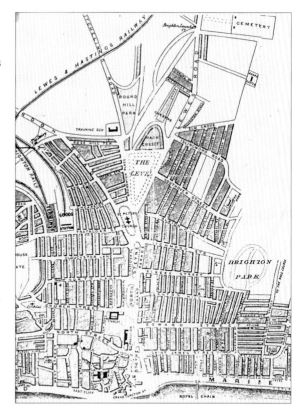

Below: This old image shows a portion of West Street where Maynard's shop stood and the Barkers had their holiday lodgings. West Street was a thriving commercial area, much as it is today. The image shows an unusual building labelled as 'The Telegraph' offices. This building, along with much of Victorian West Street, has vanished either as a result of redevelopment or air raids during the Second World War.

Left: This is one of the few contemporary portraits of Christiana Edmunds and gives a rare glimpse as to what she may have looked like. Of course, illustrators used a great deal of artistic licence when sketching criminals at trial, but from various descriptions of Christiana, this would seem a reasonably accurate illustration.

Below: The Royal Pavilion was a significant icon in Brighton. Christiana walked past the façade every time she ventured into North Street to buy poison. (*Courtesy of David Simkin, Sussex Photo History*)

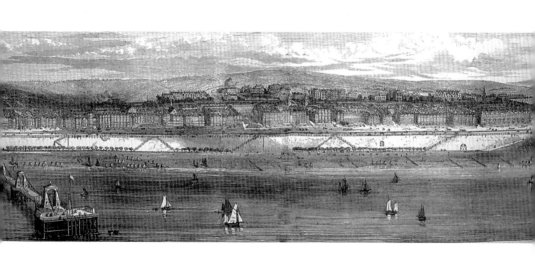

Above left and right: These two panoramic views of Brighton illustrate how the town would have looked at the time of Christiana's crimes. West Street is just visible as a wide road cutting through the centre of the old town in the print on the left. To the far right of this print is the Pavilion, its domes carefully illustrated. The view above depicts the old chain pier and the beach with its Victorian bathing machines.

Below: Brighton's population changed with the season and this could make policing extremely difficult. For Gibbs tracking criminals, he had to be aware that there were regular influxes of visitors who could cause trouble and then leave. Many of the 'visiting' criminals, especially prostitutes, congregated around the soldiers stationed near Brighton who were extremely popular as seen in this print.

This is North Street in 1870 looking up towards Bond Street. The large building on the right is Clarence Hotel. North Street was slightly more prestigious than West Street, yet it was an area of shops and business, thus the cobbled road was often filthy and the gutters clogged. Glaisyer and Kemp had their shop in North Street. (*Courtesy The James Grey Collection, The Regency Society*)

Another shot of North Street from 1870 with Clarence Hotel as its focal point. The hotel is advertising claret and port on its window, perhaps suggesting the kind of customer it was hoping to appeal to. The boys standing outside idly were a familiar sight in most towns and they were easy targets for Christiana when she needed someone to run errands. (*Courtesy The James Grey Collection, The Regency Society*)

Taking the waters was all part of a visit to Brighton and the Victorians would have rarely taken an excursion to the town without considering a dip in the waters. When the Barkers arrived in 1871, swimming would have been part of their agenda. Men and women would be expected to dress respectfully and use bathing machines to enter the water. Little Sidney Barker would have been considered young enough to venture in naked without offending anyone.

Grand Parade in 1873. The large house at the heart of the photo is Number 47. The Beard and Boys properties were slightly further along at 59 and 64. At this time, Grand Parade was still considered a very fashionable area to reside in, though some of the properties had been turned into lodging houses. Ironically, two doors down from the impressive No. 47 was another chemist's shop. (*Courtesy The James Grey Collection, The Regency Society*)

Ladies and gentlemen promenading along the front near the West Pier. It was this class of society Christiana had come from and which she believed she rightly belonged to even if her financial circumstances stated otherwise.

This is Lewes Road in 1869, just before the Kemp Town Railway was opened. Note the grand bridge bypassing the houses. The railway was extremely important to Brighton as it enabled daytrippers to visit the town along with holidaymakers from the upper working classes such as the Barkers. (*Courtesy The James Grey Collection, The Regency Society*)

The Pavilion gardens were open to the public and Christiana often walked in them. When Inspector Gibbs was trying to track her down, he found her in the gardens and tried to officially interview her there and then. (*Courtesy of David Simkin, Sussex Photo History*)

This image shows the typical assortment of people who wandered through the grounds of the Pavilion from the old woman to the respectable gentleman and the workman trying to take some rest. This was also an area for young boys to hang out as illustrated in this image and where Christiana could come into contact with her 'errand boys'. (*Courtesy of David Simkin, Sussex Photo History*)

This is King's Road in 1868, but what makes it interesting is the uniformed policeman standing by the railings. His police uniform is far from the usual image people have of a Victorian bobby. He is wearing a top hat as though he is in formal attire and his greatcoat hangs over normal trousers. It would be a policeman dressed like this that would have confronted Christiana when Inspector Gibbs went to arrest her. (*Courtesy The James Grey Collection, The Regency Society*)

Old Steine prior to 1872 showing numbers 33 and 34 which were lodging houses, similar to the Lion Mansion that the Izards owned and operated. To get to the front, it would have been convenient for Christiana to walk past these houses. Barely visible in the distance is the old chain pier. A billboard on the left advertises yet another chemist, making it clear how easy it was for Christiana to obtain her poison. (*Courtesy The James Grey Collection, The Regency Society*)

Taken just outside the Bedford Hotel, this shot of Brighton's front makes it look rather empty and deserted. Perhaps it was taken early in the morning? The horses and carriages were a familiar sight and carried ladies up and down the front. (*Courtesy The James Grey Collection, The Regency Society*)

This photograph from between 1868-1872 shows a busier scene of Brighton. The ladies are in typical Victorian attire and shielding themselves from the threat of sunshine by dark umbrellas. This is a scene Christiana could easily have fitted into. At the back is the Norfolk Hotel, yet another tourist hotspot. (*Courtesy The James Grey Collection, The Regency Society*)

Above left: Christiana considered Professor Letheby a rather frightening figure and was possibly one of the few people she was intimidated by. His knowledge of chemistry could unravel her lies and expose her crimes. Christiana had to face Letheby twice, once at the inquest into Sidney Barker's death and at her own trial.

Above right: Sergeant-at-law, William Ballantine, was to prove Christiana's arch nemesis at her trial. Not only did he have a sizeable amount of proof to seal his prosecution case, but he cast severe doubts on her defence of insanity. Ballantine never really considered Christiana insane, but he was not always right in his judgement. In the Tichborne Claimant case, he wrongly sided with the imposter at first.

The Royal Pavilion put Brighton on the map, but it also brought sex and the crimes that were associated with it. George IV had the Pavilion erected and patronised the town, but his wastrel ways, prolific love life and debauchery gave Brighton a certain reputation that was not easy to forget. Unsurprising that when Christiana's case came to trial, the papers pumped up the sex angle. It was after all a crime of passion! (*Courtesy The James Grey Collection, The Regency Society*)

Right: One of the earliest views of West Street taken around the 1850s. The image shows some of the shops at numbers 15-18. Maynard's was further up at numbers 39, 40 and 41. St Paul's Church, in the centre, is one of many churches that were constructed during the Victorian period. It is shown here with a timber roof. (*Courtesy The James Grey Collection, The Regency Society*)

Below: Brighton beach in the 1870s. The yachts were a popular part of life in the town, along with the rowboats and fishermen's boats. Note also the wooden kiosks at the back, which would be used by people to tout anything from seaside souvenirs to boat trips. (*Courtesy The James Grey Collection, The Regency Society*)

Above left: It is shocking to us today how Christiana callously targeted children in her poisoning spree. Aside from the offspring of the Beards and Boys, Christiana chose working-class children to test her chocolates on. It is possible one of the children in this picture taken between 1868-72 was one of her victims. Certainly, they would have all been told the story and warned about poisoned chocolates. (*Courtesy The James Grey Collection, The Regency Society*)

Above right: While Christiana placed herself in the middle class of society, much of her story revolved around the lower classes, such as the men in this picture. People she would have deemed beneath her and perhaps that was why she targeted them. (*Courtesy The James Grey Collection, The Regency Society*)

This would have been an utterly familiar sight to Christiana. In the distance is the chain pier and on the beach bathing huts are being pushed into the water to start the day for the daring swimmers. There are already some brave souls, apparently male, swimming in the water. (*Courtesy The James Grey Collection, The Regency Society*)

Another image of the chain pier showing how boats could be launched from it. Christiana's grandfather had fallen into trouble when he had supervised the construction of a pier in Margate that was badly damaged by storms. Piers regularly fell afoul of aggressive coastal weather. The chain pier is yet another that has vanished. (*Courtesy The James Grey Collection, The Regency Society*)

West Street was constantly undergoing change. When the Edmunds moved to Brighton in the 1860s, this was how West Street would have looked. Yet only a few years later, houses had been demolished, including the one at the centre of this picture. Brighton was an area of considerable change and expansion throughout the years the Edmunds lived there. (*Courtesy The James Grey Collection, The Regency Society*)

Left: Another shot of West Street from 1870. St Paul's is shown with a strange cap as the steeple proposed for it was considered too heavy and might collapse. Christiana's father, so renowned for his church building, would have been appalled. (*Courtesy The James Grey Collection, The Regency Society*)

Below: The Pavilion gardens in the 1870s was a popular spot for people to walk and meet. (*Courtesy The James Grey Collection, The Regency Society*)

Below right: For a number of years this was the location of Glaisyer and Kemp, perhaps the biggest chemist in Brighton. Christiana implicated them in her crimes, sending false letters in their name. This did not affect their standing in the town and they are still operating, albeit in a different location to this day.

Above left: John Humffreys Parry was acting in Christiana's defence at her trial and from the outset he knew he had a tricky case. The evidence was stacked against her and his only hope was to plead that she was insane. Ultimately, it appears Parry was acutely aware of his client's guilt. Also, he was facing Ballantine who had successfully defeated him in other criminal trials, particularly that of Franz Muller, known as the first railway murderer.

Above right: William Edmunds was influential in designing a number of properties in Margate, including the elegant and rather Grecian-looking headquarters for the Margate Pier and Harbour Company. His associations with the company, which secured him a number of prestigious contracts, were too close for comfort and he was dragged into a financial scandal. (*Courtesy Wikimedia Richard Gadsby*)

Above: This engraving from the 1860s clearly shows the close proximity of Christiana Edmunds and Dr Beard. The dot on the left marks Gloucester Place while the dot on the right marks the rough location of Dr Beard's house. (*Courtesy of David Simkin, Sussex Photo History*)

Left: Old Steine, as its name suggests, is one of the older parts of Brighton. It looks onto the Pavilion and then leads off into Grand Parade and Gloucester Place. The Beards were intimately connected with the Steine as the Izards, Emily Beards' parents, owned Lion Mansion, which was situated at numbers 36, 37 and 38. George Tatham, appointed Justice of the Peace in 1870 and yet another of Christiana's victims, also lived in Old Steine.

CHAPTER EIGHT

The Secret Love Affair

Inspector Gibbs had his theories on why people committed murder. Money was, of course, a common motive, especially when the wealthy were involved and poisoning, with its penchant for mimicking normal sickness, was a popular weapon for such crimes. Desperation was another option – the desperation of a destitute mother with too many mouths to feed. But he was not dealing with infanticide, aside from Sidney Barker, but that had been pure bad luck – the boy was not purposely targeted. Gibbs could also not see money as a motive: the poisonings were too wide and diverse and he would have expected a clear victim by now. Instead, he favoured the idea that he was dealing with a crime of passion. This was either revenge or love. What he was not expecting was for it to be both.

What he needed was a motive, but the random finds of Maynards chocolates had little logic to them, though the killer had been extremely blatant at times and at least he had a number of witnesses. He was certain the key to the matter were the parcels. They had a purpose, they had intended targets. So it was back to the drawing rooms and parlours of the victims, all notable individuals compared to the poorer classes who were the victims of the strychnine-laced chocolate. Some could therefore argue that this meant the two spates of crimes were not linked, but Gibbs thought different. Something about these six parcel victims was important. They had been chosen for a specific reason and he was convinced he was not dealing with two separate, crazed poisoners.

Initial talks with Mrs Boys, Magistrate Tatham, Mr Curtis and Mr Garrett had failed to indicate a likely culprit. None could pinpoint a particular suspect and they were mystified as to why someone would try to poison them. Tatham and Curtis could argue it was someone they had offended, either by incarcerating them or writing something scandalous, but Mrs Boys and Mr Garrett were the sort of people who lived lives without attracting enemies. They were a dead-end, but Mrs Beard was another matter. Mrs Beard was ready to point a finger at the woman she suspected.

Emily Izard had been thirty-two when she married the dashing and intelligent Charles Izard Beard in 1860 and moved with him to Brighton. Charles was a graduate of Trinity College, Cambridge, and St Barts Hospital, obtaining his BA (Bachelor of Arts) in 1852, his MB (Bachelor of Medicine) in 1855, his ML (medical licence) in 1857 and becoming a Member of the Royal College of Practitioners by 1859. Beard had worked hard all his life and certainly did not intend to stop now he had earned his qualifications. Despite his private practice in Brighton, he spent a great deal of time travelling back and forth to London and eventually managed to become the Government Inspector of Vaccination in the Midlands and West Riding areas. This effectively meant Emily spent a great deal of time by herself in the big house on Grand Parade.

Despite their time apart, they had managed to have five children. Hugh Spencer was the oldest born at the end of 1861. Arthur was born 1863, Emily Elizabeth in 1866, Frank 1868 and Edith Mary in 1869. By 1871, the house was full of children (although Hugh had been sent away to school) and the attendant servants they required. Emily also had the dubious company of Mrs Harriett Richardson, a lady of eighty-seven who was a patient of Dr Beard's and now boarded with the family as her mental condition had deteriorated. She spent a great deal of time in Emily's presence and could have been a witness to the attempted poisonings except her mind was wandering and she was deemed 'unreliable'. In 1871, she could not even remember where she had been born.

When Gibbs spoke to Emily Beard in 1871, she was a settled, upper middle-class woman with a family and a prosperous and respected husband, but her life had not always been so easy. Born in 1828 to William and Rhoda Izard, she had been the only daughter in a family of four boys: Charles, Percy, Arthur and Walter. William had started his family late in life. He was thirty-seven when Emily, the oldest child, was born. His wife, Rhoda, was six or seven years his junior, so she too could be classed, by Victorian standards, as starting her childbearing late in life.

William was a lodging house proprietor, a rather loose term that could refer to a range of social classes and people. William was at the upper end of the scale, having made his money from renting property and being classed as a 'gentleman' by the 1850s. Rhoda had two servants to assist in the house and all the boys were well educated. It is possible William is the same 'William Izard' who fitted out the interior of St Albans House in 1828. This luxurious residence (later to become a hotel) was built in Regency

Square at Brighton's height for the Duke and Duchess of St Albans. In any case, William was a respectable man who had enough money to keep his large family very comfortable.

All this was to change in the 1850s when Brighton's star briefly dimmed. In 1856, a sad notice appeared announcing that William Izard was to be declared bankrupt as of 23 February. Among the three men assigned to dispose of his property and pay his creditors with the proceeds was twenty-nine-year-old Charles Izard Beard, still currently studying at Trinity College, Cambridge (another of the three men, William Langworthy, would later also be a neighbour of the Beards in Grand Parade).

William's fortunes had faltered in line with a decline in Brighton's popularity. Ironically, he had only recently returned to the town after a brief episode as a house proprietor in Woodmancote, Sussex. At the time, Brighton was suffering from a lack of royal support. Throughout its history, Brighton's success had risen and fallen with both the patronage and popularity of the reigning monarch. It had all begun with the Prince of Wales, later George IV, who made his mark on Brighton early on and earned it a reputation as both a fashionable hotspot and a licentious bed of indiscretion. The most famous Brighton building, the Royal Pavilion, was commissioned by George IV and later used by his successor William IV. Whether the population loved or loathed him, there was no denying that the prince's presence attracted an entourage of courtly tourists who spent money in the town – not least by renting property during the 'season'. For Brighton businessmen, like William Izard, the prince's endorsement ensured them trade.

This continued, if slightly more quietly, during the reign of William and Anne, but Victoria's arrival on the throne in 1837 spelled a downturn in the seaside resort's fortunes. Initially, it seemed the new queen would be another avid supporter of Brighton. Her first visit to the Royal Pavilion in 1838 was greeted with immense festivities on a scale George IV would have appreciated. Roast beef and plum pudding was provided for 2,000 local children as part of the event. Despite this, Victoria was uncertain about the Pavilion, though by her second day she seemed charmed by its quaintness and the 'peep of sea' from the windows. However, she did not return to the town again until 1842, by which point she was married and less inclined to be 'charmed' by the town.

For the next few years Victoria suffered Brighton, but the appeal it held for her predecessors eluded her. She bemoaned the lack of privacy within the Pavilion, which was terribly overlooked by new houses on the Steine and the crowds of tourists who would follow her continuously whenever she journeyed about the roads. They were termed by the magazine *Punch* as 'unmannerly curs' and 'ill-bred dogs'. In the end, Victoria fled the teeming streets of Brighton for the seclusion of Balmoral in 1845 and did not return for twenty years.

At first the loss of a royal patron did not drastically affect the town. Older members of the nobility were too set in their ways to change their minds about Brighton, but slowly the effects of losing the fashionable 'hangers-on' that followed the queen were felt. Building projects slowed down and businesses began to feel the pinch. The Pavilion was expected to be demolished signalling once and for all that the queen was not coming back. The local people were heartbroken and a campaign was mounted to save it. By 1850, the Pavilion was public property, but that could not entirely redeem the town's diminishing popularity. There was a low period between the loss of the queen and her wealthy followers and the arrival of the new tourists and day-trippers that would appear with the establishment of the railways. In this period many faltered and William Izard was among them. He had returned to Brighton at just the wrong moment and the records of 1856 prove his mistake.

Fortunately, the family did not falter for long. Perhaps Charles was able to help out the Izards or William had money ferreted away for by 1861 he was once again a 'housing proprietor', this time owning the Lion Mansion situated at numbers 36, 37 and 38 Old Steine, just off Grand Parade. By the time of the poisonings, he had retired from business, but resided at what was now called Lion Lodge with Rhoda, three servants and his son George.

Emily's past was therefore intrinsically linked with her husband's. The Beards and the Izards were related: Charles' mother, Elizabeth Izard, was the sister of William Izard. Elizabeth married William Day Beard in 1820 a few months after her father died. She had known her husband for at least three years, but her father had disapproved of the union and prevented the wedding. So adamant was he that Elizabeth should not marry William Beard he wrote in his will of 1817: 'Residue to son and daughter [Elizabeth and William Izard] equally except that should his daughter marry, against his will, with William Beard, then she is to be paid £50 a quarter for life and if she should die without issue the said money should come back to the son.'[43]

Whatever reason caused the intense dislike between the Beards and the Izards, it was strong enough for Elizabeth's father to threaten to disinherit her should she dare to marry William Day Beard. It was clearly not enough to prevent her, however, though the union failed to have a happy ending. Barely a decade after the marriage, William Day Beard was dead in 1831 and his wife followed him a year later aged only thirty-four. They left behind five children including Charles Izard Beard. Despite their father's antagonism, William Izard had never fallen out with his sister Elizabeth and he took on the responsibility for her large family. From then on, Charles grew up in the same household as his cousin Emily.

William Izard appears to have been rather sentimental. He was fond of giving surnames to his children as middle names to remember distant branches of the family. His son was named William Chantler Izard (or Chandler), the maiden name of his grandmother. Even more confusingly, William Izard's son Charles was called Charles Beard Izard in remembrance of his sister's marriage. Perhaps it was these same sentimental feelings that had William contemplating the eventual marriage of his daughter Emily and nephew Charles. Their marriage appears to have been on the cards for a long time. However, this raises an even more interesting theory about the Beard/Izard relationship.

Inspector Gibbs could not miss the tension in the house at 64 Grand Parade, which went beyond the attempted poisonings. There was a secret problem within the household that had driven Emily into an accusatory fury. He had enough experience as a policeman to recognise a marriage that was on the verge of disintegrating.

Emily and Charles married on 26 June 1860. Almost immediately, Charles left England as a British volunteer to help Garibaldi in Italy. Garibaldi was a general, politician and patriot who helped to unify Italy with the support of Britain and America via a series of military campaigns. In April 1860, Garibaldi gathered around a thousand volunteers and marched on Sicily, taking it and declaring himself dictator there in May. The British Navy was heavily involved in his subsequent march north to Naples where he arrived in the capital city by train on 7 September. Despite the Italian public being behind him, Garibaldi had yet to defeat his enemy, the Neapolitan army, and a decisive battle would occur on 30 September.

Meanwhile, the British population were quietly cheering on the good general and an idea was raised that British volunteers should go over to help. On 31 July, *The Times* reported that a steam yacht had been bought by agents of Garibaldi for £8,000 to transport volunteers to Genoa. On 18 September, twelve days before the battle against the Neapolitans, another ship left Brighton full of volunteers to the cheers of the watching crowd. The papers at the time referred to them as 'excursionists', a term more commonly used to denote holidaymakers, which perhaps summed up the attitude of the population to the departure. It has to be wondered if they even managed to find Garibaldi in time for the battle.

Charles Beard would have been somewhere among them, either on the excursionists' ship or on the earlier steamer. In any event, he had abandoned his new wife with alarming alacrity for an adventure he was hardly prepared for. Charles had no military knowledge and, at thirty-two, would have been older than many of the recruits. He would have been surrounded by young, excited men looking for a taste of action and older war veterans looking for a final stab at glory. The young doctor would have found it awkward to fit in among these disparate groups and besides, by the time the volunteers were leaving, Garibaldi was already sitting in Naples. The atmosphere of the leaving party suggest the groups did not expect any serious fighting.

In any respect, it did not auger a happy start to the Beard marriage. Within two months of her wedding, Emily was alone in her house on Grand Parade, a pattern that would repeat itself throughout her relationship with Charles. Even at the time of her receipt of the poisoned parcel, Charles was not at home. He was visiting London reputedly on business, though the exact nature of this was never explained and he seemed rather content to neglect his private practice patients, along with his wife, for whatever allure attracted him to London. The Medical Directory of 1860 was not even sure where he lived, listing him as No. 76 Grand Parade. In fact, it was the home of a wealthy elderly woman.

The marriage was one of convenience rather than genuine affection and William's interfering hand can almost be seen in the background. Did Charles marry Emily to reunite the warring families and secure the joint Beard/Izard fortunes? Certainly, he appeared rather unattached to his wife and Emily was clearly not convinced that her husband was the picture of fidelity. She had started to open letters addressed to him while he was away – not only a breach of privacy but a clear sign of suspicion. She had found her answer in the letters. They were from a woman. Worse, they were from a friend who had spent time with Emily. When Inspector Gibbs asked her about who could have reason to harm her, she did not hesitate to point an accusing finger: Miss Christiana Edmunds.

Gibbs recognised the name as one of the other victims of the poisoned parcels. 'Why would you accuse her? She received a parcel too.' 'Because of what happened September last. We had been quite intimate with the Edmunds up until that point. Miss Edmunds and her mother were patients of my husband. We had known them perhaps five or six years and Miss Edmunds was a regular visitor. I was sitting in the drawing room with Miss Richardson when Christiana arrived that day. She had brought chocolates from Maynards and said they were for the children, but she knew full well that the children would already be in bed. She insisted on putting a chocolate into my mouth to taste. I was quite appalled at her forwardness.' Emily was still outraged by the incident. 'It was very unpleasant: it had a cold, metallic taste. I left the room and spat it out, but afterwards I suffered some very unpleasant effects from it. Saliva ran from my mouth the whole night and the next day I was attacked with diarrhoea.'

Gibbs could only nod along. The symptoms had a nasty ring of poison to them. 'You believe you were deliberately poisoned? Could it not have been an accident?' 'That is what Miss Edmunds said,' Emily admitted. 'I did not speak to her immediately, nor my husband, I was so uncertain about it all. But Miss Richardson ate the same chocolates and experienced no harm, only the chocolate I was *forced* to eat by Miss Edmunds was bad. When I did eventually tell my husband he cut off all relations with the Edmunds.' That caught Gibbs' attention. 'He was quick to assume her guilt then? Perhaps he had other reasons?' Emily looked sour. 'You would need to ask him about that.'

Dr Beard had returned to Brighton to learn that another attempt had been made on his wife and children's lives. He was a deeply troubled man when Gibbs went to talk with him, not least because he felt a burden of guilt in the case. A man full of secrets, he was more interested in preserving his reputation than rooting out the person who had tried to poison his family. 'Mrs Beard has been informing me about her suspicions concerning Miss Christiana Edmunds.' Inspector Gibbs informed the doctor, 'She says you were intimate with the Edmunds.' 'Yes, she was a patient.' Beard looked uncomfortable. 'Anything more than a patient?' 'There was nothing but friendship between us,' Beard answered hotly. 'If the lady viewed our professional relationship a little more seriously than I did, that was not my fault. Spinsters have a tendency to become infatuated with their doctors. It's natural.' 'Is it? How did you know she was infatuated?' Beard sighed, recognising his stumble. 'I received many letters from her, but my wife was intimate with Miss Edmunds and her mother, so it seemed no harm.' 'Until September last... What happened then?' 'My wife told me about the actions of Miss Edmunds,' Beard admitted reluctantly. 'And you were inclined to believe that the incident was not an accident?' 'No... I... Miss Edmunds struck me as the sort of woman who could do such a mischief and my wife was insistent I handle the matter. Sometime between 22 September and 2 October I spoke to Miss Edmunds. I alluded to the poisoning and spoke of the illness of my wife after Miss Edmunds had put the cream into her mouth. At the same time I spoke of the great use which had lately been made of the spectroscope in discovering poisons in animal tissue. I thought it might deter her from any future attempts.'

'You feared future attempts?' Beard hesitated. 'No, not as such. Anyway, Miss Edmunds denied any intention of doing mischief and said that she herself had been very ill in consequence of eating chocolates.' 'So the intimacy ceased?' 'On my part, at least.' Beard was looking more and more troubled. 'Miss Edmunds did not want our friendship to end. I was away from Brighton at the start of this year, but when I returned she told me she wished to return to the same terms of intimacy as before. But I refused as I could not help thinking she had attempted to poison my wife. When I told

Miss Edmunds this she was very indignant and the next day she and her mother called upon me to expostulate. They were very upset that I should accuse Miss Edmunds so. I put the matter off as practically I could prove nothing. My wife was put fully on her guard, but I proceeded no further as I had no proof.' 'But you were still worried. Did Miss Edmunds threaten to take action against you should you say anything publically about the poisoning?' 'There was no absolute threat, but I understood distinctly that I must retract what I had said as to the poison and I did so.'

Inspector Gibbs was unimpressed by the cowardice of the good doctor. He had been too afraid to protect his family from a mere spinster. 'Do you have any of the letters she sent?' he asked. 'I destroyed most of them, but I do have one.' He found a long letter couched in romantic terms to show to the inspector. Though it said nothing explicit, it suggested a coolness from Mrs Beard towards Miss Edmunds. Moreover, it intimated a serious relationship between the doctor and his patient whatever the former professed. It had arrived just after the inquest on the death of Sidney Barker. No wonder Dr Beard looked so perturbed and worried about the matter. His private life was about to be exposed.

Caro Mio, I have been so miserable since my last letter to you. I can't go on without ever speaking to you. What made me write so? [referring to a previous letter about breaking off the relationship] I thought, perhaps, it would be better for both of us, but I have not strength of mind to bear it.

We met La Sposa [Mrs Beard] the day after her return, and were glad to see her back again. La Madre [Miss Edmunds' mother] thought she looked very thin and care-worn; I hope she will feel the good now from her change. You must have missed her. I didn't enter on the poisoning case in the street, but I called and told her that I was obliged to appear at the inquest in a few days, and I hoped she would send you a paper and let you know; but she said 'No' she did not wish to unsettle you. However, dear, I mean you to know about this dreadful poisoning case, especially as I had to give evidence; and I know how interested you would be in it, as you told me you would give anything to know what La Sposa swallowed. I sent you the analysis, and have no means of knowing if it were sent you. Yes, through my analysis [of Maynards chocolates] the police found me out, and cited me to appear. You can fancy what I felt; such an array of gentlemen; and that clever Dr Letheby, looking so ugly and terrific, frightened me more than anyone; for, if I gave wrong symptoms, of course he would have known. You can fancy my feelings, standing before the public, looking very rosy and frightened as I was. When I saw the reporters' pens going and taking down all I uttered,

Burns' lines rushed to my memory; 'The chiel's amang them taking notes and faith be'll prent it.'

I did the best I could, thankful when I had finished. It seemed so long, and my evidence – [a blank space in the letter]. As the jury had nothing to say, my heart was thankful. When Mr Gell and Mr Penfold [defence solicitors at the inquest] attacked me – Mr G. 'Why didn't I show Maynard the analysis?' it was so sudden, my ideas all left me, and I merely said because I found Mr Maynard so sceptical and prejudiced, and I thought I had done sufficient. Oh! Why didn't I say as I meant, 'Because I supposed Mr M. would take the same steps as I had done, or else destroyed his stock, and that, if those sold to Mr Miller were from the same stock I had warned him against, then he was answerable.'

If I had only said that, for I had no friendly feeling towards Mr M. That man's chocolates have been the cause of great suffering to me. The Inspector said he wished I had spoken as I felt and as I did to him when he came to me, earnestly and energetically. But La Madre said I should be thought flippant, so you see I was subdued. It was unfortunate the woman Cole's case was dropped. The Inspector told me Dr Letheby took one of the chocolates from her bag and said, 'Good God! This is filled with strychnine.' He felt the effects of it all day; it was rash of him. You see there were two poisons. Zinc was in La Sposa's and mine. I was troubled to describe the taste. The reporters smiled when I said 'castor oil and brandy.' The coroner said - 'Ah! Your usual remedy.' I was a stupid. He is so deaf. I was told to stand close to him. I took care to turn my back on the jury all I could. They were all very polite to me, even that fierce Mr Penfold. Dr Letheby's evidence was so interesting, and showed the different sweets in one glass tube, yet separated. His physique is large and grand, like his mind. Now, darling, rest assured, through the whole affair, I never mentioned your name or La Sposa's, and if I had been asked to mention a friend, I should Mrs Dix. She is very kind and fond of me, and would come forward, had they wanted her to help me. No, the rack shouldn't have torn your name from me, and the only reason I said September was that you might see I had concealed nothing.

My dear boy, do esteem me now. I am sure you must. What trial it was to go through that inquest! La Madre was angry I ever had the analysis; but you know why I had it – to clear myself in my friend's eyes. She always says nothing was meant by you. No, darling, you wanted an excuse for my being so slighted. I never think of it; it was all a mistake. I called on La Sposa and told her how I got on. She said my evidence was very nice. She didn't ask me to come; but perhaps she mustn't. Now there is no reason. La Madre says if you were at home she is sure you would ask me just the same as ever.

Come and see us, darling; you have time now. La Madre and I have been looking forward to your holyday [sic] to see you. She wants to know how you get on and like the North. Don't be biased by any relatives; act as your kind heart tells you, and make a poor little thing happy, and fancy a long, long bacio from

DOROTHEA

CHAPTER NINE

The Missing Motive

William Gibbs had joined the police force in the 1850s at a time when the concept of policing by a specific force was relatively new. Sir Robert Peel had first called for a distinct police force to monitor and control the rising tide of crime that was resulting from large segments of the population moving from the countryside into London in 1829. However, it would take considerably longer for the various counties of Britain to establish their own forces.

Brighton was one of the earliest, perhaps due to its close links to London. Brighton Borough Police Force was created in 1838 and consisted of a chief constable, two superintendents, three inspectors, twenty-four constables and a night constable. A total of thirty-one policemen to serve a population of almost 47,000. In 1851, around the time Gibbs joined, the force had almost doubled to sixty-one men and by 1871, it had risen to 108.[44]

William rapidly shone out as a policeman. By 1861, aged thirty, he was a sergeant living at 17 Belgrave Street with his wife Emily (four years his senior) and children, William, age three, and Emma Jane, age ten months. Belgrave came under the ward of Hanover and was a mixed bag of an area. It had begun with an alms house, built in 1795 by Mrs Margaret Marriot, to accommodate six poor widows at that time in a rural area.[45] They were the only properties in the district until 1822 when the luxurious Hanover Crescent was built – nothing more extreme than these two distinct types of properties could be imagined. On the one side lived Horace Smith, writer and poet who welcomed Thackeray and Dickens to his dinner table, and Sir Rowland Hill who introduced the Penny Black stamp, while on the other lived black-dressed and bonneted widows who existed quietly except for their weekly trips to church.

Belgrave Street was several roads away from the luxurious Crescent, just off Albion Hill where Chate's Farm stood. The terrace houses were typically Victorian and housed the better-off working-class families. With their modest bay windows that extended across both floors and small but functional yards, they were a pleasant enough home for the young sergeant. Not far away was the Belgrave Street Congregational Chapel and, at a respectable distance, another of Reverend Wagner's homes for penitent women in Finsbury Road. In 1871, despite his promotion to inspector, Gibbs still lived in the modest street, though now across the road from his former house.

The 1870s was not the happiest time for the new police force. Across the country growing hostilities towards the police were causing problems and made the force deeply unpopular. Older officers could remember the 1830s and 1840s when similar problems had arisen, but to newer men this was an unprecedented condition. To Gibbs, who joined in the 1850s when the police force was on one of its quieter periods in popular opinion, this new resentment – which at its best would result in complaints and at its worst physical violence – was a surprising twist. Having just risen to inspector, he had a duty to present the police as a responsible and worthwhile organisation to a population who either hated them or considered them inept.

In general this new 'anti-police' feeling expressed itself in a lack of co-operation from the public, especially the lower classes who felt victimised following the implementation of the new licensing laws and Poor Law Policy which the police had the misfortune to enforce. Policemen felt despised and alienated from the rest of society. They complained bitterly that people would not come to their aid when they were in danger of attack. Meanwhile the taxpayers moaned that the police were failing in their duty, were not solving crimes and were a waste of money – sound familiar?

Into this muddle stepped Inspector Gibbs facing the most serious case of his career: the mass poisoning of Brighton. He had to solve this crime quickly and have the murderer safely behind bars before the public began complaining about incompetence. There was a great deal of pressure on Gibbs as he turned his attention to the potential motives behind the poisonings. He needed answers and he needed them fast.

Mrs Boys seemed the next most significant victim in the poisoning case. If the 'Christiana Edmunds theory' was true, then there must be a reason why she singled out Mrs Boys, and if that could be found then the case against Edmunds would become more solid. But Inspector Gibbs' optimism was met with confusion from Mrs Boys. Elizabeth Boys barely knew Christiana – she had once seen her in the Beards' household when she was visiting. She had no contact with her and did not entirely remember her name. But there had to be some connection. Perhaps, Gibbs theorised, her husband had dealings with the Edmunds?

That was a dead end as well. Elizabeth married Jacob Boys in December 1861 by which point he was sixty-five and retired. The Edmunds moved to Brighton in the 1860s, so they could not have had any professional dealings with Jacob that might have caused disagreement. Elizabeth had previously lived in London, so again could not have had contact with the Edmunds prior to her move to Brighton with her elder sister Mary Ann Barrack. The more he dug into the Boys' family past, the more it seemed to Gibbs they had no connection with Christiana. In fact, there was a connection, but not one that Gibbs was likely to discover unless he was able to obtain a full confession from Christiana – something that never happened.

The link between the Boys and the Edmunds was nearly sixty years old and had begun in Margate. It had all started with Thomas Edmunds (c.1741-c.1826), Christiana's grandfather, who had been Clerk of the Works for the rebuilding of the Margate pier after it was badly damaged in the gales of 1808. It was a prestigious moment for the family, unfortunately marred in 1813 when further storms caused one of the walls Edmunds had raised to form a promenade to become seriously unstable. It was obvious a large section of the pier would have to be demolished and rebuilt. The irritated Margate residents wanted someone to blame and pointed their fingers at the Clerk of the Works, Thomas Edmunds. Prominent Margate resident and solicitor, John Boys, was particularly vocal about the issue, suggesting Edmunds had departed from the instructions of the engineer who had been commissioned to design the pier, John Rennie. The backlash on Edmunds was surprisingly harsh and single-minded.

While Thomas tried to keep his head down and avoid the furore, the Edmunds women began to get vindictive – a trait that would flow down to Christiana. Mary Edmunds, second eldest daughter of Thomas and aunt to Christiana, was around twenty when the debacle started. She was furious with the criticism of John Boys: as an important Margate figure, he was listened to and his allegations were ruining her father's reputation. Outraged, Mary began her own campaign. In June 1814, a short poem appeared around Margate accusing John Boys of borrowing an iron roller from a coach master named Mummery to use on the ground at the centre of Hawley Square where he kept his offices. Rumour had it he had later sold the iron roller, despite it not belonging to him, and the poems repeated this:

Is there a heart that can be found,
With foul dishonour blacken'd round,

Whose deeds with infamy are crown'd.
Like B---s?

Lives there a man who does not hate,
The soul without one honest trait,
The damning guilt that rules the fate, -
Like B---s?[46]

And so it continued for six verses. Despite the deletion of the name, it was obvious who it was referring to and to make it absolutely clear a copy was sent to John Boys. A second libellous poem appeared shortly after, referring to a disagreement Boys had over the organ in St John's Church. It was accompanied by a drawing showing the Devil filling the organ pipes with sand.

A third poem discussed arguments over a lime kiln in Margate and suggested that John Boys was in league with the Devil. A caricature of Boys showed him conversing with Satan. Enough was enough. Boys could not allow such scandalous material to keep circulating. He must have had his suspicions about who was behind the verses and in July 1815 he brought an action against Mary Edmunds.

The trial was held at Maidstone and the main crux of the case revolved around whether or not the handwriting of the poems matched Mary's handwriting. It was a controversial matter. The handwriting had been clearly disguised and public feeling was not in Boys' favour. A cartoon drawn at the time shows a prim and respectable-looking Mary Edmunds with a veil over her head sitting calmly and smiling in court while the lawyers arguing the case smile and rain scorn on Boys.

Even so, triumphant as she may have felt, it was a bad day for the Edmunds family. William Edmunds was fifteen at the time and a significant witness in the case. He was summoned to the stand and asked to say whether the writing on the poems was that of his older sister: 'I do not believe it is,' he unsurprisingly answered. Despite favourable local feeling, the fact the case was held in Maidstone and the jury consisted of men unfamiliar with the intrigues of Margate, went against Mary. The jury found her guilty but felt sympathy towards her awarding only ten pounds damages to Boys, even though he had been suing for £1,000.

Thomas Edmunds may have been spared expensive damages, but he had incurred costs with the case from organising a defence for his daughter to the travel costs of getting to Maidstone. His Margate neighbours were distressed by this and still believed in Mary's innocence. A report on the trial from 1815 recorded:

That so well convinced are [Thomas Edmunds'] numerous neighbours
and friends of the innocence and worth of Miss Edmunds ... they had
intimated an intention of raising a subscription to defray those expenses
[of the trial]... This intention is the more honourable to the town, and
the more flattering to the feelings of the young lady, as, fortunately, such
are the pecuniary circumstances of Mr Edmunds that no such relief is
necessary.[47]

Was Mary guilty? She had the education, inclination and material to
produce the libels. John Boys was a director of the Margate pier project
and his scorn of her father had cut deep into the family. There was to
remain bad blood between the Boys and Edmunds right down to the
time Christiana was born. It seems likely, despite her neighbours' wishful
thinking, that she was the correct culprit. Whatever the case, the trial left a
bad taste in the mouths of the Edmunds. They had been scandalised before
their neighbours and their innocence questioned.

John Boys was born in 1782 and admitted as a solicitor in 1803.[48] Until
1805, he practiced in partnership with Jacob Sawkins of Margate, after
which he practiced alone until 1837. In 1811, his offices were listed as
being in Hawley Square where the firm remains to this day. At the time of
his clash with Thomas Edmunds, he was in his thirties, a man at the early
stages of his career working to make himself prosperous and respectable.
He had married his wife Martha around the time he went into single
practice, she being four years his senior. Their daughter, Sarah Maria, was
born in 1807. When Christiana Edmunds was eight years old, her family's
nemesis was just going into partnership with John Harvey Boys to create
the firm Boys and Boys. He was also soon to become Justice of the Peace
for the County of Kent. While John Boys' star rose, the Edmunds' family
fortunes continually faltered.

The last census Boys appears on is in 1851 when he was living
comfortably at St James Square with his wife and spinster daughter. In
comparison, Christiana's family had moved to Canterbury after the death
of Christiana's father, William Edmunds, in 1847. The Edmunds were in
dire circumstances. Money was tight and one of Christiana's sisters was
having to work as a governess.

John Boys died on 13 January 1861 aged seventy-nine leaving behind
a small fortune, though his will only states that his effects were under
£6,000. Martha followed him seven months later leaving Sarah Maria
under one hundred pounds. It seems John Boys had ensured his fortune
had gone directly to his daughter. It was around this time Christiana's
family suffered more blows through the loss of a brother and sister, and
she moved with her mother to Brighton. When she arrived, she learned of

another respected solicitor in the town by the name of Boys of an age that might make him young enough to have been John's son.

The story of the feud between Thomas Edmunds and John Boys had circulated among William's children. Aunt Mary had been particularly bitter about the case and resented seeing the Boys thriving. Now as Christiana moved into a humble house with her mother struggling to maintain a fragile position in middle-class society, she was horrified to discover the son of John Boys was practicing in Brighton as well. Worse, he lived in a smart house with servants only a few doors down from the home of her beloved Dr Beard. With her original victim of revenge, John Boys, dead, she turned her attention to his child.

Unfortunately for Christiana (or perhaps fortunately for John Boys), she had muddled up her families. She had taken the name and ages of the two men and come to the conclusion they were related. But Jacob Boys was not the son of John Boys. Jacob Boys was born in 1796 and baptised in February at St Peter and St Mary Church, Lewes. He *was* the son of a John Boys, but not John Boys of Margate who would only have been fourteen at the time of his birth. Jacob's father was married to Charlotte Mann and together they had at least six children, but none named John (so John Boys could not have even been Jacob's older brother). Jacob's oldest brother was William born 1786, four years after the birth of the Margate John Boys. While it is possible they were related more distantly, it seems there was no connection between the families.

What about John Harvey Boys? He was born in 1815, again not one of Jacob's siblings (Jacob was nineteen by then), and died in 1870 aged only fifty-five. His son, Toke Harvey Boys, joined Boys and Boys in the same year, but eventually went into practice alone.

While modern information proves the Boys of Brighton and Margate were not direct relations, Christiana would not have had access to such resources. Perhaps she heard that Jacob Boys was the son of John Boys and erroneously came to the conclusion that he was the son of the man her family despised. She had not been at Margate when John Boys died and it was unlikely she knew his age. It would only take a slight alteration of years to conclude he could be Jacob's father. In any case, it appears Christiana believed Jacob Boys was in some way related to her now deceased family nemesis and decided to enact a long awaited revenge on him.

Inspector Gibbs could not have known this. The only person who could have told him was his suspect. He had no idea about the Maidstone trial of Mary Edmunds or the long-running Margate feud, so he had no option but to conclude his investigation of the Boys by deciding there was no apparent motive for them to be targeted. If only he had access to today's records, he would have realised Christiana Edmunds was proliferating her heart's desire for revenge on specific residents of Brighton – on Mrs Beard for being in the way of a relationship between Christiana and Charles Beard and now the Boys due to her erroneous belief they were related to John Boys of Margate. That left only three victims for Gibbs to find motives for. Mr Garrett, chemist, Mr Tatham, surgeon and JP, and Mr Curtis, newspaper editor. However, with these men Christiana's thoughts and feelings become hazier.

Mr Garrett fell afoul of her no doubt because he had supplied the poison to 'Mrs Wood' who it now seemed was Christiana. He had also been saving the fraudulent notes from Glaisyer and Kemp and had been in close contact with the police. Christiana needed him out of the way. Make no mistake, the parcels she sent were not intended to merely make people ill, they were designed to kill. Mr Garrett had forfeited his life simply by being a good chemist.

Mr George Tatham was even more curious. Born in September 1808, the sixth child of Thomas and Susanna Tatham, he was a surgeon who spent most of his life in London before moving to Brighton in 1849 (his father died in Brighton in 1818, but it is not clear if he lived there). He later also studied to become a general practitioner and was licensed to be an apothecary. Tatham did exceptionally well for himself, eventually able to move into the prestigious Old Steine – just across from the Royal Pavilion and next to Grand Parade – and to be appointed a Justice of the Peace in 1870. Perhaps that was his 'crime' in Christiana's eyes: John Boys had been a JP too. He may also have been involved in the Sidney Barker case, but unlike her other victims, it seems to have been only association that threatened Tatham's life.

Lastly, there was poor Frederick Curtis, stationer, printer, artist and newspaper editor. Frederick was thirty-seven in 1871 and listed as a journalist and artist. He was married to Fanny with seven children. His only crime was to report the news about the poisonings.

Inspector Gibbs pieced together his new information. In 1870, Christiana Edmunds had apparently tried to poison Mrs Beard that resulted in a break with the two families. Desperate to get Dr Beard back, Christiana had written several letters and then attempted to prove her innocence. The 'Caro mio' letter was incriminating – why had Christiana had the chocolates tested? It was ten months after she had passed the bad chocolate to Mrs Beard. All logic would suggest that any similar tainted chocolates would have been already sold and eaten. No one else had been poisoned, destroying her argument that Mr Maynard was selling bad sweets. Until Sidney Barker died. Which was when Christiana started having chocolates analysed (though not informing Mr Maynard of the results) and testifying at the inquest. But it didn't work: Beard would not let her back into his life. He would not believe the poisonings were an accident. Consequently, more people suffered to prove it really was Maynards' chocolates that caused the sickness, and when that failed to work, it would appear that Christiana tipped over the edge into despair and tried her last attempt – the poisoned parcels. To prove her point, she would no longer choose random victims but high-profile people, and if it happened some of them deserved a little revenge from her, all the better. The Beards, of course, had to receive a parcel as did she to prove they were fellow victims.

Inspector Gibbs had to admire the cunning of it all. The business had been performed coldly and calculatingly, but he finally had his solution. If anything, Christiana had tried too hard to prove her point and by making herself the victim, not once but twice, had put herself slap bang in the limelight. While Gibbs had been determining her motive, his officers had been rounding up hard evidence. He had a number of witnesses who identified the mysterious lady bearing poisoned sweets from a photograph of Christiana. He had the chemical analysis of the parcels and now the letter from Dr Beard that would help him to identify if the parcels were addressed by her. In fact, he had more than enough for a Victorian criminal trial. At last his hunt was at an end.

CHAPTER TEN

The Arrest

Christiana Edmunds presented a strange picture of vanity and dowdiness when Inspector Gibbs went to speak to her. She was a short woman with hard, care-worn features. Later newspaper reports would use terms such as 'decidedly plain' and say her complexion had an 'underlying swarthiness'.[49] Words that were not kindly used against a middle-class woman. Christiana was not a beauty, but she was vain particularly about her hair, which she commonly wore parted in the centre and woven into a plaited knot at the back of her head. *The Daily News* gave a detailed account of her appearance:

> There is considerable character in [the face's] upper features, spite of the plainness; the quick flash of the large dark eye, once noted, suffices to blot out the first conception of common-place. But the character of the face lies in the lower features. The profile is irregular, but not unpleasing; the upper lip is long and convex; mouth slightly projecting; chin straight, long, and cruel; the lower jaw heavy, massive and animal in its development. The lips are loose – almost pendulous – the lower one being fullest and projecting, and the mouth is exceptionally large. From the configuration of the lips the mouth might be thought weak, but a glance at the chin removes any such impression.[50]

This was the age of phrenology – the pseudo-science that examined the features of a person's head to identify their personality. A belief was rife that certain 'bumps on the head' could determine that a person had criminal tendencies or other flaws in their temperament. The way Christiana was described was precisely to appeal to the amateur phrenologists who read the papers. Phrenology as a science had been widely discredited, but it was grist to the mill for journalists.

Christiana might not have been a typical figure for an illicit romance, but when she talked she became animated and her charm apparent. There was a spark to her eyes and an excitement in her speech that drew people in. She was the ideal person to take in and delude the Brighton population, except for those scorned women immune to her charms like Mrs Beard. Gibbs had previously written to Christiana when first beginning the case and requiring information. He now confronted her with his suspicions. She immediately denied them. Hadn't she been a victim too? But he was not fooled: she was a cunning liar and he now saw the extent of the web of deceit and harm she had woven over the town. He arrested Christiana, and as there was no magistrates court in Brighton, sent her to Lewes gaol to await her first hearing. It was September 1871.

Who was Christiana Edmunds? Christiana was born in 1829 to William and Ann Christiana Edmunds. Ann was the daughter of Major Matthew Burn (or Burns), a Second Lieutenant in the Royal Marines, who was deceased by the time of her marriage in 1827. Christiana was their first child followed by William (1830), Louisa (1832), Mary (1831) and Arthur (1842).

Despite the Boys/Edmunds family feud, William Edmunds' life looked full of promise and his wife and children benefited from a comfortable income. His father, Thomas, had begun his career as a carpenter, living in a house on the north side of Hawley Square (the same square where Boys ran his business). Aside from his work on the Margate pier in 1811, Thomas was running the White Hart Hotel on Marine Parade and was recorded as a 'surveyor of considerable eminence', meaning he charted important works in areas of the town and was also called an 'intelligent builder'.[51] Of course, the family faced troubles with the partial collapse of the pier in 1813 and the libel case against Mary in 1815. Thomas retired slightly from public life, but continued to run the White Hart Hotel until his death in 1824. William had not been daunted by the pier disaster from following in his father's footsteps as a surveyor and decided to go one step further and become an architect. Despite a brief spell running the White Hart Hotel with Mary after his father's death, William had already set his course.

His first opportunity came in 1825 when the Margate authorities decided the rise in population and visitor numbers meant the town would benefit from a second church. Churches in early Victorian Britain were a complicated business. Some were raised by subscription and places inside had to be bought, effectively excluding poorer Christians. In the early 1800s, Parliament became concerned at the number of growing towns ill-served by small and exclusive churches and passed an Act in 1818 for 'Building Additional Churches in Populous Parishes'. The Act meant that the government would pay half the cost of erecting a new church as long as half the seats inside were free for anyone to use. In Margate, it was decided to use the design of the new church as a competition and advertisements were placed in both national and local papers in May of that year. They stated:

> To Architects. The committee appointed to superintend the erection of a new Church at Margate, give notice that they are willing to receive plans for a Gothic church of the time of Henry the Third – to contain two thousand sittings – of which twelve hundred are to be free seats – and eight hundred sittings in pews. The building is to be brick-cased, with stone and slated. The cost not to exceed sixteen thousand pounds, including the Architect's commission.[52]

Architects had a mere three weeks to submit their plans with twenty-four designs sent in for consideration. Reverend W. F. Baylay was to choose the design and in the end he picked that of twenty-four-year-old William Edmunds. This early success, when William had never been commissioned to design a building before, was an immense springboard for Edmunds' career. Commenters during the height of William's professional life suggested that his '...professional success was in a great measure owing to the kindness and discrimination of the Rev. W. F. Baylay'.[53]

On 28 September 1825, William watched as the foundation stone of *his* church was laid. A procession was organised through the streets of Margate to mark the monumental occasion and spectators lined the road to watch, waving flags, cheering, playing music and beating drums. In the centre, flanked by the Archbishop of Canterbury and the MP for Kent, walked William proudly bearing his winning plans. He could not have imagined a grander spectacle for the son of the disgraced Thomas Edmunds. The bells of the old church rang out and the crowd roared in celebration. In an age when many could not afford to go to the private subscription churches, the proposed Holy Trinity Church with its free seats was cause for excitement. At last, everyone in Margate who wanted to worship could whether they were rich or poor and William Edmunds was at the heart of the project.

As excited and proud as Edmunds was, his inexperience as an architect quickly shone through when the costing of the church was reassessed. In a notebook possibly belonging to Edmunds, calculations for the new costing were scribbled. The estimated final total was now £19, 664 6s 5d.[54] A couple of weeks before the grand procession and laying of the first stone, *The Times* gave its own estimate of the final costs as being £24,000, though was pleased to announce that £18,000 had already been raised by subscription (ironically some of which came from the Margate Pier and

Harbour Company). The final cost came to £28,000, far higher than the originally proposed £16,000.

It took four long years for the church to be raised. It was consecrated in June 1829, the same year Christiana was born. Holy Trinity was a typical Gothic-style Victorian church with high-arched windows, towering pinnacles and a grand 136-foot tower. But it was also very striking with sharp lines and a minimum of excessive decoration – the bane of Victorian church design. *Kidd's Pocket Guide to Margate* gave a description of the interior:

> It consists of a nave which is fifty-seven feet high, and side aisles which are elaborately groined. The east end is terminated by a recess for the altar, having a very noble window thirty-two feet in height... The stone screen in front of the west gallery is richly ornamented with buttresses and pinnacles, and produces, a very imposing effect. The arrangement of the ceilings under the galleries, deserves peculiar notice, from not having that gloomy appearance usual to such portions of churches, which Mr Edmunds in this instance has happily relieved by spandrills and pierced arches...[55]

Edmunds' first work was perhaps his most impressive and would have been a monument to his raw talent through the centuries had not an air raid in 1943 destroyed all of the church but the tower. The ruins were eventually demolished to make way for a public car park.

While waiting to see the completion of his church, Edmunds was busy on other projects. He designed the rather grim-looking and stark Margate new lighthouse, finished in 1829 and destroyed during the 1953 floods. More picturesque was the stunning Droit House, designed to be the offices of the Margate Pier and Harbour Company. Edmunds' desire for clean lines and unfussy facades is evident in the building, which could almost be compared to a Grecian temple (or tomb) with its rectangular, austere shape, accented by four pillars at the entrance and a clock tower. Also in 1829, he completed the designs for 'Levey's Bazaar' or The Boulevard, a public building with Grecian faux columns and high-arched entrance. It too resembled a mausoleum, but was popular with the critics of the time.

> Few watering places can boast of a public building similar to the Boulevard here. Its fine classical stone entrance, which has been built under the direction of Mr W. Edmunds, commands universal admiration. Its interior corresponds with the grand entrance, and is one of the most splendid fitted up saloons in the kingdom. It now takes the lead as a

promenade, being about 200 feet long, with a corresponding height, and stone floor...[56]

Edmunds' fame was slowly spreading and he was commissioned to design Trinity Church in Dover. The heavy Gothic structure stood on Strond Street, wedged between public houses and shops. With spiralling ornate pinnacles and large arched windows, it was a distinctive feature of the pier district of the town. It was consecrated in 1835 and this time costs were kept down to a mere £7,973. Sadly, the church suffered a similar fate to its namesake in Margate and was demolished after the Second World War.

At Canterbury, Edmunds was called to design a new workhouse, the symbol of Victorian charity and poverty. The Old Blean Union Workhouse (later the Herne Hospital) opened in January 1836 and could house 420 inmates. Edmunds designed it to comprise a large formal quadrangle enclosed by two-storey buildings.[57] At the same time, he was working on plans for improvements and extensions to the Kent and Canterbury Hospital. Edmunds' fame and renown seemed unstoppable. In an age when it was firmly believed that if a man worked hard he would continue to rise and rise without hindrance, Edmunds seemed the epitome of this idea. He had cast off the shame of his family's involvement with the Margate pier and the terrible Boys libel case. In 1839, Christiana was ten and able to witness and remember a momentous occasion for her father when he was commissioned to design a temporary pavilion at Dover where a dinner for the Duke of Wellington could be held. Erected on Priory Meadows, *The Times* gave a full description of it:

This structure is composed entirely of wood, and though the decoration of the interior of the building has been, of course, the principal object of attention, yet the exterior has also a very elegant appearance. The entrance to the dining hall is by three distinct passages, all of which lead to the side opposite the chairman's table. The shape of the hall is nearly square, and the flooring of the side portions was made to rise gradually, so as to enable the gentlemen dining there to have an uninterrupted view of the entire scene. A long gallery, occupying the whole of one side, opposite the chairman, was appropriated to the use of the ladies. The chairman, with his illustrious guest, and other distinguished person, sat on a raised platform at the upper end. The decorations of the hall were exceedingly gorgeous and gay. Every part of the inside of the building, with the exception of the roof, was covered over with pink and white striped drapery; and the walls at regular distances were additionally ornamented by a variety of escutcheons, rare paintings, and tapestry. The ceiling was divided into three distinct apartments, and was supported by separate rows of pillars, likewise tastefully decorated with drapery. In front of the two first rows knights in armour were placed, and it seemed as if these mute representations of ancient glory had again assumed their mortal forms in order to assist in honouring the greatest warrior of modern times. In all parts of the hall floated a profusion of flags; and the effect of this picturesque scene, when filled with the company, and lighted by the gas chandeliers, was brilliant in the extreme.[58]

Edmunds' fortunes looked good and his work was becoming familiar. It is a crying shame that his only building that survived into the twenty-first century was the Herne Workhouse (now being redeveloped to form residential accommodation). None of his other magnificent projects remain, even the stunning Droit House that sits at Margate is a replica, the original being destroyed in the war. Perhaps there is something ironic about the insubstantial nature of Edmunds' work as his flourishing career would prove equally short-lived.

One fine morning in February 1836, a rumour reached Edmunds at his home in Hawley Square that one of his associates, Mr Thomas Cobb, had committed suicide. The news sent a shiver down his spine. For some time there had been deep-seated problems running through Margate and focused on the Pier and Harbour Company, for whom Edmunds had recently designed Droit House and acted as their town surveyor. Town gossip spread stories that the Margate Pier and Harbour Company were working hand in hand with the Margate Commissioners for Paving and Lighting to run the town for their own financial benefit. Local feeling was that no decision was made for Margate unless it was of considerable benefit to the members of the two committees.

At the centre of it all was Edmunds. As surveyor to both companies and an architect who had won several big commissions in the town for prestigious works, his position looked suspect. Adding to the calumny were allegations of serious financial mismanagement, verging on embezzlement. Director of the Company, Joshua Waddington, in an effort to save face and restore faith to the residents of Margate was determinedly rooting out the problem with the assistance of John Sterland, a proprietor of the company and a former director. He was working on bringing a variety of charges against the company treasurer F. W. Cobb and Edmunds. Edmunds was accused of forging an invoice for stone amounting to £305. The invoice was in the name of Jonathan Duncan, but Duncan claimed he had no knowledge of it and had not authorised its creation despite it having been entered into the treasurer's cash book as paid. There was no receipt to prove the payment. Mysteriously, the dubious invoice had been 'privately abstracted' from an iron safe at Droit House. Was someone trying to hide evidence that could prove bad financial dealings within the company?

In early 1836, it seemed that in Edmunds' case at least, there was no evidence to prove any wrongdoings. However, the suicide of Thomas Cobb proved a problem. Whether Edmunds knew that Cobb was behind the stealing of the incriminating invoice we will never know. Cobb apparently had a conscience, however, because he did not destroy the document and it was found among his papers after his death. For Edmunds, this was disastrous. Cobb had been dead nearly a year when a special meeting of the Pier and Harbour Company was called to consider the charges against F. W. Cobb and Edmunds. The rediscovery of the dodgy invoice was key to the case, especially as it was stated to have been made out in Edmunds' own hand. Edmunds claimed he had written the invoice under the direction of the previous company chairman, Dr Jarvis, who was also deceased and could not confirm or deny the statement. Edmunds also explained that while delivery of the stone had been delayed, it had eventually arrived and been paid for. Despite his arguments, he had still dabbled in what could at worse be deemed fraud and at best serious mismanagement of the company finances.

Joshua Waddington wanted reforms to appease the Margate population and prove that his company was not up to nefarious dealings. As part of his plans, he cut Edmunds' salary as a surveyor to the company from £200 to £100, though he was lucky not to lose his role completely. Three years later, his salary from the Paving and Lighting Commissioners was reduced from eighty-four pounds to sixty pounds. This was still a good wage considering a surveyor at Ramsgate was only being paid forty pounds, but it was a big drop in the Edmunds' family income.

It was a deep blow to Edmunds, especially as his external work as an architect had dried up after 1839. The triumph of the Duke of Wellington's pavilion was now followed by depression and anxiety. This all contributed to Edmunds' declining health. Throughout the 1840s, he was a very ill man and could do little in terms of work for the company, though it seems they kept him on salary, perhaps in deference to the large family he had to support. Edmunds passed away in 1847, leaving his family with no financial provisions.

Christiana was sent to a boarding school in her early teens and was recorded at Ramsgate in 1841 living with twenty-one other girls ranging in age from eight to twenty-one and four teachers, two of which were barely four years older than their senior girls. In her book on Victorian murderesses, Mary S. Hartman argues that the girls' boarding school was the sort of place perfect for teaching young girls the skills they would need to ultimately conceal their crimes. While that is a slight stretch, it is true contemporaries viewed boarding schools for middle-class girls as an unnecessary evil and prone to developing unhappy traits.

The girls' boarding school arose as another attempt to ape the upper classes by the rising middle ranks and to attain a higher quality 'frivolous' education for their daughters. Mothers, whose education had consisted of learning the practical elements of running a home, now desired to mask their daughters from such homely skills. They wanted their daughters completely oblivious to the practical side of life. 'The daughters were taught to turn up their noses at the domestic chores of home, and their mothers had to keep pace with them,' wrote Duncan Crow in his book *The Victorian Woman*. 'Had this escape from drudgery been satisfyingly used as the result of any real education it would have been all to the good. But it wasn't. The girls were taught to pass their time elegantly with the sort of drawing-room accomplishments that the ladies of the manor had stamped with gentility. Work was shunned and any gentlewoman who was obliged to earn her living was an object of pity to her friends.'[59]

The most famous (or infamous) example of such a boarding school appears in *Jane Eyre* by Charlotte Bronte, though Lowood School for Girls was in fact a charity school and respectable middle-class parents would not have sent their daughters there. Another example of such a type of school was mentioned by Thackeray in *Vanity Fair*. Bronte's school was a prison for girls where they languished in cold rooms falling sick one by one to a typhus epidemic. The Academy for Girls in Thackeray's work was of a higher grade, and although Becky Sharpe was a charity case, most of the girls attending the school were from wealthy families – the new emerging upper middle classes. Somewhere in-between the two fictional creations lies a representation of the school Christiana would have attended and whose principals of luxurious idleness took roost in her consciousness, never to be shaken free.

The Schools Inquiry Commission of 1864-68 described the sort of education girls were receiving at these establishments as '...fragmentary, multifarious, disconnected; taught not scientifically as a subject, but merely as so much information, and hence, like a wall of stones without mortar, it fell to pieces'.[60] This was hardly surprising as the women who set themselves up as teachers were often middle-class women who had fallen on hard times – just like governesses – and their education was unlikely to have been in any way sufficient for teaching others. Teachers used books of catechism to teach their pupils such as Mangnall's Questions first published in 1800. The questions were peculiar and hardly useful with girls learning the 'correct' answers, or rather responses, off by heart. One example saw students whizzing through the uses of whalebones, the making of umbrellas and its ancient Greek origins and travel in Italy, hardly pausing for breath or to examine their answers. Nothing was questioned or clarified. Information was expected to be absorbed without understanding, for what did it really matter when these girls were expected to be idle things sitting in parlours awaiting suitable marriages? Only the teachers could have known the fallacy of this idea as they too had once been brought up to expect such a life only to have it cruelly snatched away.

There is little information on the school in Chapel Place, Ramsgate, that Christiana attended other than it was situated in a row of respectable Victorian houses all used for the same purpose. It appears Chapel Place was the area to start a girls' school. The school was run by Miss Charris and Miss Fisher with supplemental teaching provided by Miss Turner and Miss Veronica Venetozze who was listed as being born abroad and probably taught languages.

Discipline within the schools was strict and girls were heavily monitored and restricted, even letters home were censored less they reflect badly on the establishment and the inmates learned to be deceitful. Private belongings were ruthlessly plundered by teachers checking up on their pupils. Diaries and other personal notes were far from safe unless well hidden. This need for deceit established young in the girls lasted for many into their adulthood. Christiana in particular perfected her secrecy and skills for subterfuge at school and retained them throughout her life. It could be argued that she learned some of the abilities she needed to commit murder under the tutelage of Miss Charris and Miss Fisher.

The other element of schooling was that many girls of varying ages, experiences and backgrounds came abruptly together and shared their knowledge and ideas. Far from closeting girls as middle-class fathers wanted to do, this gave girls far more worldly (if sometimes inaccurate) views. For example, thirteen-year-old girls mixing with twenty-year-olds picked up titbits of knowledge on life, love and romance that their parents would have been shocked by. From this chaotic education, Christiana developed a lifelong desire for knowledge and a mind for collecting and remembering details. She also picked up schoolgirl attitudes on romance and marriage that real life failed to dent and which fuelled her imagination when she was into her forties. But the life the schools had prepared her for was about to be swept away. In 1847, Christiana was nineteen and home from school to discover her future about to be radically altered.

The death of Christiana's father put her and her family in a dire situation. Christiana had been brought up to a life of reasonable luxury. The new idea of Victorian womanhood within the middle classes was one of idle and insipid leisure. Middle-class girls were taught accomplishments such as music and drawing, but nothing that could be considered 'practical' in the sense that it could earn them a living should the worst happen. And the worst happened all too often. Commentators of the time criticised this trend in teaching daughters to be frivolous things with no life skills which would ultimately cast them into poverty should the family fortunes diminish. They did not even know basic household management skills like their mothers: being raised to mimic the daughters of the upper classes, but without the financial safety nets those women had. If you could raise your daughter to have nothing in her head more taxing than dance steps and the latest popular pianoforte tune, then it was a sign you were up and coming in the world. You could afford to educate your daughter for enjoyment rather than learning, but the result was many women suffered when they found their 'talents' could help them little to earn a living in the real world.

Christiana had very few options when her father died but to marry well (and quickly) or become a governess – about the only occupation open to middle-class, under-educated girls. For the first few years after Edmunds' demise, his daughters were too young for either occupation. Their mother, Ann, managed to support the family in a modest manner by renting property. In 1851, she was listed as a shareholder, but it does not state which company or what sort of shares. Perhaps she retained some association with the Pier and Harbour Company. In any case, she was just able to afford the continuing higher education of her son William who was training to be a doctor.

The family moved from Margate and never returned. They spent the 1850s at Canterbury while William was a medical student in Middlesex. Christiana was disinclined towards employment. She had been raised during the height of her father's career and she was an undisputed snob. While her mother struggled and scraped by, Christiana continued to view herself as a young lady who should not have to demean herself by work. Her utter indignation at the idea of employment appears to have left her untouched by the family crisis. Her younger sisters were not so fortunate (or callous).

Mary pursued the first of two options for impoverished middle-class girls and was married in 1856. Louisa pursued the second route and became a governess. In 1861, she was living at Camberwell, Surrey, in the household of a printer. Her work at the time cannot have been arduous as his eldest child was only four, so her role may have been better viewed as unofficial nursemaid. She was twenty-seven and her prospects for the future looked grim. The life of a governess was hard and depressing. She drifted in limbo between the family ranks and the ranks of the servants – she was neither one nor the other. The tragedy of governesses came when they were either too old or ill to work and would find themselves destitute.

Charities were set up in response to this abysmal end and homes for retired or sick governesses sprung up in locations such as London, though further afield there was little provision for them. Louisa is the most tragic figure in the Edmunds dynasty. A sensitive and quiet girl, she was deeply affected by her father's death. Her life as a governess only brought her more despair and she died in 1867 aged only thirty-six.

Four years later, Christiana was living in Brighton, still styling herself as a lady and deluded enough to fancy her chances of marriage to the handsome Dr Beard, if only his wife was out of the way. She was now forty-two years old, but preferred to tell people she was only thirty-five. With her mother she lodged in Gloucester Place in a small house, but maintaining a façade of elegance that meant they could still move in the circles of wealth that contained the likes of the Beards and the Boys. She spent her days visiting and frittering away her time. She read extensively, like so many ladies of leisure, and would have favoured the lending libraries of Brighton. Her letters are pock-marked with the signs of this habit from her phraseology and views on life.

But to mistake Christiana as an uneducated wastrel would be dangerous. Deep down she had a passion for learning, even if it came out in odd ways. She was intrigued by the new forms of science and read about them extensively, proved by her advanced knowledge of poisons and the means for identifying them: not common knowledge among refined middle-class women. Christiana also knew about the crime scandals of the age and had paid enough attention to try and cover her tracks when she began her crime spree. She was a master at false names and fake letters, her cleverness fed into her cunningness. Christiana had the potential to be a dangerous criminal, not least because she did not seem to realise the harm she had caused.

CHAPTER ELEVEN

Prosecuting Poison

'Today the magistrates have been engaged from morning until evening in continuing the investigation in regard to the extraordinary poisonings which alarmed Brighton a few weeks ago...'[61] announced *The Times* on 1 September 1871. Christiana was in front of the magistrates who would decide if the evidence against her was enough to send her on to a criminal trial. Dubiously, among the magistrates present who could influence the outcome, was Mr G. Tatham, one of the victims of the parcels. There was no indication that anyone, not even the defence, viewed this as a conflict of interest. Defending Christiana was solicitor Mr Lamb who knew he had a difficult task ahead of him. The prosecution was aiming to make the attempted murder of Mrs Beard the centre of their case while also bringing separate cases in relation to Mr Garrett and Mrs Boys. Christiana '...sat in a corner of the prisoner's dock, and not unfrequently smiled as the descriptions were given of the pains taken to trace the hand administering the poisons', *The Times* added. The outcome was almost inevitable. Christiana was sent to trial and would spend the meantime in Lewes gaol. 'She made no signs of fear, and was throughout the day apparently the least excited person in the court.'

Christiana was to appear at the Winter Assizes at Lewes and it was expected she would come before Baron Martin. However, her trial had barely begun when Mr Justice Lush sent an order under the Palmer's Act that Christiana should appear at the Old Bailey instead. The Palmer's Act was created in 1856 and was known previously as the Central Criminal Court Act, but was popularly known as Palmer's Act because of the person who had sparked its invention. That was none other than Rugeley poisoner William Palmer, referred to earlier as one of the few known Victorian serial poisoners. At the time Palmer came to trial in his native

Staffordshire, it was feared that he could not expect a fair trial due to local prejudice against him. The Central Criminal Court Act was rushed through so that Palmer could be tried in London at a neutral court, thus making it impossible for him to ask for a retrial on claims that his original hearing had been prejudiced. Since then, the Act was used sparingly, but with Christiana's trial it was thought wise to move her case to a neutral setting.

Justice Lush was probably right in his view that a Lewes trial would be biased. Christiana had caused a sensation in Brighton, the story was splashed across the papers and public opinion was heavily against her. Worse, the magistrates who first saw her could easily have been guided by their outrage that one of their own, Tatham, had been caught in the poisoning scare. Christiana was moved to Newgate gaol in late December 1871. She had spent Christmas in Lewes and was unhappy and depressed about the change of scene. She was still very much protesting her innocence and trying to maintain a demeanour of respectable and lady-like grace. The warder of Newgate conveyed his prisoner by train to her new accommodation and by 1 January 1872, *The Times* could report she had safely arrived.

Newgate gaol had a notorious reputation known for its insanitary conditions, cruelty and overcrowding. For centuries, executions had taken place just outside the prison and in cases of treason, a room was set aside as a 'kitchen' for preparing the quartered bodies of traitors for display around the city. Newgate inmates lived a hopeless life in semi-destitution. Up until the nineteenth century, it was customary for them to pay for their confinement. They even had to pay a fee for entering and leaving the prison. The gaol keeper expected money for food, bedding and clothing, providing only a minimum of essentials if a prisoner was too poor to pay. Some inmates simply starved or fell ill from lying on cold, bare floors.

The prison was divided into 'poor' and 'rich' sides, along with separate accommodation for condemned prisoners and debtors. The rich side was for the wealthier prisoner who could afford to pay the fees imposed by his keeper for a single room with a decent bed and other furnishings. Successful highwaymen often fell into this category during the eighteenth century and glamorised imprisonment at Newgate. But for most prisoners the poor side was all they would ever see. Prisoners formed communities within themselves. Until the nineteenth century, there was no segregation of men and women or of adults and children, something philanthropic reformers criticised heavily. A new prisoner had to integrate quickly. As soon as they arrived they were informed by their new neighbours that 'garnish money' was expected from them. Garnish money was a form of fee imposed on arriving prisoners for anything from clothing to drink. If a prisoner could not pay they were rapidly stripped of their clothes and left to fend for themselves.

When the reformers of the early 1800s began a concerted effort to investigate the prison system, they were stunned by seeing people walking around naked, sleeping three to a bed, the sick and dead crammed in with the living. Christiana was fortunate that her imprisonment came a short time after the reformers had made inroads into improving Newgate such as separating male and female prisoners; however, Newgate was still a heinous place to be imprisoned. When Christiana left Lewes she was aggrieved and complained that her treatment in Newgate was much worse – she was probably telling the truth. County gaols were rarely full to capacity. In the later nineteenth century, many would be closed due to being virtually empty of prisoners. The keeper at Lewes had time to check on his prisoners and allow them the odd privilege, as Christiana had pointed out, much to his alarm. At Newgate, there was no such individual attention. Christiana (who would not share a room with the Lewes' matron) would have been lucky to have a cell to herself, despite Newgate supposedly adopting the American Separation System.

The 'Separate System' arrived in the 1830s along with the 'Silent System'. The two regimes had their own advocates and enemies. The Silent System enforced absolute silence on prisoners during their confinement with flogging for talking. The Separate System kept prisoners isolated at all times with their own cells. In some cases, prisoners were exercised in individual sections of the yard and forced to wear masks. In a number of prisons, the systems were combined. The idea behind both schemes was to enable the prisoners to reflect on their imprisonment and to prepare them for a more law-abiding and spiritual future. Reflection was seen by many as the key to solving criminality. They were soon to be disillusioned. In America where both systems had been taken to extremes, it was noticeable that the rise in suicides and depression among prisoners in the Separate System was exponential.

Fortunately for British prisoners, few gaols had the facilities for enforcing either system. Newgate semi-adopted the Separate System, but since it only had a certain number of single cells, many prisoners had to sleep in communal rooms in hammocks. This was the world Christiana entered. Newgate would have come as a dreadful shock. In 1850, Hepworth Dixon, historian and author of a work on the prisons of Europe[62], described Newgate as being '...surrounded by high walls, between which a scanty supply of air and light find their way downwards as into a well ... inside and outside it is equally striking. Massive, dark and solemn, it arrests the eye and holds it. Of all the London prisons, except the Tower, it alone has an imposing aspect.'[63] Just over twenty years later, almost contemporary with Christiana's imprisonment, the *Illustrated London News* ran a series of articles on Newgate in 1873:

> The prison is a stern and necessary reality in our civilisation. It is one which we cannot refuse to contemplate, though it is unpleasing as a spectacle and in the feelings associated with it.[64]

Readers were taken on a tour of the prison from the entrance hall where they could peruse a collection of plaster casts of executed criminals to the exercise yards, workshop and soup kitchens. They could also view the flogging box, still in use for punishing criminals, although no longer used on women. Lastly, the article briefly described prison life:

> [The prisoners] rise at six o'clock in the morning, and go to rest at eight in the evening; and most of them being untried, have no labour imposed on them while in this prison. They are not permitted to converse with each other when they meet in the exercise yards.

Christiana's pre-trial days in Newgate during the winter of 1871-1872 were bleak and dull. She could speak to no one, though she hardly desired to. Too poor to afford the extortionate fees for the wealthy cells yet too well-bred to fit in with the other poor prisoners, she lingered in a limbo, her only glimmer of hope was the trial that would absolve her guilt. As she had yet to be tried, she was not forced into the prison uniform that had become standard in Newgate, but retained her own clothes. She was also not forced to perform any of the hard labour other convicted female prisoners did such as oakum picking or laundry work. But she was isolated with no one to talk to and no occupation to keep her busy. Newgate was freezing cold in winter, the communal women's wards only had a single small fireplace that was fiercely fought over. There was no form of heating in the single cells and sickness was rampant. Gaol fever was the commonest sickness, but there were plenty of other conditions that would carry off a prisoner who did not have access to suitable warmth or nutrition. Despite the reformers work, the care at Newgate was haphazard at best, much of it provided by charitable individuals.

Attitudes towards prisoners and the prison system went through repeated about-faces and reversals during the eighteenth and nineteenth century, at one point extorting tolerance and gentleness, while at other times expounding harshness and brutality. Christiana went to Newgate at one of these cusps of change. Unfortunately, the system was once more reverting from liberal treatment back to medieval violence. Her life had been turned upside down in a manner Christiana had never expected.

Christiana complained very quickly about her new abode, stating that she was not treated as well there as she had been at Lewes. Statements appeared purporting to be from her in *The Times* that while at Lewes she had been allowed 'special indulgences' not usual for prisoners. This was scandalous. The governor of the prison, Mr Helby, wrote that Christiana had been treated just like any other prisoner, except for '...some trifling exceptions allowed by the visiting justices upon the recommendation of the surgeon'. These included '...that she did not occupy the same apartment with the matron of the prison, but an ordinary cell; and that the articles of cutlery said to have been in her box [a trunk of belongings she would have brought with her to the gaol] were used under the supervision of the prison officers, with due precautions against any mischief arising'.[65] They were subtle exceptions but exceptions nonetheless and must have made people wonder what manner of excuses the surgeon had given about his patient's health that she should be entitled to use her own cutlery?

Christiana had spent her time at Lewes with 106 other women inmates under committal for trial. She had her own cell and the worst element of her incarceration would have been sheer boredom. Prior to committal for trial, prisoners spent their time in relative solitude with odd visits from the prison chaplain. On Sunday, the Lewes inmates attended divine service twice, the only highlight of the rather drab and dull week. While some women used the time to rest and recuperate from their normal lives, Christiana was morose and agitated, tired of waiting and tired of the insipid routine of her new existence. Newgate was no improvement. Her only ray of light was the impending trial when she could finally voice all the scorn inside her and reveal to the world her feelings for Dr Beard.

Christiana's trial began on 15 January 1872. *The Times* reported: 'The trial excites unusual interest from the very extraordinary circumstances under which the charge is preferred and the court house was much crowded during the whole day.'[66] Christiana was to be charged with the murder of Sidney Barker. She was allowed to sit during the proceedings with a female warder beside her and she kept her head down, not wanting to see the rows of ogling ladies occupying reserved seats to watch the performance. *The Times* remarked that this was very 'becoming' and then erroneously listed her age as thirty-six. When the charges were read out against her, Christiana pleaded not guilty and then watched anxiously as the jury was empanelled.

William Ballantine was leading the prosecution as Serjeant-at-Law, an order of barrister that was destined to become defunct three years later in 1875 when it was decided to confirm no more serjeants, though existing ones could still perform their role. Ballantine was born in 1812. His father was for a time the magistrate for the Thames police and it was anticipated his son would follow him in his pursuit of the law. Ballantine was admitted to the Inner Temple in 1829 and was called to the bar in 1834. Ballantine soon went on to conduct some of the most notable cases of the Victorian age. In 1848, he was engaged at the House of Commons on a suit to annul the marriage of Esther Field, an heiress, on the grounds of coercion and fraud. In 1864, he was involved in the first railway murder concerning a banker named Mr Briggs. His prosecution of the culprit Franz Muller on controversial evidence saw him win Muller the death penalty, despite the best efforts of Serjeant Parry who was defending. In Christiana's case, Parry and Ballantine would become opposing forces once again.

In 1871, Ballantine was involved in the Tichborne Claimant case where Australian butcher Thomas Castro claimed to be the long-lost son of Lady Tichborne and therefore entitled to inherit the vast family fortunes. Ballantine led the legal team on behalf of Castro when he entered an action to establish his rightful identity as Sir Roger Tichborne, motivated by the recent death (and thus cessation of his income) of Lady Tichborne. The case, however, went hopelessly wrong and Ballantine was fortunate to extract himself before the position of his client became utterly desperate. Ironically, Castro was accused of perjury and ended up in Newgate around the same time as Christiana.

Anyone who knew Ballantine's previous career was aware that he was a dangerous adversary. He was charming, quick-witted and subtle. His success against Franz Muller with the complicated and contradictory evidence at his disposal would have given Christiana little comfort and the public would still have the Tichborne case, which had caused quite a scandal fresh in their minds. When Ballantine set out his case for the prosecution he made it clear to the jury that they would be looking at a woman scorned in love. He stated, '...she had formed ... the acquaintance of Dr Beard and his wife in consequence of his having been called to attend her in his professional capacity. That seemed to have ripened into a state of things which did not ordinarily exist between a medical advisor and his patient, and there can be no doubt the patient herself entertained very strong feelings indicating considerable affection towards him.'

Ballantine reflected on the events of September 1870 when Mrs Beard ate a bad chocolate: '...there could be no doubt there was something deleterious in the cream'. Not that any poison could be traced to the prisoner prior to the incident with Mrs Beard. 'It might occur to the jury that jealousy might have had something to do with the transaction, but they would take care that no suspicion arising out of it was allowed to bias their judgement in arriving at a conclusion on the case they were now called upon to try.'

The motive for the mass poisonings in Brighton was more complicated. Ballantine stated Christiana might have concocted them '...with the view of distracting attention and diverting suspicion from herself, she determined to pursue a course by which the blame attributed to her might be thrown upon another person. If that were so, she appeared to have determined to carry out the idea in a manner probably unparalleled in any court of justice.' Despite all the evidence he was to present, Ballantine determined to remind the jury that he would do his duty without imparting any undue prejudice. He would state the facts, but the jury would have to decide. And so the trial of Christiana Edmunds began.

'I live in Hammersmith,' Charles David Miller, the first witness stated to the court, 'and am a coachbuilder. I am the brother-in-law of Mr Albert Barker. In June last year his little boy, Sidney Barker, was alive. He was four years of age. My sister, my brother-in-law, the boy, and I were all staying at Brighton. On the morning of the 12th of June I went to Maynard's shop, in West Street, and bought some chocolate cream drops, for which I paid a shilling, and took them home.' It was seven months since that fateful day and Charles was having trouble recalling the details clearly. 'About 4 o'clock that afternoon my brother gave the boy one of the drops and he ate it.' Charles meant his brother Ernest, though in an earlier testimony he had said that it was himself who gave Sidney the deadly chocolate. 'About ten minutes afterwards the child began to cry and my sister took him in her arms. His limbs gradually became stiff and about 20 minutes afterward he had died.'

Then came a more controversial change in Charles' testimony. 'I myself had eaten two or three of the creams in the morning. About ten minutes afterwards I felt dizziness in my eyes, a coppery taste in my throat and my limbs began gradually to stiffen. I gave several starts and I became as stiff as if my bones were all one. I sat down to dinner about 2 or 3 o'clock, and felt a return of the symptoms; I had another 'start' and could not eat anything.' Charles was describing the effects of strychnine poisoning and he said he had experienced them, not after Sidney had become sick as previously had been implied, but many hours before. He could have prevented his nephew's death, had he only realised the strange illness he was suffering from was a direct result of the chocolates he had eaten. Was it guilt that made him change his version of events to suggest Ernest gave Sidney the killer sweet? Perhaps implying that he was aware of the danger but his family were not. In essence, however, his evidence was the same as before. He had bought some chocolates from Maynards and they had poisoned his nephew.

Mr Rugg came to the stand next. As the medical man who attended Sidney, his evidence was crucial, but it also made it apparent how out of his depth Rugg had been when witnessing the tragedy. 'I was called in to see the little boy and found him in strong convulsions. I wrote a prescription for an emetic, but there was no time to have it made up. The boy died in convulsions about eight minutes after I saw him.' Emetics were the stock tools of surgeons designed to make a person vomit and used for a range of conditions. To be fair to Rugg, they were standard treatment in the case of a suspected poisoning, but the state of Sidney at the time must have made it clear that purging was not going to help.

'I made a post-mortem examination the next day and found the organs generally in a healthy condition with the brain slightly congested, which would be apparent in a child dying of convulsions.' To the Victorians the term 'congestion' referred to an organ or part of the body becoming engorged with blood. 'The body was very rigid. It had been well nourished. There was nothing about it to indicate the cause of death. There was a quantity of undigested food, which I preserved. I could form no opinion as to the cause of death as I had never seen anyone die of strychnine.'

Ernest Miller came next and repeated his story of visiting Maynards that same evening to buy a second bag of chocolates which he gave to Inspector Gibbs. Then it was the turn of a key witness and one of the most important forensic experts on the case – Dr Henry Letheby. Henry Letheby was born in Plymouth in 1816 and trained as an analytical chemist, graduating from London University in 1842. He lectured on chemistry at the London Hospital and was known for his work on chemical tests, particularly strychnia. In 1856, he wrote an article for the *Lancet* on the subject, giving his professional address as the College Laboratory, London Hospital. Letheby had a mixed career. In his guise as a medical officer of health, he had been controversial for voicing his opinion that cholera was not being spread by bad water from the pumps in the city during the 1860s. But this failing did not prevent him from becoming a food analyst and examiner of gas for the Board of Trade.

Letheby wrote extensively on the subjects of chemical analysis and was known to his contemporaries as an 'exceedingly accurate technological chemist' who contributed papers to the *Lancet* and other scientific journals. His skill was realised by the criminal courts who were finding it increasingly difficult to prosecute poisoning cases without clear-cut evidence. The general public was sceptical about anecdotal evidence as well as the failings of tests and demanded unequivocal proof before they would be prepared to send a man or woman to the gallows.

Letheby came into his element during the infamous Palmer trial. He appeared as an expert witness on the eighth day of the trial in 1856, the same year he wrote about detecting strychnine for the *Lancet*. On that occasion, Letheby's evidence went in favour of the accused as he did not believe the symptoms experienced by Palmer's victim was indicative of strychnine poisoning. The judge dismissed the learned man's opinion because in his *own* experience poisoning could take many forms and did not need to conform to the expert's pattern to have taken place! That was one way to ensure that not even a lack of poison in the victim or viable symptoms could excuse a man the noose. No wonder then that Letheby felt it necessary to write to *The Times* three years later on the 'Scientific Fallacies in Courts of Law' where judges such as the one he had come across in the Palmer case abounded as did dubious 'experts'. 'Dr Letheby … shows that the existing mode of conducting an inquiry into a case of suspected poisoning is such as must often leave the results in the greatest uncertainty.'[67]

Letheby's outburst would spark a response from the man later to be his fellow expert witness on Christiana's case, but his views had validity. The unmethodical use of science within criminal cases troubled him. He was concerned about the mishandling of samples – what would now be deemed as a broken chain of evidence – that could throw doubt onto the innocent and free the guilty. While by the 1870s matters were improving, (Inspector Gibbs after all had sought out the testimony of two London experts) things were still not perfect. If Mrs Boys felt the need to have her own private tests done, then what did that say about the general public's faith in the police? And all the samples came from private individuals rather than the police. Some had passed through several hands before reaching Letheby and who knew what contamination might have occurred along the way? Christiana could perhaps take comfort that one of the experts against her would take a fair and neutral approach to the evidence he gave.

Letheby gave his evidence succinctly. He had listened to the testimony of Charles Miller about both his own and Sidney's symptoms and was convinced they were caused by strychnine. He had conducted an analysis of some chocolates provided to him by Inspector Gibbs and had discovered further strychnine, though he could not say if they were all poisoned as the chocolates were '…all broken up when he received them'. There was at least a quarter of a grain of poison in them and that was enough to kill an adult. Only a sixteenth of a grain would be necessary to kill a child of around Sidney's age. On 16 June, he received Sidney's stomach to examine four days after the death. Despite the length of time that had elapsed, he found a quarter of a grain in the contents. Sidney had stood no chance.

After Letheby came poor Isaac Garrett, not only a victim of the Brighton poisoner, but now an unhappy witness to his business practices. Garrett told how he had sold strychnine to a woman named Mrs Wood who had come down from Kingston. He repeated again and again how cautious he had been about selling the poison, how he had deferred and deliberated and only conceded after much persuasion and mention that Mrs Wood was married. Why was the husband so important in swaying him? There had been talk not many years before of restricting the sale of poisons to men, implying that women were not reliable to purchase or safeguard dangerous substances. The point had been mooted after it was remarked how difficult life would be made for the average housewife wanting to poison rats in her kitchen if she was banned from buying substances such as arsenic. Instead, the poisons book had been introduced. But there still lingered an idea that women and poison should not mix, a notion not helped by the large numbers of female poisoners on trial. Mr Garrett worried about selling poison to a single woman and Christiana recognised this concern and made it clear she had a husband who could 'keep watch' of the strychnine she bought.

Garrett seemed to have needed little persuasion and despite his protests in court, he sold Christiana large doses of strychnine on not one, but three separate occasions. Each time she took around ten grains of the chemical. If one grain was sufficient to kill an adult and Christiana's reasoning for needing the strychnine was to poison cats in her garden, it would seem that Garrett was more interested in a sale than safety. In the space of barely six weeks, Christiana bought thirty grains of strychnine, more than enough to kill dozens of cats. On the last occasion, she claimed to have needed the poison to kill an old and diseased dog. Again, she received ten grains which, given Letheby's calculations, was more than enough to serve the job. Did Garrett never wonder what happened to the remainder of the poison? Clearly not. After the last visit of Mrs Wood, Garrett received the note from Glaisyer and Kemp asking for a drachm of strychnine as they had run out. Garrett prepared the poison in a bottle, handing it to the boy who had brought the note. The lad left with sixty grains of strychnine, the quantity in a drachm! Christiana now had a supply of ninety grains of strychnine, enough to kill around one hundred adults and countless children.

After describing the coroner's note requesting the poisons book that resulted in a page being torn out (Oddly the one before Mrs Wood's entries. Did Christiana make a mistake in her haste or was she making another attempt to cast suspicion elsewhere?), Garrett left the stand to be replaced by Caroline Stone, the milliner, who repeated her evidence about being an impromptu witness for Christiana. She was also keen to emphasise her reluctance to witness the transaction and had insisted she never knew the accused was buying strychnine, only that Christiana wanted the poison to stuff birds. If only Mrs Stone and Mr Garrett had conferred they would have realised the inconsistencies in Christiana's story.

Sixty-two-year-old chemist Thomas Glaisyer came to the stand next to testify that he never sent a letter requesting strychnine from Garrett. In fact, the more the matter was discussed the more odd it seemed. Glaisyer was one half of Glaisyer and Kemp, a large and impressive pharmacy in North Street, Brighton. They were in a different league to solitary Mr Garrett with his small shop in Queen's Row. The shop had been founded by John Glaisyer, a former baker and chemist in 1798. When he died in 1813, his employee Grover Kemp was taken on as a partner to form Glaisyer and Kemp. Thomas joined the business in 1852 when he was registered as a pharmaceutical chemist. He was then forty-three, being born in 1809 and may have been the son of John, but this is not clear. He was partnered with John Kemp, registered as a chemist in 1853, and together ran the business successfully into the 1890s. When Thomas Glaisyer died in 1898, he was able to leave a substantial fortune for that time of £10,657 and Glaisyer and Kemp still exists today.

It was obvious for everyone in the courtroom that the idea that Glaisyer and Kemp would request a drug from Mr Garrett, a small chemist who would have been below their business ranking, was mildly absurd. How could Garrett imagine they would ask him? It had never happened before. Or was he flattered that his biggest rivals had made an error and needed his humble assistance? Another unanswered question in the motives of Mr Garrett, but his reputation was beginning to look distinctly soiled.

One of the most damning witnesses to Christiana came to the stand late on the first day of the trial. Adam May was eleven, but insisted to the court that he would be twelve on 1 May. It was just after his last birthday that he had first met Christiana. Adam did not know who she was at the time, but when he saw Christiana in court he recognised her as the lady who had asked him on several occasions to run errands. The first errand happened after he met her in Portland Street. She asked him to go to Maynards and buy sixpence worth of large chocolate creams for her. She gave him 6d and Adam hurried off, but when he brought back a bag of creams, she said they were the wrong sort and sent him to return them and fetch more. This would be but one of many occasions when boys would buy and return chocolates at Maynards arousing suspicion in the staff.

As far as Adam could tell he had returned the same bag he had originally purchased, though he admitted it was possible it had been switched. It was doubtful he was watching very carefully. Eventually, Adam brought Christiana a box of chocolate creams that she was happy with and gave him a piece of chocolate from a paper she had in her hand. Adam was lucky that this apparently was not a poisoned piece. He watched her walk up North Street and thought little more of the matter. Three months later, Christiana came across Adam in King Street and asked him to run another errand for her. For some unexplained reason, Adam hesitated and said he would need to ask his mother first. This he did and received permission to run the errand.

Expecting to be sent for more chocolates, Adam was surprised to be given a note to take to Mr Garrett. He did not read it and had no interest to. When Garrett read the note, he bundled up a book and gave it to Adam to carry away. Christiana had wandered from the original spot where they had spoken and eventually he found her in Duke Street. She was pleased with him and gave Adam 4½d. He spotted Christiana again on only one further occasion. This time there was no errand, but she gave him a bag of 'bulls-eyes'. Cross-examined as to his identification of Christiana, Adam stated, 'I had always said the prisoner was like the lady who sent me for them [the chocolates].' While it was not a positive assertion that Christiana was one and the same with the lady he ran errands for, it was persuasive to the jury and Christiana's defence knew it.

Two more boys, George Brooks and William Guy, gave similar evidence of running errands for a lady, though neither was so clear in their assertion that Christiana was their employer. George explained that the lady he had bought chocolates for was the same one he had later seen in the police court and William made no assertion whatsoever. It was fortunate the prosecution had Adam.

The day's evidence could not be completed without the appearance of Mr Maynard and his staff. His life had been turned head over heels by the case, though fortunately the accusations of Christiana had not stuck as badly as they might have. His staff could confirm the suspicions they had had about the number of boys buying and returning chocolates for a lady. In consequence, Charles Schooley had been sent to follow one lad to see who he gave the chocolates to and had seen Christiana.

John Goddard Maynard looked a frail figure as he came to the stand. He was nearly blind, despite only being in his fifties and so spent less and less time on his shop floor. His wife helped out in the shop at busy periods such as Christmas, but Maynard was becoming a background figure. Yet whatever his outward appearance, his mind was as sharp as ever. 'I have carried on business as a confectioner in West Street, Brighton, for more than 25 years,' he told the court. 'I do not make the creams myself. Mr Cadbury and Mr Ware manufacture them for me. I have sold such creams in large quantities in Brighton for many years – ever since they were introduced. In February or April last, the prisoner made a complaint to me about the creams, which she said were bad, and had nearly poisoned one of her friends. She said a gentleman, a friend of hers, intended to have them analysed. I said I wished she would. My wife, on that occasion, ate one in her presence. I never heard if the prisoner had them analysed. I have never had in my establishment strychnine or poison of any kind and I could not say how poison had found its way into any of the creams.'

Mr Ware, whose chocolates were the ones in question, was equally keen to assert that he kept no strychnine at his factory and could see no way in which his product could have become accidentally tainted. Mr Cadbury, whose name remains as a brand of chocolate, did not require being called as his chocolates had never been suspected.

Mr David Black, coroner, was called forward. Black was the man whose name was used to obtain the poisons book from Mr Garrett – another link in the chain leading back to Christiana. She would not have known many coroners, but Black had presided over the inquest of Sidney Barker. Curiously, Black took to the stand to reiterate evidence that Christiana had given at the inquest. One has to presume this came from notes taken at the time considering the detail Black remembered, but this was not stated and it has to be wondered how fair such evidence presented by a far from impartial witness was. Nonetheless, Black told the court what had been said by Christiana on that sad day in June:

She said 'I bought some chocolates at Mr Maynard's in September last. A young woman now present [at the inquest] sold them to me. I ate two of those which I bought. I did not notice any bad taste, but I had violent internal pain and burning in the throat which came on about an hour after eating them. I took some brandy, which made me worse, and then some castor oil. The pain and burning in the throat continued for about 20 minutes. In March last, I bought some more chocolate cream, pink and white at Mr Maynard's in West Street. I ate a portion of one, but it tasted so bad that I did not eat the remainder. It had a metallic taste; it took away my taste. I felt very ill about ten minutes after taking it; my throat felt burning hot, and I was strange all over, and had a feeling of tightness in the throat. I took some brandy and water which made me worse, and then some castor oil. About 3 or 4 in the afternoon I felt better, and went and called on Mr Maynard and saw him in his private room. Mrs Maynard was also present, and I told them how ill I had been from the chocolate. Mr Maynard said it could not be that, and that the metallic taste I complained of must have come from something else I had been eating. They brought several from the shop to try, and I tasted a very small piece of some of them but they were free from the peculiar taste I had perceived in mine. I said I should like to know what was in them, and Mr Maynard said I was at liberty to have any analysed out of the shop. I told him to try and find one like that I had for if he once tasted it he would believe what I said. He said he was obliged to me for coming and would write to his French agent [Mr Ware]. I gave one to a lady at the same time I partook of one myself; she ate it, and it made her ill like myself, but she took a glass of wine, which made her sick, and she soon after got better. I took the remainder of the chocolates I had left to Mr Schweitzer[68] and told him how I had felt, and I wanted to know how so small a portion of chocolate cream could have made me so strangely and suddenly ill. Mr Schweitzer treated it very lightly. He thought I was nervous and fanciful, but he altered his opinion after he tasted one himself, and he said he would make an analysis, and he gave the result in writing. I gave it to Mr Rugg, but did not mention Mr Maynard's name. Mrs Maynard ate several from the shop, and tasted one of those I had left. Some of those I had left were good, but others I am convinced were bad. I did not communicate the analysis to Mr Maynard, as he seemed so sceptical. My object in going to him was to warn him.'

Christiana's inquest evidence is both suspicious and enlightening. First is the weird convolution of facts. She talks of a lady, presumably Mrs Beard, as taking a chocolate cream and then a glass of wine that made her sick. This did not occur: Mrs Beard merely spat out the chocolate. Then there is the analysis she says was handed to Mr Rugg. The surgeon never mentioned the analysis Christiana had commissioned, nor did Miss Edmunds ever elaborate on the findings personally. Which leads to the poisoning symptoms. Just what type of poison was Christiana describing? In her own letter to Dr Beard, she stated her 'tests' had resulted in finding zinc in the bad chocolate Mrs Beard had eaten. She then described her symptoms after eating another chocolate from the same batch. They fail to tally with zinc poisoning.

The symptoms of an overdose of zinc include a persistent metallic taste in the mouth, the first thing Mrs Beard noticed when the chocolate was forced upon her. Then aches and pains, sometimes followed by vomiting and diarrhoea, exactly as Mrs Beard described. In serious cases, feverishness, chills, fainting, difficulty of breathing, problems urinating, yellowing of the skin and eyes, and seizures follow, ultimately putting the body into shock and killing the victim. Christiana described only internal pain and a burning sensation in the throat (which is not a common symptom of zinc poisoning) after eating the first chocolate. With the second chocolate, she did describe the metallic taste associated with zinc, but excluded any other distinct symptoms.

Was she describing the effects of strychnine, the poison she subsequently tried on Brighton? Her description of the foul taste of the chocolate when she first ate it is an indication of strychnine – the bitterest of all minerals – but her body's reaction with a burning sensation in the throat (though sometimes found with strychnine cases) was more associated with arsenic poisoning, especially as she failed to list other strychnine symptoms. Wherever Christiana had obtained her knowledge of poisons, it was incomplete and a skilled chemist such as Dr Letheby would have realised this. She could not have been describing a genuine poisoning. Her 'symptoms' were muddled and the effects of whatever she had supposedly eaten were far too mild. Mrs Beard had merely tasted and spat out the zinc-laced chocolate, but was ill for over twenty-four hours. Christiana ate the chocolate but was ill for only twenty minutes and a few hours respectively. Christiana's testimony at the inquest was not just suspicious, it indicated either a hypochondriac who presumed herself poisoned, an attention-seeker or worse. A poisoner trying to cover her tracks...

When Harriet Elizabeth Cole came forward to give her testimony, she had new information that had not been revealed to the press. Harriet explained that in March, Christiana visited her husband's grocer's shop and when she left a bag of chocolate creams had been found. Harriet thought nothing of giving them to her daughter and a young female friend staying with them at the time. Both girls ate some of the chocolates '...and were very sick and bad.'[69] The incident, however, was quickly forgotten. In June, a similar find was made after Christiana had been in the shop: a bag of chocolate creams and a bag of lemon bulls-eyes in a zinc pail. Harriet had no hesitation in giving the creams to her daughter and trying a bulls-eye for herself. Mistress Cole tried one of the creams and instantly spat it out, disliking the taste. Harriet gave this little thought and passed the bag to a little boy. Master Walker took the kind gift home to his mother, the unfortunate Caroline Walker who reiterated to the court her terrible sickness after eating a piece of the chocolate. She was one of the few victims after Sidney Barker and Charles Miller to experience severe strychnine poisoning. Fortunately, she had not eaten enough to kill her, but she was ill for a week.

Thirteen-year-old William Henry Halliwell told the court a similar story. He was more civil-minded than the Coles and tried to return the creams to Christiana. She denied they were hers and instructed him to eat them. Out of the dozen chocolates in the bag, it was only the last one that tasted odd and made William ill. At the age of thirteen, William was probably just robust enough to avoid death from his consumption of the chocolates; however, it would have been a close call and he could easily have succumbed. As it was, he was sick for ten days until the poison had finally left his system. William caused the court some humour when he said that around a week after he had recovered, Christiana appeared in the shop again and another bag of chocolates was left behind. William told the court that this time he did not eat the chocolates and a ripple of laughter ensued.

As compelling as this evidence was, it was circumstantial. There was no direct link of seeing Christiana leave the chocolates that later caused the sickness: she just happened to be in the same place at the same time as they were left. The conclusion was obvious, but it would be torn to pieces in a modern court of law by the defence. Gibbs was also aware that this might be a sticking point in his case, so was relieved to have subsequent witnesses who could make that vital connection.

On 4 March, fifteen-year-old Henry Diggens told the court that he was in the Spring Gardens with his friend Benjamin Caulthrup when a lady approached them and spoke to Benjamin. She gave him a paper bag with Maynards written on it. Inside were several large chocolate creams. Benjamin gave his friend one of the chocolates and ate twelve of them himself. Henry was a more careful eater and tried a portion of the cream: '...it had a hot taste'. He did not like it and threw it away. Benjamin was not so fussy and did not notice anything wrong with his treats as he gulped them down. Within half an hour both boys felt ill. Henry was giddy and sick. Benjamin had a burning sensation in his throat and his body had gone so rigid he could hardly walk. He made it home to his mother who fetched him a powder (probably a purgative) to little effect. The next day, Benjamin was taken to hospital and was an out-patient for a week and had not fully recovered for a month. Like William Halliwell, he had come very close to death. Benjamin and Henry identified Christiana from a photograph – of course, witness identifications are always awkward and can be proved fallible. It is not described whether they were shown more than one photo, but it seems probable they were merely asked if the woman in a certain picture was the one who had given them the chocolates. Was that a fair identification? In the 1870s, it was considered reasonable and prominent evidence. In any case, the boys were not challenged on the matter, other than to confirm they had never seen Christiana before that day in March. The testimony of Benjamin and Henry was damning.

Yet what came next was worse. Emily Selina Baker, described as a pretty child of ten, was just leaving school when Christiana asked her if she liked sweets. Promptly Emily responded that she did and was handed a bag containing a mix of chocolate creams, lemon drops, acid drops and cough drops. Emily was not fond of hard sweets but liked chocolates and took the bag home to her mother. Mrs Harriet Baker did not question the origins of the gift, but picked out the chocolates for her daughter from the bag. Emily ate five or six, but one tasted exceptionally bitter. Within half an hour, the strychnine was at work and the little girl was sick and ill. Emily remained unwell for two days. About eight or nine days after her daughter's sickness, Harriet had a strange visitor at the door who she would later identify as Christiana Edmunds. The well-dressed lady on her doorstep was asking the oddest question: had anyone in her house or in the street been ill recently? Harriet said her daughter had been unwell.

Christiana said no more and went away. It was a bizarre encounter that would stick in Harriet's mind, though she developed the idea that perhaps her daughter was not the person Christiana was asking about.

The thought springs to mind as to why would Christiana put herself more and more in the picture and risk suspicion? The answer was simple: Christiana's earlier, subtle campaign of poisoning was not working. People were not coming forward and fusses were not being made at Maynard's shop, which is clearly what she hoped for. She wanted to be exonerated by the public for any attempt on Mrs Beard's life, but despite her poisoned chocolates being dotted about the town, no one seemed to be noticing. Worse, Dr Beard was not responding as he should be. He should be glad and even grateful that his beloved was not a poisoner and that suspicion fell elsewhere. Instead, he was ignoring Christiana.

She had to accelerate her campaign. First, she did this by ensuing the chocolates came into the most promising hands – children. Children would eat chocolates without thinking. They would not react like adults and, perhaps more sinisterly, Christiana knew strychnine would have a very dangerous effect on them. Was she trying to force another death like that of Sidney Barker's to clear her name? It seems very possible. However, her results were limited. Where was the gossip going around Brighton that children were sick and dying? Where were the complaints about bad chocolates? So desperate was Christiana for proof that her scheme was working, she risked everything to visit and question one of the children she had poisoned. If she had remained anonymous it would have taken longer to pin her down, but Christiana was about to make her most fatal mistake.

One Sunday in August of 1871, Inspector Gibbs received a message to visit Miss Edmunds at 16 Gloucester Place. It was just at the time when poisoned parcels had been sent to a number of notable residents and Miss Edmunds was claiming she had also been a victim. Gibbs had been quietly investigating the case for some time and was beginning to grow suspicious of the spinster, Miss Edmunds, who seemed to turn up at the centre of all poisonings in the town. He did not have all his hard evidence yet, but his instincts were telling him that Miss Edmunds was not simply another victim of a mysterious poisoner. Gibbs explained to the court how he arrived at Gloucester Place and found Christiana lying on a sofa just within the door. She appeared quite pale as she spoke. 'Here I am again Mr Gibbs, nearly poisoned. You have heard I had a box sent to me with some fruit in it. It came on Thursday evening by post. It is evidently no one well acquainted with me or the sender would have known my address and how to spell my name correctly.' She had not, of course, retained the packaging for comparison with the others. 'The box contained some strawberries, two apricots and a pair of new gloves. Mrs Edmunds, my mother, had the strawberries, which were all right, and I ate one apricot, and found it so bitter that I had to spit it out.' Christiana explained keenly, 'Is it true what I have heard that Mrs Beard and Mrs Boys have received one as has also Mr Curtis, editor of the Gazette in North Street? It is very strange and I feel certain you will never find out the culprit.'[70]

What a blatant challenge! This was not the first occasion Gibbs had spoken with the strange Miss Edmunds. He had also interviewed her in the gardens of the Royal Pavilion and was starting to understand her character. She liked being at the centre of attention and considered herself extremely clever. Christiana was now informing him that she was cleverer than him! It was a gesture that could not be ignored. On 17 August, he returned to Gloucester Place and arrested her on a charge of attempting to poison Mrs Beard. 'I, poison Mrs Beard?' Christiana said in astonishment. 'Who can say so? I've been nearly poisoned myself!' With this last testimony, the court had heard all the witness evidence, aside that is from the stories of those who received the parcels. Strangely, however, the supposedly key witness, Mrs Beard, was not to be summoned. Baron Martin presiding over the case felt that neither Dr or Mrs Beard should be allowed to testify. 'I have read their depositions,' he said, 'and a good deal of their evidence I should not admit at all.'

Could it be that Baron Martin believed the victims would sully a fair trial? That Mrs Beard was so angry with Christiana that she might exaggerate her story? Or that Dr Beard was so ashamed of his conduct that he would not be truthful about his relationship with Christiana? Whatever the case, the Beards, amazingly, would not testify in court. No matter for Gibbs, he felt he had made a substantial case and had his 'expert' testimony to present. Victorian science was about to doom Christiana.

CHAPTER TWELVE

Experts on Trial

Henry Swayster was not used to standing up before a large crowd such as the one pressing in to the Central Criminal Court. He was a humble boy, son of a bird stuffer, living in Queen's Road, Brighton, who had stumbled into the poisoned chocolates case quite by accident. Henry's father, like many in his trade, relied on donations of animal bodies to supply their stock. During the end of May 1871, the Swaysters received a message to say there was a dead dog they could have at a house in Gloucester Place. Henry was sent over to collect it.

It was a pitiful story Henry was told as he collected the dog's body. Half an hour before its death, the dog was fit and healthy. In fact, it had been playing quite merrily with one of the ladies residing in Gloucester Place, Miss Edmunds. Then it suddenly grew sick, dying in great agony. As it was handed over, Henry was told it might have been poisoned, but there seemed a limited amount of concern over the matter. Henry took the dog to his father who was not interested in the corpse – he was, after all, a *bird* stuffer – so the dead dog was passed on to a fellow taxidermist, Robert Bragnor.

A taxidermist might not have seemed the obvious choice for an expert witness, but in an age when surgeons required no qualifications, the evidence of a man who routinely dealt with dead animals as well as chemicals was as valid as anyone else's. Bragnor would have spent his life dealing with dangerous poisons, in particular arsenic, which was a common preservative for stuffed animals. Arsenical soap for cleaning skins before tanning and hopefully preventing insect damage was regularly used and strychnine was another chemical popular for pest control. Poisons might also be used to kill specimens but leave no marks. Therefore, Bragnor had an equal knowledge to the effects of poison as Mr Rugg.

Bragnor told the court that after receiving the body of the dog, he opened it to remove organs and tissue and was certain the animal had been poisoned, 'but not with prussic acid,' he added.[71] Bragnor noted '...the peculiar rigidity and inward bending of the backbone and the limpness of the muscles. I have dealt with the bodies of dead animals for many years, but never saw a body in the state this particular dog was, and there was saliva about the throat and mouth of an offensive character. The pupils of the eyes were double the size they ought to have been.' The poor creature had died in misery from strychnine poisoning. It seems Christiana was experimenting with her new drug before moving her scheme onto human victims.

By far the most fascinating of all the expert witnesses was Frederick George Netherclift who came to the stand as a self-professed handwriting expert.[72] Any science involving handwriting was fairly new, bearing in mind that for a large chunk of human history, vast sections of the population have been illiterate. Observations on handwriting had first been made by Aristotle in ancient Greece, but it was only in 1622 with the publication of a book on the subject by an Italian physician and professor of philosophy that wider interest was gained. Even so, it would not be until the late 1800s that intellectual Abbe Michon coined the term 'graphology' for the study of handwriting and began publishing books on the topic. Netherclift was therefore ahead of his time and so unique he could be rightly considered the only professional handwriting expert in Victorian England. In the latter half of the nineteenth century, he reappeared time and time again in court cases, and his word was virtually gospel.

Prior to the 1860s, handwriting was not considered as valid evidence in a criminal trial. The example of Henry Jumpertz in Chicago in 1859 is a prime example. Jumpertz admitted to dismembering and disposing of the body of his lover, but denied killing her, claiming she had committed suicide. As evidence of this a letter with suicidal overtones was produced. The prosecution argued the letter was in Jumpertz's handwriting and produced a receipt from the dead lover as proof that her handwriting differed to that in the letter. But significantly there was no expert to verify the claims, the judge and the jury had to make their own minds up. In the end, though Jumpertz was initially convicted, he was set free on appeal due to the handwriting evidence being inconclusive.

But with the growing literacy of the world written evidence started to become more and more important at trials and there was a need for experts who could explain the subject of handwriting comparison. But who was to fill this gap? Writing masters were a popular first choice because they spent their days looking at handwriting, but they had not studied the subject as a science and people with greater technical knowledge were necessary. It was also around the 1850s that Joseph Netherclift appeared on the scene as England's first handwriting expert. Joseph (born 1792) was the father of Frederick and a noted lithographer, an art that requires a great deal of skill and care and, not least, the ability to copy a drawing precisely. Joseph had a fascination with handwriting. He published several books on the subject, usually collections of facsimile letters. In the days before photography to reproduce such work, a lithographer would carefully copy them. Joseph therefore learned to forge the hands of famous people throughout the ages! He taught his son Frederick the skills of a lithographer and by the 1840s, they were publishing books together. One example is *Facsimile Autographs* published in 1849 when Frederick was thirty-one. It is not clear what prompted Joseph to take his hobby more seriously and to become an expert witness in court. He may have been approached by a defence counsel who had read his books and needed someone to look at forged letters in a case. It is less likely he put himself forward, but somehow he came onto the scene and by the 1850s, while still officially a lithographer, he had an interesting sideline in expert testimony.

This set Britain ahead of the Americans. Even so, it is surprising how long it took recognised experts to appear in courts when cases involved suspect handwriting, especially considering how often trials revolved around documents. Disputed wills were a favourite. How to prove a person wrote the paper unless a witness to the creation of the document could be found? Courts often brought in friends or relatives who could testify that certain writing appeared to be that of a deceased loved one, but it was a rough science and easily open to abuse and error. Still, it remains a mystery why it took so long for someone such as Netherclift to come forward and approach the subject logically and without bias.

Perhaps one answer comes from *how* you define and create a handwriting expert. Even today the subject is disputed, but in the 1850s and even the 1870s when Frederick Netherclift stood up at Christiana's trial, there was no means of quantifying his talents. He had no recognised qualifications and he was effectively self-taught: in essence he was voicing an opinion. He might argue an educated opinion, but even so his testimony perhaps did not deserve the blind acceptance many judges and, of course, juries showed. Sir Henry Hawkins, Queen's Counsel, first met Netherclift when he was a junior just beginning his law career. As a young upstart defence lawyer, he had a necessary scepticism for Netherclift's talents since they regularly came up against him. He remembered one particular case in his book *The Reminiscences of Sir Henry Hawkins* (1904) and it is worth looking at his views at length on handwriting evidence, since it was so key to Christiana's case. Hawkins wrote:

I always took great interest in the class of expert who professed to identify handwriting. Experts of all classes give evidence only as an opinion; nevertheless, those who decide upon handwriting believe in their infallibility. Cross-examination can never shake their confidence. Some will pin their faith even to the crossing of a T, 'the perpendicularity, my lord' of a down-stroke, or the 'obliquity' of an upstroke.[73]

By 1904, handwriting experts appeared regularly in court, but perhaps Hawkins was thinking of Netherclift when he described their belief in their infallibility.

Mr Nethercliffe(sic), one of the greatest in his profession, and a thorough believer in all he said, had been often cross-examined by me, and we understood each other very well. I sometimes indulged in a little chaff at his expense; indeed, I generally had a little "fling" at him when he was in the box.

In days long gone by, the eminent expert in this science had a great reputation. As I often met him, I knew his peculiarities, and how annoyed he was if the correctness of his opinion was in the least doubted.

He had a son [Frederick George] of whom he was deservedly proud, and he and his son, in cases of importance, were often employed on opposite sides to support or deny the genuineness of a questioned handwriting. On one occasion, in the Queen's Bench, a libel was charged against a defendant which he positively denied ever to have written.

I appeared for the defendant, and Mr Nethercliffe(sic) was called as a witness for the plaintiff.

When I rose to cross-examine I handed to the expert six slips of paper, each of which was written in a different kind of handwriting. Nethercliffe took out his large pair of spectacles – magnifiers – which he always carried, and began to polish them with a great deal of care, saying –

'I see Mr Hawkins what you are trying to do – you want to put me in a hole.'

'I do, Mr Nethercliffe; and if you are ready for the hole, tell me – were those six pieces of paper written by one hand at about the same time?'

He examined them carefully, and after a considerable time answered:

'No; they were written at different times and by different hands!'

'By different persons, do you say?'

'Yes, certainly!'

'Now Mr Nethercliffe you are in the hole! I wrote them myself this morning at this desk.'

He was a good deal disconcerted, not to say very angry, and I then began to ask him about his son.

'You educated your son to your own profession, I believe, Mr Nethercliffe?'

'I did sir; I hope there was no harm in that, Mr Hawkins.'

'Not in the least; it is a lucrative profession. Was he a diligent student?'

'He was.'

'And became as good an expert as his father, I hope?'

'Even better, I should say, if possible.'

'I think you profess to be infallible, do you not?'

'That is true, Mr Hawkins, though I say it.'

'And your son, who, as you say, is even better than yourself, is he as infallible as you?'

'Certainly, he ought to be. Why not?'

'Then I put this question: Have you and your son been sometimes employed on opposite sides in a case?'

'That is hardly a fair question, Mr Hawkins.'

'Let me give you an instance: in Lady D---'s case, which has recently been tried, did not your son swear one way and you another?'

'He did not deny it, whereupon I added: It seems strange that two infallibles should contradict one another?'

'The case was at an end.'

Hawkins had successfully argued that not only was handwriting expertise an inconclusive form of evidence, but that it could be wrong and depended on the point of view of the expert. Fortunately for the Netherclifts, few others saw matters this way and continued to use the men in their cases – as Hawkins had said, perhaps rather tongue-in-cheek, it was a lucrative business for them. By 1881, Frederick was able to list his occupation purely as 'professional expert in handwriting'.[74] It might have still seemed dubious in some people's minds, but it was a 'science' that the Netherclifts dominated and made their own. Joseph died in 1863, leaving Frederick the sole handwriting expert. From the moment Frederick took the stand, the case against Christiana became concrete.[75]

Frederick George Netherclift told the court that he had been known as an expert in handwriting for the last thirty years. He had been given the packaging the parcels of poisoned fruit and sweets had been wrapped in and was asked to compare the handwriting on them with that of Christiana Edmunds. Without a shadow of a doubt, he stated, they were one and the same. He had examined the parcel wrappers and they had all been written by a single person and that person was Christiana Edmunds. There was an instant objection from Christiana's defence: surely this evidence was wandering from the specific charges levelled at her which were administering poison with the intent to murder? There was a want of evidence to show 'personal administration' and this could not be 'supplied by evidence as to the receipt of parcels by other persons'.

The objection was partially accepted, except in the case for the parcel sent to Mr Curtis as there was another witness who could link Christiana directly with the parcel. This was an unnamed maid who worked in a boarding house in Margate. Christiana had paid a visit to her old hometown in 1871 and while there had been seen with a parcel. The nosy maid had snuck a peek at the box when it was briefly unattended. It was addressed to a Mr Curtis and contained fruit and sweets. There was no defence to this as Christiana had handled the specific parcel that had contained poison. The next question was whether any attempt had been made to disguise the handwriting. Netherclift affirmed that an attempt had been made on all parcels, but there were certain distinctive characteristics in the writing that appeared on both the wrappers and in the Beard letters. This would have been the peculiarities of writing that Sir Hawkins had thought so little of and criticised roundly as evidence. His own experiment, had it been remembered, would have showed that a disguised handwriting was not so easy to identify.

There was very little Christiana's defence could do but try to cast doubt on expert testimony in general, inferring that it was an opinion and not necessarily accurate. This was an old tactic that Frederick was used to. Blithely, he answered that he had been involved in cases of all matters and was always cautious in his reports to avoid assumptions or dangerous inferences. It seemed that settled the matter.

Gibbs had proved to his satisfaction that Christiana had sent the parcels. Netherclift would be recalled several times to testify that various other papers (including the letters sent to Mr Garrett) were all in Edmunds' hand. Now all he had left to prove was that the cakes were deliberately poisoned and he had a glittering array of experts to demonstrate just that. First in his arsenal was Professor Rodgers. Julian E. D. Rodgers was born around 1816 and by the age of twenty-five was a surgeon with a special interest in chemistry. Most surgeons, as mentioned before, were apprenticed, so it was slightly unusual that Julian diverted his career to study medicine to become a qualified doctor. By 1851, Julian boasted his MRCS and his general practitioner's licence. He was also recognised as a professor of chemistry. His success had not diminished his memories of harder days when he had struggled as a surgeon and to become recognised as a doctor. When Dr John Propert began fundraising for a benevolent college[76] to provide accommodation for pensioned doctors or their widows, Rodgers was quick to become a subscriber paying an annual amount of £1,1s. Perhaps at the back of his mind he was considering his new wife Frances and what might become of her if he was to die.

Julian had married Frances in the early 1840s and she had quickly provided him with three sons: George, Julian and Frederick. Frances (b. 1821) was a native of Heligoland, a regularly disputed little island forty-six kilometres off the German coastline. Denmark and Germany both laid claim to it and for centuries the island had jostled between them. In 1714, Denmark finally had enough and captured the island. It would remain in Danish control until 1807 when Britain captured the island during the Napoleonic Wars. Presumably, Denmark was tired of the little island it had owned for nearly a century, for in 1814, they officially ceded it to the United Kingdom in the Treaty of Kiel. Thousands of Germans began to emigrate to Britain, their new master country, and many joined the King's German Legion to fight Napoleon.

By the time of Frances' birth, island life had changed considerably for the remaining Germans. Throughout its history, Heligoland had supported itself via fishing. However, it now became a tourist hotspot and seaside spa, attracting upper-class Germans who liked the freedom of the British-ruled island. How Julian met Frances is open to speculation, busy as he was in the 1840s becoming a professor with little time for travel, but meet they did and they were married for nearly forty years. The 1850s were a good time for Rodgers. A bust of Julian by James Scurry was exhibited at the Royal Academy in 1850 and his articles on strychnine poisoning regularly featured in the *Lancet*.[77] In 1857, he was asked to be the professor of chemistry for a proposed new university in Wales. With a salary of £500 a year, equivalent to that of a professor at Oxford or Cambridge, it would have been a boost to Julian's career – if only the project had got off the drawing board. Instead, he remained a chemist at St George's Hospital in London.

Meanwhile, his family continued to grow with Elizabeth (1849), Jane (1853), Edward (1856), Frank (1861), Jessie (1865) and Adelina (1868). By the time Julian came to testify at Christiana's trial, he should have been a settled and well-respected family man, but things were not that simple. Julian had secrets when he stood up in court, not least that his wife had left him. This was scandalous in Victorian Britain. Divorces were still extremely rare and separations, though they occurred, were invariably hushed up. At some point after Adelina's birth, Frances left her husband and moved from their fine house in Belgrave to a small villa in Clapham, Surrey. Evidence for this appears in the census and at first glance it could be assumed Frances was merely on a holiday – husbands and wives did take separate trips at times. However, noted next to her name was the odd comment 'with separate maintenance' under occupation. Frances was not on holiday, she had moved away. But the split could not have been too volatile as Julian was providing her with an income, something many Victorian gentleman would have not considered when their wives left them.

Frances could not have expected to take her youngest children with her, even in divorce cases children were expected to remain with their fathers. It was why divorce could be seen as so scandalous and disreputable to a woman: she was abandoning her children when she left the matrimonial home. Her eldest sons Julian and Frederick did go with her. They were adults and could not be prevented from going with her. Curiously, her daughter Elizabeth, aged twenty-two, did not go. For some reason she preferred to stay with her father.

Elizabeth is curious for another reason. She does not appear in the list of family members for the 1851 census when she would have been around two and should have been at home. Between Elizabeth and Frederick's birth there was, at most, the span of a year. Not uncommon in Victorian families, but where was she in 1851? It should also be noted that she was not born in the same place as almost all her siblings who were born at Pimlico. She was born at Marylebone along with her sister Jane. Not so odd if we assume that was where the family were living at the time, except Frederick, born between the two sisters, has his birthplace listed as Pimlico. So in 1872, as respected an expert as he was, Julian Rodgers had some skeletons in his closet as he tried to concentrate on giving his expert testimony. Could the defence have used these to discredit him? Probably. Separation was a contentious issue and the scandal would have overshadowed any evidence Rodgers gave. Either Christiana's defence did not know about the curiosities in Rodgers' private life or he was not prepared to stoop so low to quash his evidence.

Rodgers had received a sample of cake from Gibbs in August. This sample had a dubious journey. It had been handed to Mr Glaisyer (of Glaisyer and Kemp, again not unbiased witnesses as they had been implicated in the poisoning, even if it was only loosely) by Mr Boys. Glaisyer examined part of the cake and gave the other part to Gibbs who sent pieces to London and to Professor Rodgers, along with two other samples. Rodgers told the court:

> I have analysed the contents of these packages [numbered 5, 6 and 7]. All the three cakes in the parcel contained a large quantity of arsenic – a dangerous quantity of the poison in each piece of the cake. I have made a quantitative analysis of the packet No. 7 and the arsenic contained in it weighed a grain and a quarter, the poison being the white arsenic, a proportion of 11 grains and two-tenths of arsenic to an ounce of cake. I cannot say whether the poison was or was not added after the cake was made in the case of No. 7 package, as the cake was so broken; but my impression is...

At this point Rodgers was interrupted as 'his impression' was not suitable evidence for the court and he said no more. One wonders if he was about to say he believed the cakes had been poisoned afterwards, which would indicate deliberate rather than accidental contamination.

With Rodgers uncertain, it remained up to Dr Letheby to conclude the case against Christiana. As has been mentioned before, Letheby was a well-known face at such trials and Christiana had found him frightening. Letheby had a presence about him and was not afraid to speak his opinion. Dr Letheby reiterated his previous testimony on analysing Sidney Barker's stomach and several chocolate creams, all of which contained strychnine. There was enough of the poison to easily kill a child and possibly an adult. Even more important, Letheby had been provided with two packets of chocolate creams, both bought at Maynards. However, only one packet contained poisoned chocolates and these creams appeared broken and mixed as if they had been handled prior.

Letheby had also analysed the remainder of the chocolate cream that had been partially eaten by Mrs Walker and made her so ill. The white filling of the chocolate contained a grain of strychnine to every twenty grains of cream and '...while half a grain was a poisonous dose, a grain was regarded as a killing quantity. One large cream of those handed to [Letheby] contained six or seven grains.'[78] This was a dangerous testimony because, even though circumstantial, there was a direct link to the chocolates left at Mrs Cole's shop which then found their way to Mrs Walker and Christiana.

Lastly, Mr Ware came forward and gave his opinion (as a chocolate manufacturing expert) as to how the poison was placed into the chocolate. He had been in his business for thirty-two years and manufactured French creams exclusively – the same creams that the killer exclusively chose to poison, but there was a good reason for that as Ware explained:

> There is a great difference between [French and English creams]. English get hard in the centre, but the French are soft when warmed by the hand, and anything may be pricked in and the puncture glazed over again with the finger. This was the character of chocolate creams purchased by the prisoner.[79]

Gibbs had virtually proved his case. He had pinned down the motive and had shown Christiana had the opportunity and the means to poison chocolates. Serjeant Parry might try and convince a jury that evidence against his client was circumstantial and nothing really conclusive (as long as he ignored the testimony of the children who had accepted chocolates direct from Christiana that had made them ill), but he knew it was a long shot. The jury would take a great deal of convincing to be swayed from the opinion that Christiana was a cold-blooded killer. He only had one option left. He had to argue Christiana was insane and spare her from the noose.

CHAPTER THIRTEEN

A Plea for Insanity

Insanity was an unpopular concept among the Victorians. Recent inroads into the processes and symptoms of mental health problems had left people feeling decidedly uncomfortable – it seemed anybody could be insane and, worse, they need not show their madness by overtly violent or eccentric behaviours. This disturbed a population brought up to believe insanity was both obvious and easily identifiable. As Mary Elizabeth Braddon wrote in Lady Audley's Secret, the sensation novel of the century, '...how many minds must tremble upon the narrow boundary between reason and unreason, mad today and sane tomorrow, mad yesterday and sane today'.[80] Braddon voiced a worry that faced many as madness seemed to become more and more prevalent in Victorian society.

The concept of insanity also raised awkward questions about criminality and guilt. Surely murder in itself, the ultimate of crimes, could be considered a form of madness? But if so then, where did guilt and consequence lie? Should all murderers be treated as insane and thus spared the noose?

Punishment was a paramount element of social control in Victorian Britain and the idea that murderers might be 'let off' because they were simply insane at the time of the crime troubled the public. It was a different matter when dealing with traditional madmen: those that raved, acted violently and displayed a lack of humanity. These creatures, demented as they were, could be afforded sympathy and treated with kindness by being sent to an asylum. It was the quiet madman, the person who seemed totally normal at first glance and who, on closer acquaintance, might be simply described as a little odd who worried the public, police and the court system alike. Where was the line between insane and sane? These ordinary madmen, who could spend their lives without raising an eyebrow until the time of their crime, baffled juries and were a nightmare for judges.

Christiana was a prime example. She had lived for forty years among normal society, showing no outward troubling signs until the moment she snapped and began poisoning strangers. If that was insanity then surely anyone was at risk both from madmen and madness itself!

The philosophy of insanity filled column after column in newspapers. To try and comfort a frightened readership, editors offered causes for insanity – from excessive drink to sexual neglect – and pointed out that insane criminals were more likely to come from the lower classes with their poor living conditions, lax moral standards and easy access to alcohol. Do not fear middle and upper classes for you are immune to insanity proclaimed the papers! Of course, they were dreadfully wrong – in some cases there was a tendency for hereditary insanity in the nobility due to years of inter-marriage. The insanity of King George III is one famous example, but there were plenty of other families troubled by inherited madness. Today, we would recognise these strains of insanity as symptoms of untreated hereditary illnesses. To the Victorians they were baffling and frightening.

The pseudo-science of phrenology briefly seemed to offer a solution. Though it was quickly disregarded by scientists and many medical professionals, it was taken to heart by the public and particularly the newspapermen. Throughout Christiana's trial, lengthy descriptions of her were published in the papers, describing every detail of her appearance for the benefit of amateur phrenologists who could read madness and criminal tendencies in the angle of an ear or the length of a nose. The gist of the science was that the inner workings of the mind were reflected in the outward appearance of a person, a theory that can be argued to unconsciously affect our perception of criminals today.

Certain areas of the brain, argued phrenologists, if overused would cause a portion of the head to become more pronounced. By studying the contours of the head and how they interrelated with the features of the face, a true idea of the person's personality, inclinations and desires could be formed. Of course, phrenology rapidly became used to identify the criminally inclined. But the bumps on the head were no sounder a method for finding a madman than any other method the general public might employ. It was merely a comforter to a scared populace.

However, for those involved in the legal system, there was more to disturb them than the identification of insane criminals – it was what to do with them that bothered so many. While in the past insanity was a defence, but not necessarily one that would spare a perpetrator the noose, the Victorian humanitarian movement pushed the courts to spare criminals who were insane. Insanity meant a person could not be responsible for their actions and so the death penalty was not only pointless but cruel. Sympathy should be bestowed on those who had succumbed to madness and who had been failed by society prior to their crimes. If only they had been identified as insane sooner not only would they have gained the help they needed (as much as there was in Victorian Britain), but their victim would be still alive. Thus it was society's fault the crime was committed, not the madman. Such thinking was very new and not always popular, but it was having an impact on courts that would become fundamental to Christiana's future.

One May evening in 1800, ex-soldier James Hadfield entered the Theatre Royal in Drury Lane with a loaded pistol. As the National Anthem was played and King George III stood in the Royal Box, James aimed his gun and shot at his majesty. The bullet missed, possibly deliberately, and James cried out, 'God bless your royal highness. I like you very well, you are a good fellow.'[81] James was quickly arrested and sent to trial for treason. This proved deeply significant as the severe charge enabled him to be represented by counsel, a privilege not afforded to most criminals. Representing James was Thomas Erskine (reputedly the most brilliant attorney of his day) who quickly realised that his client's only defence was insanity.

James, in modern terms, had a good case. At the battle of Roubaix in 1794, he had been dreadfully injured, suffering eight sabre blows to the head which left permanent disfigurement and probable brain damage. He was subsequently captured by the French, though somehow made his way back to England. Lost and abandoned, James fell under the influence of a millenarian cult who were predicting the imminent return of Christ and thus the end of the world. James was deeply taken by the idea and slowly became convinced that he could speed up events by sacrificing himself to the state. In his damaged mind, he reasoned that judicial murder by the state would cause Christ to return faster and the most obvious, and simplest way, to achieve this was by making an attempt at treason. No one knows if James meant to kill the king or wanted to be tried for attempted treason. It was probably the latter as James, despite it all, seems to have been quite a gentle soul.

Erskine was convinced his client was deranged, but legally he would have problems making a case. Insanity had been a defence since the medieval period, yet it was carefully defined and a madman had to exhibit a complete loss of humanity to the point of bestiality. In other words he must be '…lost to all sense … incapable of forming a judgement upon the consequences of the act which he is about to do'.[82] There were several reasons why James did not fit this criteria. He had been able to obtain a pistol, know where to find the king and picked a spot within the theatre that would give him a perfect line of fire. He had also repeatedly made it clear that it had been his intention to shoot at the royal highness. This clearly made him far from 'lost to all sense' and he had indicated he had a firm idea of the likely consequences of his actions. Erskine chose to challenge the traditional definitions of madness. Complete loss of all reason, he argued, would render a person incapable of committing any act, criminal or otherwise. Instead, he suggested that a true delusional nature was one '...unaccompanied by frenzy or raving madness ... the true character of insanity'.[83]

Erskine brought in two surgeons and a physician to explain the injuries James had sustained and which they concluded had caused his insanity. The matter was helped as several of the sabre scars were still clearly visible on James' scalp. But Erskine's best argument was James' ludicrous association and belief in the millenarian cult. The testimony was persuasive and Lord Chief Justice Kenyon realised the case was progressing in a manner both unparalleled and politically hazardous. His hands were tied. The law stated that if a defendant was found to be completely deranged, he had to be acquitted and Erskine proved his client's insanity, despite having to go against most of the traditional views of madness. That left a difficult situation. Kenyon had to acquit James and that meant he would simply walk free, yet that would also leave him free to try again. James was too insane to be hung, but also too insane to be let loose on the public.

Parliament acted swiftly. The king's life could be in danger and with unusual speed they passed an emergency bill – the Criminal Lunatics Act 1800 came into existence. In simple terms, this introduced a new court verdict in special cases: not guilty by reason of insanity. Instead of a standard acquittal, the new verdict meant the person would not be executed, but would spend the rest of their life in an institution for the insane. No longer could a person walk free from committing a crime simply by claiming to be insane.

James Hadfield spent the next forty-one years locked in a cell at Bethlem Hospital (except for a brief spell when he escaped and was taken to Newgate). For the man who had wanted death so badly, his incarceration was infinitely worse. He died at Bethlem aged sixty-nine in 1841. Hadfield's case had several impacts on the court system, not least the Criminal Lunatics Act that made juries and judges feel more comfortable with finding a person insane. In the past, dangerous and delusional criminals had been treated as normal because no one wanted to see them gain an acquittal and go free. Erskine had compelled the jury at James' trial to open their minds to the possibility that insanity need not present itself as bestiality, but could be something more subtle. A twisting of morality, even a belief that what was wrong was right. These alterations in thinking have had a lasting impact to this day and the idea of what does and does not constitute insanity remains a challenging concept to modern juries.

For centuries, Bethlem had been the home for the mad. Often referred to as 'Bedlam' because of the chaos that ruled inside and the appalling treatment of the inmates, it was gradually changing its image in the nineteenth century. Though like Newgate goal where Christiana had her first taste of London institutions, the changes were often half-hearted or ineffective. When James Hadfield entered Bethlem in 1800, it was still customary for visitors to pay a penny to view the inmates (there was free entry on the first Tuesday of every month). Close to 100,000 visitors toured Bethlem in 1814 alone. At least the inmates were now referred to as 'patients' and were separated into different wards – the curables and incurables.

The number of people being sent to Bedlam, particularly with the new Act, was making it plain the old buildings were no longer suitable or big enough. Therefore in 1815, the new Bethlem Hospital was opened at St George's Fields, Southwark. In the first winter, there was no glass in the windows and the patients (now called 'unfortunates') shivered their way through the colder months. Perhaps it was partly this act of cruelty, designed to reduce unpleasant odours in the asylum, that caused head physician Thomas Monro to resign in 1816 under a scandalous cloud. He was accused of 'wanting humanity' towards the 'unfortunates'.

It was the scandals of Bethlem that influenced Victorian writers when they conjured up desperate images of frightening lunatic asylums. Charles Reade, Victorian sensation novelist, was particularly fond of dreaming up disturbing and arcane institutions where his suffering characters could tremble and quake with fear at their treatment. Lunatic asylums in general had become quite a fetish for Victorian writers. They were the 'in-thing', the most famous example being in the *Woman in White* by Wilkie Collins.

Christiana could not have been unaware of these stories as they appeared in the papers, journals and novels she would have read. There is little indication of what she felt or thought about her defence plea of insanity. It is unlikely she had much say in the matter as defendants rarely did in those days. But in her mind she would have been wondering what was to become of her. She had already had a sample of life in confinement at Newgate and her knowledge of asylums would have been shaped by the fictional works of the day, even if they were largely exaggerations. The prospect of being declared insane and sent to an asylum was an equally terrifying prospect as the noose. Charles Reade had thrilled and frightened readers with stories of the brutal methods of restraint used on the 'unfortunates' and the abuses perpetrated on them. He had been writing sensationalism, but he based a great deal on truth. Christiana had to be aware of the awful fate she faced and she had to be scared.

There was at least one saving grace for her. She just might avoid Bethlem as it was now one of three hospitals serving the criminally insane. The other two were Fisherton House Asylum (opened 1849) and the brand new Broadmoor Criminal Lunatic Asylum opened in 1863. If only she was not being tried in London she could have expected to end up in a county asylum which were smaller and generally quite respectable places (they had to be due to regular inspections). Instead, she was at the Central Criminal Court and her prospects were grim. Yet first, she still had to be proved insane.

Erskine had muddied the waters of criminal lunacy quite unintentionally when he defended James Hadfield. The problem remained: what was actual insanity? Even today, the question is open to debate. The Victorians found themselves at the forefront of a new era in the understanding of mental illness and they were increasingly struggling. There simply were no real definitions of what was madness. Insanity was a catch-all phrase that included those who were deemed lunatics and mentally unsound to those with a mental deficiency or medical problem.

When a pauper felon needed to be deemed insane, a medical man (and this could be a loose term in itself) would be called to certify him mad. If this was accompanied by papers by a Justice of the Peace or clergyman and a relieving officer for the poor laws, then the accused would find himself carted off to an asylum instead of a prison. Judgement was therefore largely based on a surgeon or doctor's opinion. This was all very well for minor cases, but in the criminal courts where matters were more serious, just the opinion of a doctor was not enough. Something clearer and irrefutable was needed to enable judges and juries to understand just *why* a person was being declared insane. The matter was not really moving forwards until the case of Daniel MacNaghten in 1843.

In January of that year, Edward Drummond, private secretary to Sir Robert Peel, was confronted by a well-dressed Scot who promptly proceeded to shoot him. Drummond died five days later. It would have been no comfort to him to know that the Scot, Daniel MacNaghten, had really been after the prime minister but had not known what he looked like and mistook Drummond for someone important. By March, MacNaghten was at the Central Criminal Court on a charge of murder and being defended by another celebrated counsel, Alexander Cockburn. Cockburn was determined to argue his client's insanity by claiming that he was possessed by a powerful delusion that the Tories were his deadly enemies. The prosecution, while accepting that MacNaghten may have been delusional about politics, argued that this did not mean he was incapable of understanding right from wrong and as such should be responsible for his crimes. Cockburn called nine medical experts to prove his client's insanity and when this went unchallenged by the prosecution he won his case. MacNaghten was deemed not guilty by reason of insanity.

While similar verdicts had been recorded in less sensational cases over the last four decades, it was the cold-bloodedness of MacNaghten and the calibre of his crime that brought the defence of insanity into question again. The public and even the queen were disturbed that such a man could be deemed insane and escape justice, and they feared this paved the way for other madmen to feel they could commit crimes with no fear of any real judicial retribution. MacNaghten did not seem all that mad. He was rather radical in his politics and, of course, he had shot a stranger, but it was rather slim evidence compared to that of James Hadfield. Hadfield at least had physical scars to prove the cause of his delusions (Victorians liked things they could see) and it was decidedly strange to think you could sacrifice yourself to encourage the second coming. Interestingly, modern academics are now questioning if the public and the queen did not, in fact, have a point. Some now believe MacNaghten was not mad at all.[84]

The resulting controversy generated a debate in the House of Lords. It was decided that judges would be asked to state criteria which a jury could use to decide the criminal responsibility of a defendant. The MacNaghten rules, as they became known, were in essence a test of 'right-from-wrong'. Juries had to decide if an accused was of such a deluded nature that they were either unaware of what they were doing or unaware that it was wrong. Simplistic in its form, the 'right-from-wrong' rules were far too narrow in reality, but they provided a jury with something they could understand and grasp on to. The result was many genuinely insane prisoners being judged responsible for their crimes. Ironically, a genuine madman might be judged sane by a criminal court and sent to prison while a non-offender would be deemed insane and sent to an asylum. This was the sort of situation Serjeant Parry was up against when it came to defending Christiana.

As for MacNaghten, whether he was feigning madness or not, his fate could have been deemed worse than death. He was sent to Bethlem and spent the next twenty-one years in an eight-and-a-half by ten-and-a-half stone cell. In 1864, he was transferred to Broadmoor, but died the following year due to heart complications. He was entirely forgotten by the public and *The Times* failed to record his passing. On the other hand, the MacNaghten Rules were now standard in the court system and would remain so in Britain until 1957.[85]

In 1863, there were 877 criminal lunatics in custody and in 1880, 1,280 individuals[86] were classified as criminal lunatics or ex-criminal lunatics (we have to assume the latter as they were either deemed 'cured' or of no further harm to anyone). That seems quite a low figure, but it would have not accounted for those who had failed the MacNaghten test and had been sent to an ordinary prison. There still remained an open question as to the best way to deal with the insane criminal. Placing them in asylums put them out of harm from the public's point of view, but it was very disagreeable to the asylum staff and other patients who were now sharing their quarters with often dangerous and violent individuals. Bearing in mind that at this period the inmates of an asylum varied from those with behavioural or learning problems (lumped under idiocy), to epilepsy, depression, hysteria or the general term of mania which covered a wealth of issues including anxiety and nervous conditions. These patients did not wish their peace to be ruined by criminal lunatics.

For the most part, however, there was very little option. Bethlem, Fisherton and Broadmoor were only for the worst cases and the majority of convicted madmen found themselves at county asylums. Roughly speaking, county asylums held 50 per cent of the criminally insane throughout the latter half of the nineteenth century. Discussion was also raging as to the validity of MacNaghten's rules. As Christiana came to trial, the legal authorities, led in part by prison doctors who had firsthand experience of the insane who had been wrongfully sent to them, were beginning to understand the mixed bag that insanity was. There had still been a prevailing idea that the insane felon was identifiable by his violent and seriously disordered mind. However, closer attention was being paid to the weak-minded felon who was equally insane, yet due to his less spectacular symptoms did not afford the sympathy of the jury. These 'weak-minded' individuals found their way into the ordinary prison system and were often identified as repeat offenders who simply could not help themselves. In 1869, it was estimated that one in every nine prisoners was 'more or less insane'.[87] At Perth prison, Dr James Bruce Thomson gave a similar estimate that 12 per cent of prison inmates would be deemed insane to various degrees.

More significantly there was a new theory about there being such a thing as 'born-criminals'. This came from the concept of progressive degeneracy '...in which ever worsening moral and physical defects could be passed from one generation to another...'[88] Effectively, this fed into the idea that insanity was hereditary and that if madness affected a person's ancestors, at some point this would reach a peak in subsequent generations, producing the criminal lunatic. It was a challenging concept, but it fixated on previous ideas about family traditions of insanity.

It was on this point that Serjeant Parry would rest his defence case. Physically, there were no obvious signs of mental deficiency in Christiana. She did not show violent tendencies or any outward abnormalities. She was not prone to fits (she did faint in court but a doctor from Newgate testified that this was not due to epilepsy, a blow to the insanity defence as epilepsy could be a symptom). She spoke and acted perfectly reasonably. She refrained from outbursts during her trial and gave the appearance of being wholly respectable. What a blow to Parry! He needed evidence his client was quite mad. The MacNaghten test could be awkward, Christiana after all had proven time and again that she was aware that poisoning the population of Brighton was wrong. She had made all those protests to Mr Maynard and called in the police – not the actions of someone who could be claimed to have no idea that lacing chocolates with strychnine was a crime.

She did not take opium or morphine (Victorians understood the mental consequences of drug addiction) and there was no sign of alcoholism, another blow as alcohol was seen as a cause of insanity as well as a symptom of it. Only the weak-minded, after all, would become addicted to drink. In essence, Parry had only one choice. He had to prove that Christiana was a victim of progressive degeneracy, or at least a variation of it. He could not state she was a born criminal, but that her family history inclined her to insanity. For the Edmunds family, every skeleton in the cupboard was about to tumble out as Parry determined to prove his client was utterly and totally insane.

CHAPTER FOURTEEN

Family of Lunatics

John Humffreys Parry was born in 1816 and, compared to many of his contemporaries, had an odd career to the bar. He was the son of an antiquary and received a commercial-based education at the Philological School, Marylebone, with the expectation he would go into trade. He briefly spent time in a merchant's office, but disliked it so much that he was delighted to accept a post at the British Museum in their printed books department. He was effectively a library assistant and began the mammoth task of cataloguing the museum's vast numbers of books, writing everything out by hand.

He was not a man without ambitions, however, and in the best tradition of the Victorian idea of an 'improving man', he spent his free time listening to lectures at the Aldersgate Institution and studying for the bar. He was called to the bar in 1843 aged twenty-seven and rapidly became a prominent figure at the Central Criminal Court. He was made a serjeant-at-law in 1856, a massive career move as it gave him access to better (and more profitable) work within the civil courts. He was very successful '...thanks to an admirable appearance and voice, great clearness and simplicity of statement, and the tact of a born advocate'.[89] Sadly, it was also in 1856 that he lost his first wife Margaret New, though barely a year later he was remarried to Elizabeth Mead Abbott.

Parry was an advanced liberal in his political views, an awkward position that put some noses out of joint around the conservative law courts. He felt sympathy for the first chartist movement, though was against the extremes of some of its members and was also one of the founders of the Complete Suffrage Association in 1842, a radical movement open to everyone and appealing to the working classes. This mattered little to Christiana. She was more interested in Parry's criminal court career where he had starred in a number of high profile cases including that of Franz Muller in 1864, the Manning trial of 1849 and the Tichborne claimant case.

In 1872, as Parry prepared his insanity defence for Christiana, he was a settled family man with two sons (John who would become an actor, but died aged only twenty-nine in 1891, and Edward who became a successful judge, author, dramatist and theatre producer dying during the Second World War) and two young daughters. He was fifty-six and at the height of his career. He was easily a match for Ballantine with whom he was on good terms. If only the case were not so clear-cut...

For Parry, proving Christiana insane was not easy. She presented a calm, outward appearance in court – she seemed rational, intelligent and above all, perfectly ordinary. There was no obvious sign of madness to present to the laymen of the jury. She did not rend her clothes or rant gibberish or attack her gaolers violently like the quintessential crazed person of the past. Christiana's madness was far more subtle and sinister. It loitered in the background causing her to concoct ghastly schemes while Christiana appeared to be the picture of respectability. Parry's only hope was to show that her family had a streak of madness running through it that had coagulated into Christiana and turned her into a poisoner without conscience. Parry opened his defence for Christiana by first trying to pick holes in what was proving to be an extraordinarily water-tight case:

> ...the only course to be taken was that of placing before the jury every fact in reference to the prisoner, of commenting upon the evidence already given, of pointing out to them the real issue, and then of leaving the matter in their hands and those of his Lordship ... The issue was, in fact, an extremely narrow one, and the evidence directly and immediately relating to that issue lay in the smallest possible compass.

Parry was admitting it would be difficult to defend his client against the charges before he even began. It seems a rather negative approach.

> The prisoner was charged with the murder of a child of tender years, whom she had neither known nor seen, and against whom, therefore, she could not entertain either malice, hatred or dislike. On the part of the prosecution it was said that she was in the possession of poison which she distributed broadcast over the town of Brighton in portions sufficient to take away human life, and if by her agency that poison was given to the child and caused his death, she was as much guilty of wilful murder as if she had entertained towards the boy the deadliest and most abominable malice, and had administered the poison with her own hands.

[Parry] could not deny that the prisoner obtained strychnia from Mr Garrett ... but he confessed he was astonished to find that gentleman, in that short time, supplied the prisoner on the most flimsy pretences with poison capable of killing 60 or 70 people...

He again could not deny, for it would be futile to do so, that the prisoner had been found delivering chocolate creams containing, if not poison, some deleterious matter, to a number of children, of whom six or seven had become more or less ill in consequence. But the jury, before convicting the prisoner, must be satisfied beyond doubt that the chocolate which caused the little boy's death came to be given to him, directly or indirectly, through the agency of the prisoner.

...was that fact proved clearly, unmistakeably, and beyond all doubt ... The lad May was undoubtedly sent by the prisoner to get some chocolate at Maynard's shop at the end of May or the beginning of June and received it in a bag and handed it to the prisoner ... It was then alleged that she opened it, and either sent that same bag, into which she had slipped some poisoned sweets, or another bag which she had substituted for it back to the confectioner's. Now there was an entire absence of proof that the prisoner did any such thing. On other occasions, when the prisoner sent boys for sweets in the same way it was not pretended that she had returned them in an altered or a poisoned shape.

It was remarkable that the chocolates in question were not purchased until ten or 12 (sic) days after the transaction in which the prisoner had used the lad May, and during that time the case in the shop from which they had been taken must have been emptied and refilled half a dozen times ... On the Monday morning when the witness Miller bought the creams the shop woman nearly emptied the compartment to serve him , and it was afterwards filled up. But, strange to say, the sweets that were subsequently purchased by Ernest Miller, his brother which would have been taken from the top of the new heap and not from the bottom of the compartment, where his brother's had been got, also contained strychnia. That fact alone proved almost to demonstration that the poison was not put there by the prisoner, and the matter was worthy of their most grave and serious attention.

This was a complete distortion of the facts by Parry. Firstly, the shop staff from Maynards had made it clear in their testimony that during the summer there was a downturn in the sales of chocolate creams and this resulted in the cases not requiring refilling so often. So the returned chocolates, once jumbled in with the rest, could have easily sat there for ten or twelve days before being purchased. Secondly, it is normal practice in the stocking of perishable goods to ensure that the oldest products sit in front or on top of the newest. When the case was refilled, the remaining old chocolates would have been removed before the new ones were added and then placed on the top of the new stock. Otherwise, the same chocolates would remain at the bottom of the case indefinitely. It was therefore completely logical that the chocolates Ernest bought should be poisoned even though they came from the top of the case as they had previously been at the bottom. Parry can be forgiven this slip as he probably did not know the normal practices of such shops, but his contradiction of the evidence of the Maynards staff was a clear attempt to manipulate the truth to save his client. Parry was indeed desperate and he knew all too well that this niggling at the finer points of the case was far from enough. He moved on to the case for her insanity.

> He had thought it his duty, in addition to commenting upon the evidence, to give [the jury] a history of the prisoner's career, and in doing so he should endeavour to prove without doubt that she was of impaired intellect. He frankly confessed that the whole of the case rather baffled him; he did not know how to deal with it. In his experience at the bar – now not a short one – and in his reading of the criminal annals of this and other countries, he did not remember any similar case, and he felt completely at a loss to know how to place it before them in the way of argument.
>
> He would prove that the father of the prisoner died at mid age in a lunatic asylum, and that for years before his death he suffered from that form of insanity known as suicidal and homicidal mania; that her brother died in the prime of life an epileptic idiot at the Earlswood Asylum; that both her grandfathers were of unsound mind; that her sister suffered from constant hysteria, and that other relatives were afflicted with insanity. She herself, when about 24 years of age, was seized with paralysis under most painful circumstances, and her conduct for some time past had excited attention among her friends. About 12 or 15 months ago a great change came over her, and even now she had the idiotic vanity to deny her real age, which, instead of being 34 was 43.
>
> The nature of that insanity was in her case the entire destruction of her moral sense, and he believed that she could not fully distinguish the difference between right or wrong, or recognise the quality of the act she was committing.[90]

This was the crux of the matter. If Christiana could be proved incapable of knowing right from wrong, she would be spared the noose, though she would spend the rest of her days in an asylum. To do this, Parry had to go on a crusade of character assassination for her entire family, stripping them of their respectability and sacrificing whatever reputation remained to the surviving Edmunds. It was a costly price to pay for what could only be described as a desperate gamble.

It had to begin with Mrs Ann Christiana Edmunds, Christiana's mother, who took the stand miserably and in great distress. She was about to fight for her daughter's life, but at the expense of her family secrets and privacy. For a proud Victorian woman like Ann, it was horrific to imagine all the private problems she had kept hidden would now be broadcast across the country in the daily newspapers for the avid digestion of the sensation seekers of the day. She would be the subject of gossip and derision, and it would have only added to her depression to know that her testimony would be transmitted across the pond to America and printed in the New York papers. The Edmunds scandal was about to become trans-Atlantic to the misery of all involved. A large portion of the defence rested on the alleged insanity of William Edmunds and his behaviour that had, perhaps, been inherited along with madness by his daughter. Ann had to start her testimony with the horrible account of the final years of her husband's life.

In 1843 my husband became insane, and was sent to a private asylum at Southall, where he was confined until August 1844. He was very strange in his manner a long time before he was sent there. He raved about having millions of money, and attempted to knock down his medical man with a ruler. He had to be confined in a straightjacket before going to the asylum. He had two attendants before he was sent there. In August 1844 he returned home from considerations of expense. He was better and remained at home until March 1845, when he had to be sent to the Peckham Lunatic Asylum. He remained there until March 1847, when he died in the Asylum. For a considerable time before his death he was paralysed, though he could move. He was all drawn on one side. He was about 47 when he died.[91]

Parry claimed William Edmunds was suicidal and homicidal. But what was really going on with William in the 1840s when Christiana was just becoming a young woman? There is evidence that during the 1830s, William had been involved with some shady deals with the Margate Pier and Harbour Company and William was in the thick of it. The scandal involving a missing invoice (that led in part to the suicide of Deputy Chairman Mr Thomas Cobb) suggested fraud was at the heart of the matter. There were, after all, a few too many bankers and businessmen involved in the company to make financial carelessness believable. Charges were laid against William along with others, but were dropped in 1837. Even so, Williams suffered a pay cut and a stain on his reputation.

It was around this time William's mental health started to suffer. The result of the charges would have been acute anxiety for his position, possibly leading to depression. Dr Steward was the medical man at Southall and gave evidence on Edmunds' mental state when he saw him.

> He remembered receiving into it [Southall] Mr William Edmunds about 1843, on the usual medical certificates that he was of unsound mind and a proper person to be confined. He was described in them as 42 years of age. The idea of having immense riches was stated in the certificates to be one of the evidences of his insanity. He was also described as fond of good living, but did not drink hard. It was a case of acute mania, [with] all the customary characteristics ... Affection of the brain with increased action of the blood throughout, was one of the incidents of his disease producing congestion, and resulting in this case in apoplexy. There was general incoherence of speech and sleeplessness. He talked all manner of nonsense. Those were not the exact symptoms of *delirium tremens* [alcohol withdrawal].[92] The father did not suffer from that. It was one of the cases that the witness thought reducible by medical treatment. Dr Henry Armstrong of Peckham Lunatic Asylum produced the original medical certificates for the court which had resulted in William being put into his care. William's death was certified as being due to "general paralysis, extending over three years".

This was all very convincing, but there was a twist in William's story that failed to be produced in court. In the early 1840s, it seems the trials of the Margate Pier and Harbour Company were about to resurface again. William lived the high life and the almost immediate poverty his family fell into after his committal to an asylum suggest he was careless with his money, spending it while the good times reigned. The last thing he, or his family needed, was another exploration into his financial dealings. We will never know exactly how deep William was involved with the dubious activities behind the scenes at the company, but he benefited heavily from them and he kept quiet about the oddities arising in the company's books. If William thought this could last forever he was sorely mistaken. In 1842, one of the Directors of the Company broke under the strain and committed suicide. Robert Pringle, it emerged at the inquest, had long '... laboured under a deep-rooted delusion, in reference to something going on at the Margate Pier – that he was under confinement for something he had there committed, but was unable to state what; that all the clocks and bells in the town had been stopped until the verdict should be given; that he was sensible it would be against him, and that he should be dragged to the place of execution. He appeared quite rational on every other subject, but as soon as any allusion was made to the Pier, he would commence crying and giving himself in custody.'[93]

Pringle was viewed as insane at the time of his death, but what was a man under a terrible strain of keeping a secret and who was close to confessing it? Aside from his talk of extreme punishment, the rest of his words could be taken as genuine and rational – it was only because people did not believe there was a problem at the Margate Pier that they took it as the ravings of a madman. Was Pringle so torn between his conscience and loyalty to his friends that he became unhinged and took his own life?

We cannot be certain, but perhaps someone was as this all coincided with William's decline. Did William fear another scandal such as what had happened in 1836? William's actions now become of interest. He started to sell his assets. He advertised a house for sale or let in *The Times* around the same time as Pringle was contemplating suicide. The house never sold and this was stated as the trigger for William's initial breakdown. Why would a house sale falling through so disturb a successful architect unless his fortunes were not so favourable?

Suddenly, luck no longer seemed on William's side. Timelines now become crucial. Pringle's inquest when news of his fears of suspicious dealings occurred in September 1842. The house sale fell through early 1843 and William became insane shortly after and was in Southall asylum by the end of the year. Ann Edmunds claimed he had been peculiar for a while, but he cannot have been very odd as he was able to write a detailed and comprehensive will in 1842. Was William wrapping up more of his estate before troubles struck him? It seems far too coincidental that all these events could occur and not affect William. Which raises a further, intriguing, suggestion. It was admitted in court that William liked the high life and drank, though it was denied he was a heavy drinker. However, the only people to deny it were those who were on the defence's side. The last thing Parry wanted was the jury to believe that William Edmunds had become crazed because of drink as that would rule out hereditary insanity in Christiana's case. But Ballantine was suspicious that William's demise was the result of alcoholism.

It would be hard to imagine that a man like William, under intense emotional strain, would not consider drink as an option to drown his sorrows. It would start gradually, but all too soon he would be consuming more and more to ease his anxieties. William liked his drink and he would have turned to it in hard times. Alcoholism would explain his changing behaviour, erratic outbursts, violent moments and ravings. Ballantine was convinced William was an alcoholic because he asked whether he was suffering from withdrawal symptoms at the Southall asylum. Dr Steward said his symptoms were not those of the delirium tremens, but was that accurate? Delirium tremens is a severe form of alcohol withdrawal and usually affects people who have either been heavy drinkers for more than ten years or those who drink four to five pints of wine or seven to eight pints of beer a day. Symptoms appear seventy-two hours after the last drink, so roughly the same time as William entered the asylum. They include shaking, agitation, confusion, delirium, excitement, restlessness, seizures, anxiety, depression, insomnia and headaches.[94]

William was confused and delirious. He also suffered from acute sleeplessness and seizures, which Dr Steward attributed to 'congestion of the brain' – inflammation of the soft tissue that can also cause acute headaches. Dr Steward was inaccurate in his statement: William's symptoms clearly matched those of a person suffering alcohol withdrawal. The seizures are particularly significant and in a delirium tremens patient can be extremely violent and result in partial paralysis of one side of the body lasting for minutes or hours. 'He was all drawn on one side,' Ann stated about her husband. It seems William Edmunds was a victim of alcoholism rather than genetic insanity. Ballantine believed as much and Parry was desperate to avoid the topic being raised. The sudden onset of his condition at a time of significant crises in his life, along with never before showing any symptoms, all point to an outside factor playing a role, rather than the mental snapping of an unstable person. Still, the events were traumatic for the young family and would have left lasting effects. It is also possible from other accounts that Edmunds was a sensitive soul who did not cope well with pressure and some of his children inherited this trait. However, sensitivity would not help Christiana and Parry had to push for more evidence of a family afflicted by madness.

'I had a son named Arthur Burns Edmunds,' Ann Christiana continued. 'He was subject to epileptic fits from a child. In February 1860, we could not manage him. He was very violent at times and was at length taken to Earlswood Asylum where he remained until 1866 and died there.' Born in 1842, Arthur was Christiana's youngest sibling when everything began to go wrong for the Edmunds family. Christiana was thirteen and attended a boarding school, so she did not see a great deal of Arthur until he was older, by which time it was clear he was an epileptic. Epilepsy was misunderstood by the Victorians and treated as a form of insanity. Radical cures were suggested from surgically removing the clitoris in affected women to the ingestion of various toxic substances to illicit a cure. The *North Wales Chronicle* of 1835 reported one case of epilepsy cured by the taking of increasingly large doses of Iodine. Indigestion was readily linked with the condition and even suggested as a cause as was excessive sexual passion (largely in women) and unhealthy activities resulting from it such as masturbation.

The idea of a link between insanity and epilepsy is more obvious. People subject to epilepsy in a period when it was impossible to control their seizures would have fitted violently and uncontrollably, often falling and striking their heads repeatedly. The result was brain damage from every fit and, if the epilepsy began in childhood, the effects would have been accumulative and drastic. Many epileptics eventually became 'imbeciles' in Victorian phraseology, simply from the damage caused during fits. However, the cause and effects of this form of 'idiocy' was not understood and assumptions were made that it was a pre-existing form of insanity that caused the epilepsy, and that it was the unstable personality that induced fits. A person who was epileptic, therefore, was also deemed mentally impaired. In criminal cases, epilepsy was sometimes used as proof a person was insane and also as an excuse for their actions. Defence lawyers argued crimes were committed when a person was in the clutches of an epileptic sensation and so the person could not be responsible for their actions.

Juries, unfortunately for the epileptic criminal, were not convinced. They rarely accepted seizures as evidence a person was not responsible for their crimes, not that it stopped lawyers trying the excuse time and again. In 1890, Eleanor Mary Wheeler (also called Mrs Piercey) was found guilty of murdering Mrs Phoebe Hogg and sentenced to death. Her solicitor Mr Palmer was determined to get her off as insane and even wrote to the Home Office citing Wheeler's past history of suicide attempts and hallucinations as proof (he was probably correct as to her mental state). All this was reported by the *Blackburn Standard* and *Weekly Express* under the headline 'Epilepsy and Murder'. Quite obviously, the Victorians saw a link between the illness and a dangerous personality. Therefore, Arthur Burns' epilepsy was, at least in Victorian thinking, evidence of insanity in the family. But there was more enticing evidence to modern minds that mental instability was rife in the Edmunds' clan.

'I had a daughter, a sister of the prisoner,' explained Ann Christiana. 'She is now dead. She suffered from hysteria and attempted when in a fit to throw herself from a window. She was about 36 when she died. She was always excited and suffered from hysteria.' This is the mysterious Louisa. She was two years younger than Christiana, making her eleven at the time of their father's sudden illness. Unlike her older sister, she was at home when William Edmunds fell into his alcohol-induced madness and bore full witness to the deterioration of her father. Perhaps this had a harsh impact on the sensitive Louisa. Hysteria was a broad term and could easily relate to anxiety or nervousness. Louisa, in many respects, appears to have been like her father in personality and may have suffered the most during his sickness.

Louisa is a fleeting presence in the records of the day. She disappears in 1851, not appearing with the rest of the family who were in Canterbury for that census year. She then reappears in 1861 working as a governess for a family in Surrey. Despite her hysteria, she seems to have been quite capable of taking care of herself and was the only sister to earn a living. This adds another dimension to Louisa. Unlike her sisters who stayed close to their mother, Louisa was more inclined to move far away. She took her first position in the area where her elder brother William resided when he was a medical student (it is possible he found her the job), but this is the only sign of contact between Louisa and her family. There are tantalising glimpses in the dry records of the day that there was a rift between some of the Edmunds children. William and Louisa made every effort to distance themselves from their mother and siblings. Louisa maintained her distance as a governess, eventually dying in Surrey. William travelled to South Africa, ironically to work in a lunatic asylum, as the head doctor. He never returned home. In comparison to Christiana and her sister Mary, who remained close even after the trial, the actions of William and Louisa, and the fact they almost vanish from family records, is a stark contrast.

But what really happened to Louisa? We do not know when she made the attempt on her life, but as she was living away by 1851, we can presume it occurred during the course of her father's illness and internment in an asylum. Today, we could argue the emotional stress of the events in her young life were the cause of this outburst, which may have been more the dramatic actions of a teenager in distress than a genuine suicide attempt. She was only twenty in 1851, yet self-possessed enough to live away from her family and maintain a position as a governess, not the actions of someone who was emotionally unstable. The life of a governess was hard. She was caught in an awkward limbo between the servants of the house and the family – she was neither one nor the other. Loneliness, unhappiness and hopelessness were often complained of by the women who fitted into this role. There were little prospects for the future. Louisa would expect to work until she was either too old or too ill to continue. She would then be in a dreadful position of homelessness and poverty.

During the Victorian period, it was recognised how appalling the life of a governess could be. Even working for a nice family she was isolated and it was far from an easy career choice. Many women found themselves unable to cope. In contrast, Louisa stuck at it. She maintained her position and, by all accounts, was a governess at the time of her death aged thirty-six. Was that the actions of an unstable or emotionally weak person? Louisa had a resolve in her character that can also be seen in Christiana (though it came out in very different ways). Her stressful and emotionally-charged younger years may have made her mother call her hysterical, but in truth she was a strong, determined and adept young woman – to use her as a case for family insanity is ludicrous. However, Ann Christiana was clutching at straws and any event, however far back and circumstantial, was brought to the surface to save Christiana. What, we have to wonder, would Louisa have thought about her character assassination?

There was one last close relative who could be used to prove a pattern of insanity – Major John Burn or Burns, Christiana's maternal grandfather. Ann Christiana was clear about her father's madness. 'My father, Mr Burns, was a Major in the Army. He died at the age of 43. He was paralysed before he died, he died in a fit. He had to be fastened in a chair, and was quite childish before he died.' John Burn was born circa 1770 and by 1793, was a Second Lieutenant in the Royal Marines. The RM is usually given an official foundation date as 1755, though there had been soldiers on English naval vessels before then. When John Burn entered the force, he would have trained as an infantry man, but would have spent his time either stationed at a sea port or aboard a Royal Navy ship. The Royal Marines' role was to act as the fighting arm of a ship's force, repelling boarding attacks by enemy sailors and leading their own assaults with volleys of musket fire. It was a dangerous role. Not only did Marines have to contend with the normal hazards of infantry combat, but there was always the risk of their ship being lost while at sea and the constant issues of short supplies and disease.

Despite these issues, the Royal Marines were not entirely appreciated and it was not until 1771 that an RM officer was able to obtain the rank of colonel, prior to then they could only reach the rank of lieutenant colonel. Marines also had a difficult time with the sailors they spent their days alongside as they fell awkwardly into the hierarchy of the ship's crew. They were not full sailors, yet were a vital element of the ship's complement. As a fighting force, they left the crew free to safeguard the ship, but that also meant keeping the sailors out of the main action and taking glory for themselves. They were not entirely welcome and Navy sailors gave them the derogatory nickname 'lobsters' due to their red uniforms.

John Burn's early days in the Marines were relatively quiet, the American War of Independence being just over and the Napoleonic wars yet to begin. He rose to first lieutenant in April 1795 and became a captain in 1803 at the same time as Britain went to war with France. Eleven years later, he was made a major just before retiring on full pay. This suggests something unusual and a logical assumption is that John had been injured in conflict making him unable to continue his duties, but had served so well that a consideration was made for him and his family that he should retire with pay. That he was promoted just before his retirement indicates a careful fiddle to ensure he would get more money than he was technically entitled to.

Shortly after his promotion and retirement he appears to have had a stroke and was dead within a year of obtaining his new rank. In all likelihood, John Burn had been a victim of one of the brutal conflicts of the closing years of the Napoleonic wars and had suffered severe injuries. While no mention of physical deformity is ever mentioned (i.e., loss of a limb), something terrible had happened that resulted in him being permanently out of action. The swiftness of his stroke suggests a potential head injury, which would explain his odd condition, mental impairment, fits and death.

Again, this was not well understood by the Victorians. What Ann Christiana saw as a hereditary mental illness in her father was the result of his fighting career and could have no impact on Christiana's proposed insanity. But few people of the time would have entirely realised this and the evidence did seem conclusive that Christiana had a wealth of mad relatives in her family. That all their conditions were either medical or induced by an outside influence and therefore not genetic was simply beyond the understanding of the time.

What of Christiana? Her mother had plenty to say:

[My daughter] in 1853 suffered from an illness, and was sent to London. On her return she was paralysed on one side and in her feet. She could not walk. Mr Prettyman, a surgeon now dead, attended her. Besides paralysis, she suffered from hysteria. She would come from her room at night into mine, and say she had had a fit of hysteria and could not breathe. She suffered from it for several years, and even now at times. As a child she walked in her sleep, and I was obliged to have a button on the outside of a door to prevent her walking out in that state. Recently, and for some time back – ever since she has known Dr Beard – I have noticed a great change in her demeanour.

Dr Humphry attended [my daughter] after she came home from Margate in August last. I believe she had been poisoned after eating some fruit. I begged her when she had a piece of a peach to put it out and to remember the poor little boy Barker. She said she thought she was poisoned. I did not suggest to anyone at that time there was anything the matter with her mind. It was a delicate subject to speak of. In consequence of statements made by Dr Beard, I demanded a retraction from him and threatened to put the matter into the hands of a lawyer. [Christiana] was greatly excited by those statements and I could not restrain her. She said the Beards had never spoken to her since the matter of the chocolates. She went about the room quite mad. She behaved with kindness to people in the house. She was beloved by everybody.

She is now about 43 years of age and I have always had a dread of her in relation to that time of her life; she is so very like her father.

In 1853, Christiana was twenty-two. Her father had been dead six years and her brother William and sister Louisa had recently moved away. Epileptic Arthur was eleven and was beginning to become extremely difficult to deal with when he was taken by a fit. The family had moved to Canterbury to leave behind the scandal of William Edmunds' madness and death along with the unspoken suspicions against him involving his role in the Pier and Harbour Company. Money was tight and her younger sister Mary was contemplating marriage as a solution to her circumstances. Where did this leave Christiana?

Under great stress, emotionally and practically, she could no longer live the life she had become accustomed to. She was as close to being poor as she could come while still being deemed a middle-class lady. Louisa had moved away to become a governess and relieve her family of one burden. There was unspoken pressure for Christiana to do the same, though her mother was concerned at how her eldest daughter would cope away from home. Life was full of unpleasant upheavals and changes. Arthur's illness was taking a toll and as the oldest sibling, Christiana was expected to help care for him. It simply became all too much. Christiana suffered a nervous collapse. In modern psychiatric terms, she was affected by conversion disorder: '...the emergence of physical symptoms as an unconscious attempt to resolve a painful psychic conflict. The advantages accruing from the adoption of the sick role contribute to perpetuate the disability.'[95]

In short, Christiana suffered from paralysis due to extreme emotional stress, probably developing over a number of years since the sickness of her father. There had to be a specific trigger, but exactly what it was remains unknown. Conversion disorder is still recognised and extensively studied today. It is an involuntary condition: the patient is not feigning the symptoms, but genuinely cannot move a given part of the body. Modern brain scanning techniques indicate this is due to the inhibition of prefrontal regions of the brain involved in 'willed' movement (as opposed to unconscious movement). Even today, psychiatrists have a lot of unanswered questions about the condition. In Christiana's day, it was lumped with other nervous conditions and completely misunderstood. Conversion disorder is linked to anxiety and depression, both of which Christiana was liable to. Her night-time hysteria attacks were, in modern terms, panic attacks and she seems to have been a person prone to acute anxiety – unsurprising considering the family circumstances.

That all this constituted her as insane is, of course, ludicrous. Insanity has nothing to do with conversion disorder. Considering the horrors the Edmunds family had been through and were still going through in 1853, it does not seem remarkable that younger members of the family found themselves struggling emotionally. Louisa suffered a fit of despair and eventually found it necessary to move away – a move that appears to have helped her enormously. Stuck at home, Christiana was surrounded by the on-going trauma of her family life. If it is accurate she was like her father, it can now be seen how William Edmunds succumbed to the overwhelming stress and anxiety his life had stumbled into. No wonder he turned to drink. It might even be argued that some of his symptoms were the result of conversion disorder and that raises yet another possibility. Were Christiana's symptoms in part driven by those of her father? Just like her father, she could not cope and he had escaped his duties by becoming mad and paralysed. When the situation became too much, she did exactly the same. But that was nineteen years ago and, as mentioned above, hysteria is not the same as insanity. So what about the Christiana of 1872? Was she driven by madness in her murderous actions or something else?

Reverend Thomas Henry Cole, chaplain at Lewes gaol, became a crucial witness for the defence. Despite not being a medical man, he was charged with the awkward duty of reporting any prisoner he thought showed signs of madness to the gaol governor, surgeon and visiting justices. He had a chance to observe Christiana between 19 August 1871 when she arrived at the gaol and Christmas Day of that year.

[I] observed in her a peculiar formation and expression in the eyes and a vacant look at times in her features. [I] had many conversations with her and they were perfectly coherent. They struck [me] as extraordinary, considering the circumstances under which she was placed. [I] expected to find in her great excitement and dejection, and found much calmness and exceeding levity. [I] spoke to her about the position in which she was, and she broke into an extraordinary laugh. [I] tried to fix her mind on its gravity, and she seemed to have no power to do so. She burst into tears, and from tears she would rapidly pass to laughter. That was frequently the case. From what [I] observed [I] believed she was of unsound mind.

Then there was the testimony of Alice and George Over who had known Christiana for six years, two of which she had resided with her mother in their house.

[Christiana's] general demeanour was ladylike, quiet and good in every way. From about a year ago [Alice] noticed she had not been so quiet, and latterly she felt she was going mad. That was about March or April last year, or a little earlier. She was very strange. [Alice] said to her she seemed unhappy, and she replied she felt uncomfortable and sometimes as if she were going mad. Her eyes were large and rolled, and her appearance made [Alice] uncomfortable.

George Over added that when Christiana visited his house about twelve months before the trial she '...was a little strange ... Her eyes were very full, and there was wildness in her look. Her manner, too, was a little more excited than usual.' Parry's most important witness, however, was Dr William Wood MD who was the physician at Bethlehem asylum. He, along with Dr Lockhart Robinson, Dr Maudsley and the surgeon Mr Gibson, visited Christiana while she was at Newgate. Dr Wood explained:

> [I] was very much struck with her absolute indifference to her position and [I] failed altogether to impress her with its seriousness. [I] believed her to be quite incapable of judging between right and wrong in the same sense that other people would... She knew the object of [Dr Wood's] visit, and might have known who and what he was. He told her that he, and those with him had come to ascertain the state of her mind. She appeared to understand... [I] conveyed the idea to her that it was with a view to the trial, and she seemed to understand that. [I] said among other things 'do you know the consequences of a conviction?' She said she would rather be convicted than brought in insane. [I] concluded from that she did not know the position she was in or the gravity of the charge... [I] asked whether she thought it wrong for a person to destroy the life of another because she believed that the husband of that person wished to get rid of her. After some hesitation, she said she thought it would be wrong, but she did not say it in such a manner as to lead [Dr Wood] to believe she really thought so.

Abruptly in the midst of Dr Wood's testimony, Christiana stood and told the court that she remembered the questions he had asked. She had no chance to elaborate on this (perhaps she wanted to deny her insanity defence) as the judge told her she could not speak and she had to resume her seat. Unflustered by the outburst, Dr Wood concluded:

> [I] judged by her demeanour and appearance rather than by the answers she made... [I am still] under the impression that she was not in a state to judge right from wrong as other persons were.

Dr Charles Lockhart Robinson was less convinced. He remarked to the court that he had visited Christiana several times while in Newgate and that:

> ...he had very great difficulty coming to any conclusion. He regarded hers as a case on the borderland between crime and insanity. He thought her intellect quite clear and free from any delusion, but that her moral

sense was deficient, as in the descendants of insane parents... Coupled with the history of the case, he was led to regard her as morally insane... He believed she had the intellectual knowledge that it was wrong to administer poison in order to kill a person.

Not so good for Christiana's defence, Lockhart Robinson was suffering from the same issues that challenge doctors today when trying to define a person's mental state in a criminal case. And just as he had no clear answers, so today we still struggle with the concept of just what constitutes insanity. Dr Henry Maudsley was equally unhelpful and as the last witness for the defence, probably put the nail in Christiana's coffin. He stated he concurred with Dr Robinson that Christiana lacked a sense of morality and when asked to elaborate on the subject by Ballantine really ruined the defence argument:

> [I] meant by impaired moral sense a want of moral feeling as to events or acts regarding, which a perfectly sane person might be expected to exhibit feeling. [I] should say everybody who committed crime exhibited some want of moral feeling.

This was a disaster for Parry. At the last moment, his final two expert witnesses had denied Christiana was any more insane than the next criminal. He wrapped up his defence with a stirring speech reflecting on the origins of the recent insanity laws and playing on any doubts the jurists had about Christiana's state of mind. Unfortunately, they had no doubts. Christiana was a coldblooded murderess in their minds. The verdict came back rapidly. Christiana was guilty of the murder of Sidney Barker.

CHAPTER FIFTEEN

A Pregnant Verdict

Despite her nonplussed statements to the doctors, Christiana was disturbed by the verdict of the court. Up until the last minute, she had never really imagined she would be found guilty and the horror of the reality had her reeling from the effect. How had she gone from respectable middle-class lady to murderess in such a short span of time? While Christiana wrestled with her options in the confinements of Newgate, she had a surprising champion outside of court in the form of Dr Lockhart Robinson. Writing to *The Times* shortly after the trial he was fuming at the verdict of the jury:

> The conduct of the prosecution [Robinson referred to them as using bullying tactics at the trial] has more strongly than ever forced on me the conviction how unfitted for the elucidation of truth is the present method of procedure in cases of criminal lunacy. Every admission made by [the doctors] in our anxious desire to submit the whole scientific evidence in this difficult case to the court was treated by Serjeant Ballantine as an effort to pervert the course of justice. If we had been called to advise the court as scientific experts I can hardly think that our opinions would thus have lightly been set aside. For example, the learned Serjeant, 'on account of the feelings of high consideration and respect' which he was pleased to say he entertained for the profession of medicine, 'felt the more indignant when men used the honourable character attaching to that profession to propound views before a jury...'[96]

Lockhart Robinson was furious. He felt his whole professional evidence, not to mention his ethics, had been called into question. But it was an unsurprising response when courts in general and the majority of the public were unconvinced by insanity as a defence for murder. He was also angry that the rules governing what made a person insane were still so pathetically inadequate.

> The dictum of English law which makes, not insanity, but knowledge of right and wrong the test of responsibility, undoubtedly excludes cases like Miss Edmunds; but it is the opinion of all persons practically conversant with insanity that this test is alike faulty and unscientific.

He also contradicted a statement made by Baron Martin that insanity was only used as a defence when well-to-do prisoners were at the stand and that the poor were never insane. Perhaps the Baron had seen one too many cases of wealthy prisoners using insanity as a defence for their crime when it was quite obvious they were sane (and, let's face it, even today, defence counsels will often resort to insanity when they can find no other means to defend their client). Lockhart-Robinson snapped:

> I can only say that the prisoner is poor, and that I gave my time and evidence without fee or reward of any kind.

Finally, the good doctor put in print his personal views on Christiana's mental state:

> The most marked symptom is the utter insensibility shown by the prisoner to the position she is placed in and the danger she runs. Her whole mind is centred on her letters to Dr Beard, on his conduct in allowing his wife to read them after all that had passed between them, and on the horror she would feel, not at being tried for murder, but at these letters being read in her hearing in court. She further dwelt on her certain belief that Dr Beard desired the death of his wife even by poison; that, though too cautious to speak of it directly, he had hinted at it; and that if so she knew he would marry her, etc. There was no emotion or anguish shown during my two searching examinations.
>
> From these facts I concluded that, while the prisoner has in the abstract without question the knowledge of right and wrong, and knows that to poison is to commit murder, she is so devoid of all sense of moral responsibility that she cannot be regarded as conscious of right and wrong, or morally responsible, in the sense in which other men are so. Her family history of insanity, epilepsy, idiocy, etc., points to the insane temperament, and is consistent with the scientific deduction that the prisoner is morally insane, to use the familiar term.
>
> Counsel will judge how far a jury are likely to understand or discriminate between the intellectual soundness of the prisoner and the

absence of all moral sense to guide and regulate her conduct, and on which alone any defence of insanity can rest. I am bound to add that, except in conjunction with the evidence furnished by the crime, I should not on my examination alone have felt justified in signing a certificate in lunacy.

Meanwhile, Christiana was being sentenced for her crimes.

The scene that was enacted on Tuesday evening at the Old Bailey ... was one of rare occurrence, and for its romantic ghastliness, was almost unexampled even in the annals of the *Newgate Calendar.*

Christiana certainly knew how to fix herself at the centre of attention!

The old and dingy-looking court was densely crowded... The prisoner sat unmoved and seemingly unconcerned. A female warder of the prison, who sat behind her in the dock, exhibited far more emotion and looked far more wretched. The prisoner wore no bonnet, but her hair was carefully and even coquettishly arranged in heavy folds across her head. She was dressed neatly, with a black velvet cloak and well-fitting gloves of some dark colour.

After the verdict of guilty was read out, it was remarked by the reporters present:

...the bonnet-less woman in the dock neither moves a muscle nor changes colour in the least degree during the dreadful proclamation. 'Silence while sentence of death and execution according to law is passed upon the prisoner at the bar.'

Has she anything to say? Yes, she has... Amid profound silence her voice is heard, clear, musical and steady as if the awful moment was one of the most ordinary occasions of her life. She desired, she said, to be tried upon the other charges that had been brought against her, in order that the jury and everyone should know the nature of her intimacy with Dr Beard, of the treatment she had received, and how she had been 'brought into this dreadful business' – those were her words.

To the very end, Christiana blamed Dr Beard and even hinted that the poisoning of his wife had been his idea. Perhaps he had bemoaned his wife – it seems a particularly loveless marriage – but Christiana took his words and warped them into a belief he wanted rid of Emily, by poison, if necessary. Now as her life hung in the balance, all she wanted was to talk about the man she had fallen in love with – was this one last sign of her insanity? Her delusion? Her complete misinterpretation of the seriousness of the consequences to her crimes? She still showed no remorse for little Sidney. It never even occurred to her in those final moments to offer her apologies to his family. She was utterly consumed by her own woes and failed to see how she had poisoned a child because of a failed romance. She had ruined lives, left people in agony and all she wished was that she could have talked more about her relationship with Dr Beard! Despite the dramatic narrative provided by the papers, it is doubtful that many felt sympathy for the cold-hearted creature on the stand.

> Baron Martin was much overcome with emotion, and at the dreadful words 'hanged by the neck till your body be dead,' he broke down and hid his face, during a pause when a pin might have been heard to drop.

The reporters knew how to sell a story and the artistic licence exhibited in their description of the trial (some of which was absurd) could have come straight from one of the sensation novels that were all the rage at the time. But even they could not have hoped for the new revelation Christiana was about to announce. It was customary for a female prisoner to be asked before a date for the execution was set whether she was pregnant or not. In English law, a pregnant woman could not be hanged until after the birth of her child. It was a reprieve of sorts, if only temporary. The Clerk of Arraigns asked the question and it had become another part of the standard court rigmarole. However, when he asked Christiana, expecting the usual 'no', she whispered to the female warder beside her and it was announced to the court: 'She says she is, my Lord.'

It was ludicrous, of course, despite the fact Christiana was a respectable spinster who (despite her murderous tendencies) would never have scandalised her reputation by falling pregnant out of marriage. She was also forty-three, an age when it was highly unlikely (though not impossible) for a Victorian woman to fall pregnant for the first time. She was also implicating Dr Beard in yet another scandal.   Twenty minutes after the announcement that had stunned the spectators and excited the reporters, a hasty Jury of Matrons had been empanelled. The women came from the crowd in the courtroom. One journalist remarked that they were '...a dozen well-to-do and respectably dressed women – who could have supposed that a dozen such were to be found in such a place?'

The 'Matrons' had the onerous task of deciding whether Christiana was indeed pregnant. After being sworn, they retired to a private parlour with the prisoner to try and decide. The women struggled, asked vague questions about her condition based on their own experiences and generally tried to make a decision when they were hopelessly out of their depth. After half an hour, they conceded defeat and asked for a doctor. Once again the court was searched for a medical man and one was brought forward and escorted to the parlour. Another half hour passed and the spectators were becoming impatient; however, the doctor was equally struggling as he was lacking his medical equipment and made a request for a stethoscope. A policeman was sent out for one only to return with a telescope! Christiana's trial was starting to turn into a farce. A stethoscope was eventually found and the crowd waited impatiently as the doctor continued his examination and the 'Matrons' made up their minds. Finally after much delay, Christiana returned to the dock and the Jury of Matrons stood forward and declared when asked if the prisoner was pregnant – 'Not.' It was an unhappy moment and the reporters, now firmly with the bit between their teeth, saw an opportunity for moralising on the court system.

> The humanity of the rule of law which leaves this delicate matter to the decision of 12 women accidentally present in the court during a murder trial… is… very questionable, and the result has on more than one occasion proved to be very fallible. The sort of women who care to be present at such sad scenes are not presumably the most intelligent or best educated of the community, and the question which they have to investigate might in modern days of medical science be answered far more satisfactorily by a medical man.

The reporters quietly ignored the fact a medical man *had* been present at the time of Christiana's examination along with disparaging any female who attended a trial (though for men it was perfectly acceptable). Despite it all, the verdict of the Matrons had been passed and it is unlikely anyone who had had close contact with Christiana could have really thought they were wrong. But why did she put herself through such an ordeal?

Desperation was probably the prime factor along with Christiana's dreamy view of the world that detached her from reality. Christiana would have heard about the plea either from her fellow females awaiting trial or, more likely, through some of the popular literature of the day which had latched onto the new fashion for following criminal trials. Sensation novels, aimed frequently at the female-reading public and available to many through the new initiative of circulating libraries, explored previously taboo subjects for their readers. Courts started to play a pivotal role within their pages and regularly plots revolved around criminal proceedings. Poisoning was a favourite topic causing many critics to decry the books as encouraging murder. But there were other sources where Christiana could have obtained the idea. Newspapers flourished in the

Victorian period and they loved to indulge in lengthy descriptions of trials, using legal terminology so readily that they clearly expected their readers to be familiar with it. Papers were full of crime and Christiana could easily have stumbled upon another case of a woman claiming pregnancy to forestall her execution.

What is for certain is that Parry would never have suggested such a defence. He knew it was not only hopeless, but would result in an intrusive and embarrassing episode in the courtroom. Then again, perhaps after all, Christiana was taken by the spur of the moment and said yes to the clerk's question without having considered it properly. In the end, it was a pointless exercise. Christiana was not pregnant and she delayed her fate by an hour at the most. Escorted back to Newgate, she now left behind the privileges of the prisoner who had yet to be convicted and faced life, however brief, among the hardcore elements of the prison. She had to exchange her own clothes for the prison garb and the few advantages she had enjoyed in her pre-trial prison existence now evaporated. She was expected to work while awaiting her execution, and though campaigners had been trying to improve prison labour for decades, this meant either working in the hot, suffocating prison laundry or picking oakum.

Coupled with this humiliation and tedium, Christiana now had to face the full extent of her sisterhood within the prison. It was a hard life: bullying and fighting was rife. There was little sympathy for a new arrival and, at worst, Christiana could expect to be stripped of her clothes and left naked by her fellow inmates if they took against her. Despite attempts to break the system of payments that operated among the prisoners, it still carried on and 'fees' were demanded of new inmates. In short, Christiana had to quickly ingratiate herself with the other women or suffer the consequences.

For Baron Martin, the situation of Christiana's trial and subsequent conviction was deeply troubling. Sir Samuel Martin (1801-1883) was born in Londonderry, Ireland, and graduated from Trinity College, Dublin, in 1821. He was a Liberal MP for Pontefract and became a judge after the retirement of Baron Rolfe in 1850. Martin was known for his astuteness in court as well as his fairness. Though not opposed to handing down heavy sentences on criminals, he also had a natural kindness that often led him to seek mitigation on a defendant's behalf. Just two years after Christiana's trial, he would have to retire due to increasing deafness. Martin was not a man who would stifle his concerns about a case and clearly with Christiana's he had several. Though the jury had found her sane, he was more convinced that Parry had proved her otherwise and his emotion on the day of her sentencing showed how intensely he felt condemning her to death was wrong. After the trial, Martin could not rest easy and he expressed the opinion publically that Christiana should not be executed and that her state of mind should be thoroughly and professionally investigated. As a result, Sir William Gull, MD and Dr Orange, the superintendent of the recently established Broadmoor Criminal Lunatic Asylum, were asked to intervene and examine Christiana.

Sir William Gull (1816-1890) had recently come to the attention of the public after attending the Prince of Wales when the latter was made severely ill by typhoid fever in 1871. Gull had been a physician at Guy's Hospital until 1865 when he withdrew to a consulting role due to the demands of his private practice, but would later become a governor of the hospital. Gull was known for his skill as a clinical physician, based around acute observation of a patient, an excellent memory for details and careful study of all the details of a case. He was hard-working, constantly questioning and re-examining medical practices and was against dosing patients with drugs unnecessarily. His groundbreaking work on anorexia and the pattern of fevers won him acclaim, even though he never published a book in contrast to many of his contemporaries. But he was not entirely beloved. Gull was controversially an advocate of vivisection for medical science and his sarcastic manner and dogmatism alienated his colleagues. Beloved by his patients, he was often disliked by his fellow physicians.

Dr William Orange in contrast was a lesser-known celebrity, though his name had come up sporadically in the daily papers for his work at the newly established Broadmoor Criminal Lunatic Asylum. Opened in 1863, it was created in a direct response to the new attention being given to insanity and the criminally crazed offender. Orange had led a relatively quiet existence compared to some of the men now touting Christiana's madness, but he was nonetheless an expert in his field. His firsthand experience with a range of challenging inmates, some of who were not just difficult but highly dangerous, placed him in a position to understand the nuances of insanity far better than most.

On 23 January 1872, Orange travelled with Gull to Lewes prison where Christiana was once again residing. It had become customary for criminals to conduct their sentence and execution in their home county except for the most notorious criminals who still choked their last at Newgate. At least the return to Lewes enabled Christiana to escape the confines of Newgate with its overcrowding and horrors. She was near her mother and had the sympathy of the Lewes warders who made her existence bearable. Even so, she was a woman awaiting her death. Dr Orange wrote in detail about the first visit that resulted in a letter being sent to the Home Secretary stating that Christiana was insane:

The plan we had considered best was to make the fullest examination into the mental state of the convict by personal communication and then should the result be unsatisfactory... to supplement it by such collateral inquiries as might aid us to a right conclusion.

This [examination] has conclusively shewn(sic) us that Christiana Edmunds is a person of unsound mind. This woman appears to have led a tranquil easy and indifferent childhood and womanhood up to a period of about three years ago when or rather since which time there is evidence of mental perversion and defective memory.

The crimes of which she has been convicted were no doubt committed by her but an examination of the circumstances of her mental state gives us the assurance that the acts referred to and acted by her were the fruit of a most marked insane character.

The crime of murder she seems incapable of realising as having been committed by her though she fully admits the purchasing and distributing [of] the poisons as set forth in the several counts against her. On the contrary she even justifies her conduct and in an insane way tries still to give a justification of it. We have no doubt that the mind is insane and that she ought to be treated accordingly.[97]

Christiana's case had now caught the imagination of the general public and appeals were being made to spare her. A petition by her friends and said to have been signed by two of her victims – Mrs Boys and Mr Garrett – was sent to the Secretary of State. The *Manchester Times* reported large crowds of strangers in the city, which they took as a sign that a memorial in favour of sparing Edmunds life was being considered. Why this would be done in Manchester instead of London or even Brighton was not highlighted by the paper.

In essence, Christiana had succeeded in gaining public sympathy. Some might argue it was slightly undeserved, but she was a middle-class, respectable woman making her a prime candidate for empathy rather than disregard. It has to be emphasised that status was intrinsic to the sympathy (or lack of) a convicted criminal might receive. Had Christiana been working class from a slum area or less respectable (i.e. a whore or drunk) it is doubtful she would have gained the same public support.

But Christiana was middle class, from a good family and by all accounts a 'beloved' person. That she could go insane and kill people struck at the heart of Victorian society, especially when the papers began hysterically claiming that it was inevitable that the suppressed feelings of a forty-year-old spinster should boil over into murderous thoughts. If Christiana could turn public opinion in her favour, what about other respectable-seeming middle-class ladies? Mothers thought of their unmarried daughters and those daughters thought of themselves. The trial and case had fallen unpleasantly close to home and people began to put themselves in Christiana or her mother's place. What if it was them? What if it was their daughter? So they transposed the crime onto themselves and therefore sought a reprieve for the poor woman. In the end they got their wish. Christiana had her reprieve and the papers announced it with delight. However, this did not mean freedom, far from it. No one wanted a mad woman who could not see anything wrong with poisoning the public set loose.

Dealing with insane criminals was a nightmarish problem for the Victorians. Misunderstanding, a lack of concern and the Victorian obsession with guilt and punishment meant that a great number of mentally ill patients were incarcerated in prisons. Looking at records, it seems as if there was an epidemic of insanity raging through Victorian society as the great and the good feared. Prison inspector, William John Williams, wrote in 1839: 'Every tour of inspection [of prisons] affords me fresh examples of the inconvenience of retaining in prisons individuals acquitted of crime on the ground of insanity, but ordered to be detained during pleasure.'[98] This was a laughable understatement. In 1842, a fifteen-year-old boy would be kicked to death by an insane prisoner at Preston. The situation was untenable. Not only were gaolers and other prisoners living in fear of the insane convicts, but the mentally disturbed were thrown into an environment that exasperated their condition. A prison governor's report of 1846 writing of one convict who had been sent to him from Preston under the description 'perfectly insane' stated: 'I am quite at a loss to understand why ... the Preston authorities have not effected(sic) his removal to an Asylum ... and ... avoided the painful exposure of an unfortunate and irascible being in a Court of Justice.'[99] Out of thirteen visits to local prisons paid by the Kirkdale authorities in 1844-45, seven were to deal with insane prisoners. It seemed madness was on the rise.

In fact, it was more a case that the first slow understandings of mental illness were emerging, meaning gaolers were finally starting to recognise the no-goods from the mentally troubled. Even so it was worrying times. While public asylums were being built, it was still debatable where an insane criminal might end up as Janet Saunders writes in her essay on the Victorian criminally insane: '...the superintendents of the new asylums and a growing number of prison medical officers began to realise that many of their ordinary charges might easily have found their way into either institution'.[100] It would not be until 1889 that the Home Secretary issued specific directions to magistrates that the criminally insane could be sent straight to asylums. Far too late for Christiana...

She languished in Lewes prison through the remainder of the cold winter, the fine spring and early summer. She had been in prison for nine months and the furore of her trial had died down and other crimes caught the attention of the sensation-seeking public. Behind the scenes, Christiana waited and wondered. Finally, on 5 July 1872, it was agreed that she should be transported to Broadmoor and she arrived at the newest Criminal Lunatic Asylum not realising that this was to be her home for the rest of her days.

CHAPTER SIXTEEN

The Victorian
Sex Sensation

For the papers, Christiana's trial gave them an excuse to delve into talk of sex and sensation. Despite it overtly being a taboo subject, sex was frequently discussed in lesser papers in association with crime and scandal and clearly figured heavily in Victorian minds.

> [Edmunds] was riddled with insanity and other nervous diseases, and living an involuntarily single life while struggling with hysteria and suppressed sexual feeling, it would be almost impossible to go on to the critical age of forty-three without actual derangement of mind.[101]

What a statement! Christiana was doomed because she had no opportunity to use her sex drive or so was the opinion of *The Lancet* which printed the above passage. Yet if the leading medical paper of the day was suggesting female hysteria and celibacy was a source of insanity, what could the layman or local surgeon reading it think but to believe it! Other papers portrayed Christiana as an evil vixen of a woman who had manipulated the court by her feminine wiles to escape the noose. The *Derby Mercury* printed a letter from 'A Medical Man' that portrayed her as thoroughly without humanity:

> ...that inhuman tigress, Christiana Edmunds, has escaped her well-merited doom... Miss Edmunds was defended on the old plea of insanity, and as usual found plenty of mud-doctors ready with all the old stereotyped bosh, which the judge very properly stigmatised. Here, we have a bold, unscrupulous woman, making a deliberate attempt to poison a lady, whose husband she coveted... [after the trial] with the most charming 'consistency,' the same judge who had snubbed the 'mad

doctors' on the trial, subsequently orders 'two fresh mad doctors' (perfect strangers) to visit the lady in prison, and the result is, Miss Edmunds escapes her sentence.[102]

The old controversies had been stirred up yet again. Some sources considered Christiana a woman whose passions had derailed an already disturbed mind, while others saw her as nothing more than a wanton woman and a coldblooded killer. The matter was not helped by links being made between Christiana's case and the recent trial of a certain Reverend Watson who was found guilty of killing his wife, but spared execution due to being found insane. John Selby Watson (1804-1884) had a reputation in academic circles for his scholarship and skills as a classical translator and wrote a number of books on various topics including biographies, religious histories and even one entitled the *Reasoning Power in Animals*. Despite this he was dreadfully poor, just surviving with his wife Anne on his income as headmaster of the Stockwell Grammar School. Then, in 1870, having spent nearly thirty years at Stockwell, he was sacked without a pension due to falling pupil numbers. It seems this final thrust into destitution was too much for the good reverend.

In October 1871, Ellen Pyne, the Watsons' servant, found her master unconscious after taking prussic acid. Beside him lay two notes: one contained Pyne's wages, the other was a murder confession. 'I have killed my wife in a fit of rage to which she provoked me.' Mrs Watson was found battered to death in a bedroom. Watson's case stirred a mixture of emotions, not least because he was a respected clergyman now in his late sixties. At his trial the jury found him guilty, but recommended mercy. He was sentenced to death nonetheless and, in a near identical echo of Christiana's situation, protest letters were sent and the judge on the case, Mr Justice Byles, had a pang of conscience and asked the Home Secretary to have Watson's mental health investigated. The result was that Watson was found to have been temporarily insane when he killed his wife and his sentence was commuted to life imprisonment. Because his insanity was deemed transient, he did not warrant going to an asylum. He spent the next twelve years at Parkhurst Prison before falling out of his hammock and dying aged eighty.

Watson and Christiana were both having their sanity (or lack of it) publically discussed in January 1872 and the similarities of the cases naturally linked them. Was it coincidence that both judges on the separate cases felt the need to reverse their earlier opinions? In Watson's case, it has been argued that Victorian sentiment made the thought of hanging an elderly Church of England clergyman seem particularly crass and unacceptable. However, as the legal system did not offer any levels of lesser punishment for murder, there was no other option but to warrant the death penalty. Was insanity used as a loophole in the English legal system to spare the embarrassment and public furore of hanging a respected reverend? Very likely and unfortunately this reflected badly on Christiana who was experiencing the same processes of legal wrangling at the same time.

However, insane or not, there was one thing the various writers agreed upon. Edmunds' murderous spree was based fundamentally on sex – passion for and lack of – and this gave every hack journalist a chance to write on their favourite subject. Female sexuality, the newest topic of debate in Victorian Britain. Considering the typical perception of the Victorians as repressed and prudish, they did discuss sex far more frequently than originally believed. The discussions often followed two themes: the scientific pseudo-medical discussions on the topic or the outraged puritan views of perceived sexual content from paintings to the latest fashions.

Quite frequently, these talks revolved around women. The sexual woman was a prickly subject for Victorians. A passionate woman did not fit well with the parlour room ideal of a maiden oblivious to sexual wants and desires. There was something perverse, even abnormal about a woman who wanted or enjoyed sexual relations. Yet while this was the view of influential men *and* women, others were realising that sex sold, particularly those in the rapidly expanding printing trade. Papers were now being filled with tittle-tattle about affairs, sex scandals, passionate crimes, adultery and divorces, and they sold extremely well. Despite what the critics might argue, that decent women did not attend or show any interest in criminal court cases or scandalous news, the truth was middle-class and upper-class women were lapping up the latest controversy with rapidity.

Fermenting in the midst of all this 'real news' was the work of the sensation novelists. Sensation novels emerged in the 1860s and existed roughly for a decade before merging with other forms of literature. In their prime, they were widely panned for their wickedness and reliance on ever-increasing extremes of human nature to captivate readers. In many respects they formed the basis of our modern books, placing, as they did, the plot as a central part of the story. Part adventure novel, part crime story and part romantic fiction, characters in a sensation novel jumped from one disaster to the next, each more elaborate than the last until the story finally culminated (often unhappily). Murder, sudden demises and accidental deaths were the staple of the dramas and they can be seen as a Victorian form of soap opera printed as they often were in episodic format. Mary Elizabeth Braddon was the queen of sensation with her bestseller

Lady Audley's Secret delighting the reading public and scandalising the literary critics. Unsurprisingly, her most famous novel revolved around insanity and sex. 'Most of the sensationalists include sexual passion in all its irregular aspects,' writes Winifred Hughes in her work about the rise and fall of the sensation novel. In a genuine sensation novel, it becomes in effect an obligation to incorporate a liberal amount of seduction, bigamy or even prostitution, preferably in connection with the heroine.

Reviewers profess themselves scandalised by the general threat to morality, but the main objection can be narrowed down to a distaste for female passion and sexuality, most explicitly stated in one of Mrs Oliphant's articles for *Blackwoods* [a Victorian periodical]:

> What is held up to us as the story of the feminine soul as it really exists underneath its conventional coverings, is a very fleshly and unlovely record... She [the heroine] waits for flesh and muscles, for strong arms that seize her, and warm breath that thrills her through and a host of other physical attractions, which she indicates to the world with a charming frankness... were the sketch made from the man's point of view, its openness would at least be less repulsive. The peculiarity of it in England is... that this intense appreciation of flesh and blood, this eagerness of physical sensation, is represented as the natural sentiment of the English girls, and is offered to them not only as the portrait of their own state of mind, but as their amusement and mental food.[103]

Poor deluded Mrs Oliphant. If only she realised how women, young and old, lapped up these new novels as an antidote to their staid existences. Fiction was finally appealing to the masses and acting as a form of escapism.

It is feasible Christiana spent a portion of her time reading such novels. In fact, her behaviour and later statements indicate precisely that: she had very strong notions of romance, love and happy-ever-afters. Most women read sensation novels and recognised them as pure escapism, but in cases like Christiana's, it can be argued that her views on life were warped into impractical and incredulous notions. Critics were constantly arguing that sensation novels influenced girls to behave unnaturally to emulate their favourite heroines. Braddon partially satirised this belief in her 1864 novel *The Doctor's Wife*, based quite heavily on French author Gustave Flaubert's *Madame Bovary*, which had yet to reach a wide English audience. *The Doctor's Wife* was Braddon's attempt to produce a 'literary novel' that the critics would love in contrast to her usual sensation works, but she could not resist working in her own brand of humour and making fun of the very critics she was trying to impress.

Her heroine, Isabel Gilbert, is cast as a dreamy girl who wastes her days absorbed in novels and imagining her own life in a mirror image of the books she reads. Throughout the story, Isabel compares her life to that of her favourite fictional characters and conjures up dramatic scenes in her mind to emulate them and to alter her own quaint but boring life. In essence she is the sensation critics' worst nightmare brought to life – a woman who believes what she reads. Braddon has her character, Sigismund Smith, a budding sensation novelist, sum up Isabel's plight.

'She reads too many novels.' [states Sigismund Smith]
'Too many?'
'Yes. Don't suppose that I want to depreciate the value of the article. A novel's a splendid thing after a hard day's work, a sharp practical tussle with the real world, a healthy race on the barren moorland of life, a hearty wrestling match in the universal ring. Sit down then and read *Ernest Maltravers,* or *Eugene Aram*, or the *Bride of Lammermoor*, and the sweet lulls your tired soul to rest, like the cradle-song that soothes a child. No wise man or woman was ever the worse for reading novels. Novels are only dangerous for those poor foolish girls who read nothing else, and think that their lives are to be paraphrases of their favourite book.'[104]

It is tempting to imagine Sigismund's words in connection with Christiana. She was distanced from reality, unable to fully comprehend her situation and, above all else, a big believer in true love. Something she had believed she had found with Dr Beard if only Mrs Beard would kindly and conveniently pop her clogs. Which brings attention to the next flaming arrow critics regularly launched at sensation novelists – that their work inspired murder. In another of Sigismund's reflective moments, he remarks upon how he would write about a murder in one of his stories: 'I daresay some people would cry out upon it, and declare that it was wicked and immoral, and that the young man who could write about a murder would be ready to commit the deed at the earliest convenient opportunity. But I don't suppose the clergy would take to murdering their sons by reason of my fiction...'

One can develop quite a fondness for the cynical Sigismund. Yet, ironically, Christiana's case was the sort of prime stuff a sensation novel was comprised of. In fact, she was almost a living Isabel Gilbert, deluded and living in a fantasy world where Dr Beard *would* marry her as in the best scenes of her favourite novels. And just as in those same novels, she was prepared to resort to poison to speed up matters – the heroines of sensation novels were all too frequently picking up poison bottles and contemplating murder, some even committed it, though on the whole they were 'undone' by their crimes. Christiana could easily have been the example the critics of sensation novels were looking for, except the big days of the sensationalist were drawing to a close with newer forms of fiction appearing on the horizon. Even more ironic, it was the very way that Christiana was treating her life like the plot of a good novel that ultimately proved her insane. Christiana was deluded, but she was also a very passionate and emotional woman.

Female passion was a controversial topic as Mrs Oliphant's words clearly prove – it was acceptable for a man to be driven by his sexual passions, but not a woman. In some regards, this was due to women being viewed as more practical in their thinking and not liable to being manipulated into behaviour by their sexual feelings. But largely this was based on the old notion of the 'pure' woman, the maiden who remained aloof from such things as desire and temptation. Only wanton, fallen women expressed an interest in sexuality. A respectable woman saw physical relations as a part of her duties as a wife and did not take pleasure in them – or at least that is how many would like to imagine the situation.

In reality, the day-to-day lives of the Victorians quickly cast scorn and ridicule on this ideal. With the new divorce laws implemented in the latter nineteenth century, a whole new world of scandal was open to an eager public as divorce hearings were neither delicate or private. Divorce could only be sought on the grounds of adultery and this meant a couple's dirty laundry being aired very publically in court and then reprinted in the national papers. As divorce was and is a costly business, it was exclusive to the wealthy meaning only the very prominent or celebrity couples came to court and there was nothing the Victorians liked better than the scandal of their supposed superiors. However, if daily life proved that women were not unfeeling when it came to sex and desire, there was still a great deal of debate and conflict over the result of a sexualised woman. The *Lancet* declared Christiana was bound to go mad because she was suffering '... with hysteria and suppressed sexual feeling' and this was a typical medical attitude where hysteria and sex were intrinsically linked in the Victorian doctor's mind.

Female hysteria was a historic condition, first described by the ancient Greeks in works such as the Hippocratic Corpus, which became a reference tool for later doctors.[105] Plato described the female condition of a 'wandering womb' where the woman's uterus travelled about the body and caused disease, blocked vital passages and hampered breathing. The Greek word for uterus translates into English as 'Hystera' and it is suggested that this is the source of the word hysteria, making the term intrinsically linked to women and problems with the sexual organs.

Second-century physician Galen described the connection between sexual deprivation in passionate women and hysteria, noting it was particular common in virgins. The usual prescription for the condition was more sex if the person was married (in cases where a person was single, marriage was advised) or if this treatment was not possible, pelvic massage, quite simply vaginal massage, by a doctor or midwife inducing relief (i.e. an orgasm) was prescribed.

The question has to be asked exactly how far did Victorian doctors hold to this treatment? Masturbation was, after all, considered an evil and it is hard to conjure up the image of a refined Victorian lady allowing herself to be pleasured by the family doctor. There had been 'sex doctors' advertising freely since the eighteenth century, perhaps better described as sex therapists (though occasionally they crossed a thin line to male prostitution), and Victorian illustrations show forms of medical treatment being directed at female genitalia, but it was an awkward subject for medical men and they discussed it in veiled terms. A great deal of controversy was caused by the book *The Technology of Orgasm* by Rachel Maines, later turned into the film *Hysteria* that made the claims that pelvic massage, essentially doctors performing masturbation on female patients, was widespread in Victorian Europe and in the US as a treatment for hysteria. This was then said to have sparked the creation of the first vibrator. Maines' work was based largely on secondary sources, which perpetuated the sex treatment myth, and the reality is a good deal less dramatic.

The Household Physician; for the use of Families, Planters, Seamen and Travellers published in 1859 gives a description of hysteria by US doctor Ira Warren featuring the typical ideas concerning hysteria and its treatment:

> The sexual system is doubtless the centre of the reflex nervous derangement, called hysteria. It has been sufficiently demonstrated that hysterics are dependant for their existence either upon organic disease, or upon simple irritation of the sexual organs. Sir Benjamin Brodie mentions cases of the hysteric paroxysm, produced by pressing upon an inflamed and tender ovary.[106]

In other words, hysterics were inclined towards masturbation and Sir Brodie induced a form of orgasm (or at least sexual excitement) by tenderly touching his patient. Warren continues: 'Whatever develops and excites the sexual system, and at the same time weakens the constitution, lays the foundation of this malady.' A reference again to masturbation that was deemed unhealthy and liable to weaken body and mind; however, Warren's terms for treatment are quite typical Victorian medicine. He makes no mention of pelvic massage, but suggests treating a patient for inflammation of the womb or for 'diluted blood and weakened nerves' with doses of iron and quinine. He also suggests patients can be broken out of a nervous fit by cold water being poured over their heads. In Henry Newell Guernsey's 1860s book on the use of homeopathy in obstetrics, he makes very clear the Victorian medical attitude to sexual issues. 'The labia, vulva and other organs belonging to the external genitals of the female, are liable to several forms of disease, either from morbid influences to which they are directly exposed [masturbation], or from the extension to them of disorders from the internal parts.'[107] Among these disorders he listed nymphomania of which '...the principal seat is in the vulva, nymphae and clitoris' and could result in '...actual insanity of monomania on this single subject of sexual intercourse'. He then links the disease to hysteria, '... and in fact what is this disease [hysteria] but a most violently aggravated hysterical affection, or morbid excitement of the entire sexual system of the female'.

Guernsey was convinced that female hysteria was rooted in the woman's reproductive or sexual system. He was against the idea the uterus (the wandering womb) was the source of the condition, but believed the ovaries were the chief cause of hysteria: '...the fountain head of all hysterical affections. Thus pressure on the ovaries will invariably bring on hysterical attacks in persons predisposed or subject to the disorder'. A description that echoes the experience of Sir Benjamin Brodie. Guernsey emphasised the condition was hereditary and that it could, in certain cases, develop into permanent insanity. But while he linked hysteria to sexual repression, his treatments were again quite typical involving purges and various drugs including arsenic, belladonna, mercury, magnesium, sulphur and zinc. Pelvic massage certainly did not feature. In fact, the more the subject is looked into the more extraordinary it seems that any Victorian doctor would consider using a method that was not only socially unacceptable, but was medically frowned upon as the root of many evils.

That is not to say that non-medical men did not consider the treatment. Thure Brandt of Sweden drew attention in the 1890s for his methods of pelvic massage – the closest that can be found to the claims of Rachel Maines, which he had developed from his time in the army. Brandt had started his experiments using not only massage, but various Swedish gymnastic movements that he encouraged his patients to use to strengthen or 'rearrange' their internal organs. His first success was on a soldier with a prolapsed rectum and he then went on to work with women who had suffered a prolapsed uterus, problems with the reproductive organs or sterility. He did not normally deal with hysteria, except as a symptom of a physical problem and his techniques were not designed to cure hysteric women.

Brandt's methods remained exclusive to him, deemed as he was by the medical profession as an uneducated quack. It was not until the late 1880s that gynaecologists took his work seriously and copied his methods. Brandt's methods involved '...acting upon the genital organs and their circulation, by direct and indirect movements'.[108] Patients were assembled in a large room that acted both as a waiting room and treatment area. Patients watched the treatment of others, '...thus having an object lesson which alone serves to teach the sometimes very complicated movements which precede and follow, and thus form part of each treatment'. The woman were laid down on a couch, their knees drawn up and the 'operator' as the practitioners were termed, sitting on a stool to their left, '...his left index finger in the vagina or rectum as is usually done in virgins and the right hand on the abdomen. The outer hand does all the work while the left index finger does not move but only acts as a support. The duration of treatment is from ten to fifteen minutes, except in cases of chronic exudates, half an hour to forty minutes.'

However, it is quite apparent that Brandt was keen to explain this was not about manual sexual release, but physical rearrangement of the internal reproductive organs or improving their health. It seems the idea of Victorian doctors treating hysterical women with 'pelvic massage' to aid sexual frustration must remain a myth. Nevertheless, that does not change the fact that hysteria was firmly linked in Victorian minds with passion (appropriate or inappropriate) and that sexual repression had a devastating effect on Christiana Edmunds' mental stability. Quite simply, not getting enough (or any!) could send you insane.

CHAPTER SEVENTEEN

Insane, but still Alive

'The whole of the lunatic murderers of Great Britain – those who had been "acquitted on the ground of insanity" and ordered "to be imprisoned during her majesty's pleasure" – are confined in the great Broadmoor Asylum,' wrote the *Blackburn Standard* in 1865. Rather inaccurately, the paper reported that 'Broadmoor now contains nearly 500 inmates, about 400 men and 50 or 60 women. With a few rare exceptions, nearly all are homicides, and the victims of their united crimes would probably amount to nearly 1,000.'[109] As dramatic as the statements of the *Blackburn Standard* were, it was true that Broadmoor housed some of the most dangerous and insane prisoners of the age. Any who had escaped the noose despite their horrendous crimes would end up in the asylum along with more simple characters such as mothers accused of infanticide. The *Blackburn Standard* reported on a few:

> The once terrible Capt. Johnson (who murdered the crew of his ship, Tory,) is here now, cured to a mild and inoffensive indiotcy(sic); and here, too, is Macnaughten(sic), as really mad as when he killed Mr Drummond. Here is a non-commissioned officer, whose murder of his wife and family some years ago shocked all England. His only anxiety is about his good conduct medal. Here, too, are several who have been in asylums before for attempted murder, who have then been discharged as cured, and having then perpetuated murder outright, have been committed to stay here for evermore.

This was the world Christiana Edmunds had entered alongside the dangerous, crazed and the unfortunate. It was a far cry from her life in Brighton.

It is only a very small proportion that can be trusted with such implements as spades, knives, scissors or even needles and thread. In the quiet wards the patients have blunted knives and forks, just enough to keep up appearances and enable them to cut and eat their vegetables. In the 'Strong Block' the food is cut up, and the inmates have only a smooth horn knife and spoon with which to feed themselves. It is in the 'Strong Block' where the most dangerous of all the male lunatics are confined, that what may be called the terrors of Broadmoor and its fearful collection of patients culminate. Here are confined the men whose murderous propensities and love of bloodshed seem almost inextinguishable. Into the refractory wards of this 'Strong Block' never less than three warders enter, so that in case of any attack by which one should be struck down there are always two left to grapple with the maniac.

Broadmoor presented a very mixed appearance. On the one hand it aimed, like all Victorian asylums, to cure its inmates and eventually release them back into the ordinary world. However, on the other, it was swarming with insane cut-throats, lunatics, psychopaths and schizophrenics who had been unidentified by society until their illness had reached its extremes. For most of the Broadmoor population, release was impossible. As the *Blackburn Standard* mentioned above, attempts had been made to 'cure' individuals, but upon release they had committed even worse crimes. The depths, foibles and contradictions of insanity were beginning to become apparent to the various authorities working at Broadmoor and curing the depraved began to seem more and more impossible.

In fact, this was a view that was beginning to dawn on many doctors who dealt with mad patients even within ordinary asylums. In an age with limited medicinal aids for improving mental health, many of the patients asylum keepers saw were not possible to 'cure' or even help with the poor means they had at their disposal. The governing theory in Victorian treatment of the insane was that by removing them from the stresses, pressures and anxiety of the ordinary world, this would enable the troubled mind to relax and restore itself naturally. In the cases of certain conditions, such as mental exhaustion and postnatal depression, this was a feasible cure and a few patients with conditions of this nature spent brief sojourns at asylums before returning home 'cured'. But for incidents where the problem had a physical origin such as epilepsy or was a product of mental illness such as schizophrenia, the 'wait and see' cure was going to have no effect. Slowly, Victorian doctors began to realise that the majority of insane individuals in asylums were never going to be fit for release and, as more and more were diagnosed, the asylums rapidly became overcrowded. It seemed an epidemic of insanity was at hand and the Victorians started to feel that asylums were as much a curse as a boon. The more they built the more insane patients they found!

Professor of Sociology Andrew Scull has argued convincingly that this dramatic increase in madness was in part due to the changing attitudes of the Victorian public towards those deemed abnormal. In earlier times, individuals who were either 'not quite right' or behaviourally difficult were maintained within a community, usually in among their family. However, with the rapid industrialisation of the eighteenth and nineteenth centuries, this became more and more problematic. The communities that had once existed for generations were now fragmented as people migrated to towns and cities, joining other diverse strangers in seeking work. Living in close quarters, as many of the poorest did with an ever changing mass of strangers, unusual or improper behaviour was less tolerated. In situations like this, abnormal individuals became an increasing burden. Equally they could restrict a family's ability to find employment. People became torn with earning a wage to live, but having to risk leaving a difficult individual alone or staying with them and starving to death.

The concept of asylums did not swell from a vacuum: they were a response to changing attitudes to mental health and the need to control and protect abnormal citizens struggling to survive in an urban environment. At the same time, once they existed, it became less acceptable for people to maintain their mentally ill relatives at home. It seemed unnecessary and even selfish in the sense that it placed a burden on the surrounding community. The end result was that, although the asylum had been meant for the truly desperate, it now became a dumping ground for 'useless' members of society.

In many cases, the criteria for a patient entering an asylum were too vague so that the sane and insane were institutionalised. Today, we would not think of placing an elderly relative who was becoming senile in a mental hospital, but vast numbers of such people who suffered from dementia, etc, made up the wards of the insane asylums. Quite obviously these were not individuals who could be 'cured', but at the same time were not in immediate danger of dying. So they existed within the environment of the asylum for years, perhaps living longer than they would have done in the poorer conditions of their homes.

In a similar sense, Broadmoor had expanded dramatically from its originally perceived requirements. Part of the issue was the limitations of the law. When execution was the only option for a sane murderer, the temptation to find him/her insane was strong, especially when cases were driven by desperation and poverty. Infanticide was probably the clearest instance of this. Women often found their way to Broadmoor due to murdering their children, in many cases just after birth. While some were cold-hearted, many were driven by despair, either because the child was illegitimate or they were in the depths of postnatal depression. Extreme poverty added to the burdens and some women found themselves driven to desperation due to social attitudes, constant childbirth and starvation. Juries found it hard to judge such women and, if they could, chose to find them insane rather than send them to the gallows. As a result of the limitations of the law, and also because insanity among the criminal fraternity was at last being recognised, Broadmoor's wards quickly clogged with prisoners.

Detention at Broadmoor was very different from a prison sentence at Newgate. Dr Orange, a driving force at the asylum, believed his patients were suffering from an illness that dictated their actions and, as such, should not be condemned to the life of a prisoner because of something they could not control. Broadmoor inmates were treated very much as if they were residents at a high-class lunatic asylum. 'Here one may occasionally see a female croquet party on the lawn,' wrote the *Blackburn Standard*. 'The players in which have been guilty in the aggregate of some thirty murders; or on the men's side, playing at bagatelle, a little group, with each of whose crimes all England at one time rung.' It can also be argued that the Victorians were suddenly feeling a great deal of social guilt about the way the insane had been treated in the past. An egalitarian and philanthropic view of modern patients was now in progress, coupled with the idea spreading in prisons that industry was a better way to improve inmates than casting them into a cell for the term of their sentence. Even so, Broadmoor took this social attitude to new lengths, treating its inmates more as guests than as criminals – albeit lunatic ones.

At the same time, the asylum was hoped to be self-sufficient with the inmates providing the labour required to sustain it. In some respects, this was loosely characterised as occupational therapy, though in truth it was also a vital part of keeping Broadmoor running. 'Under the eye of vigilant attendants a few are trusted to work in the garden. There is a cobblers' shop, in which everyone at work, save the superintendent, has killed one or more people. You can pass through a row of tailors, where all are quiet and busy, but where all have a history of crime – where the earnest looking man in the midst, whose very spirit seems absorbed in the movements of his sewing machine, is among the worst, and, if mad crime is to be taken as a proof of danger, the most dangerous of all. Outside are a small group of gardeners labouring with the minute labour of love upon the patch of ground committed to their care; and again you come upon a few painters, with Edward Oxford, who attempted to murder the Queen, now a fat elderly man, at their head, all busy and Oxford himself carefully graining a door in beautiful style ... A small pecuniary reward is given to those who labour well as an inducement to others to do likewise, and this money they are allowed to spend in any harmless way they please. Oxford has between £50 and £60 carefully saved.'[110]

The women's ward, mildly quieter than the men's domain as it contained far fewer inmates, still had its strange characters. 'In the women's ward, the first person we meet with here in the corridor ... is a gaunt Irishwoman, always violently abusive but not dangerous. The instant Dr Meyer and one of the kindest and most careful governors of the asylum, Sir William Hayter, make their appearance she assails them with fierce abuse and threatens to do for them what she did for Ned Taylor – the man for whose murder she is now restrained. In the dark padded cell is a young girl, rather a dangerous lunatic, but who when her fits of violence and screaming come upon her, as they often do, at once runs off to this dark quiet haven, where an hour or two of self-sought confinement never fails to restore her to serenity and cheerfulness.'

These were the 'typical' lunatics of the Victorian era, the sort of maniac that could be understood to be deranged. It was therefore no wonder that *The Times* article, which was as much about good publicity for the new building as to restore public faith in the criminal court system, would focus on such 'mad' individuals. They were the people that were expected to be consigned to an asylum and who satisfied the public need for demonstrable insanity – there was no denying they were clearly unhinged. But the quieter patients, less expressively violent and unhinged, were a troubling element within Broadmoor as they failed to fit the pattern and outnumbered the abusive inmates than *The Times* article suggests. In short, the quiet lunatics, as mentally unstable and dangerous as their violent counterparts, heavily populated the Broadmoor wards, but failed to arouse the same satisfaction in public minds that they deserved to be there rather than dangling from a rope. This was just the sort of lunatic Christiana was.

Life in the women's ward had the potential to be quite peaceful and was certainly far removed from time in prison. 'Nearly all are quietly engaged in sewing or reading, while many, young and old, are walking rapidly to and fro in the airing ground beneath the window.'[111] Christiana's new life was hardly different from her old. Aside from the obvious lack of freedom, she was still able to pursue the pursuits she would have enjoyed at home. For many of the poorer inmates, for the first time in their lives they experienced an existence without constant drudgery and worry. Broadmoor had all the mod-cons of the best Victorian establishments. It originally contained indoor water-closets, something many inmates would never have experienced. Unfortunately, a belief that they were unhygienic and spread fever caused them to be changed prior to Christiana's arrival.

They were replaced with dry-earth closets, which were deemed 'healthier', but made them more suited to being positioned outside.

In many respects, considering her crime, Christiana had landed on her feet. She was spared the noose and kept in one of the newest and best-run asylums in Britain at the time. Broadmoor operated on the new system of non-restraint and rewards of indulgences to encourage good behaviour in inmates. As such, prisoners were offered all manner of entertainments and pastimes to not only keep them occupied, but to induce them to remain amenable. Only a small handful proved impossible to manage by this system and had to be confined to their cells. This was criticised in 1869 by the County Lunatic Commissioners as it implied a form of restraint.

Christiana did not have to worry about confinement. She was not wilfully violent or dangerous that would have necessitated her being locked up most of the day. Instead, she could spend her time reading, painting or producing needlework. However, she was not happy and it seems that Christiana could not fathom why she was in Broadmoor. Christiana believed she had done nothing wrong. Dr Orange maintained a record on all his patients, but in Christiana's case it was good to establish that his original assessment had been correct. He wrote in August 1872: 'Her brother [William] who was superintendent of the asylum at Robben Island has recently died and upon the news being communicated to her she appeared quite unable to experience any feeling of sorrow although she tried to look grieved.'[112]

It could be argued that as Christiana had little to do with her brother and had not seen him for at least a decade, she no doubt did not feel a great deal of sorrow. Dr Orange also gave an indication of her appearance that was shocking in contrast to the description given by the courts: 'When admitted she was wearing a large amount of false hair and her cheeks were painted. She also has false teeth and she is very vain.' Vanity was deemed another symptom of hysterical mania.

On 21 August 1872, Ann Christiana Edmunds visited her daughter. It was a lengthy trip and far from easy on her strapped finances, but she came to discuss the death of William. She reported afterwards to Dr Orange: '[Christiana] has never once expressed sorrow for the trouble she has caused to her family and that [Ann] would regard her want of feeling as shocking if she were not insane. [Ann] also says that [Christiana] was not truthful as a child.' Christiana's true nature slowly became apparent within Broadmoor. She was deceitful but also highly manipulative. Her sister Mary suffered at her hands the worst. Mary was now married to a Reverend Foreman, but she maintained the closest correspondence with her sister. Mary felt sorry for Christiana and as a younger sister had been in awe of her. Even with Christiana in Broadmoor, Mary was reluctant to go against her wishes and behaved in a manner that could have brought herself into trouble.

November 2nd. Yesterday it was found that in an envelope of a letter addressed to her sister... [Christiana] had very ingeniously fastened a single scrap of paper covered with extremely small writing. In this communication she asked her sister to bring some articles of wearing apparel clandestinely at her next visit and also half a crown which was to be given to one of the attendants. On being acquainted with the fact of this clandestine portion of the letter having been observed she exhibited neither surprise nor shame.

Christiana still maintained her acute vanity and, to a degree, her snobbery. She hated that her patient garments were identical to the other women on her ward and constantly beseeched her sister to do something about it. '1873 Sept 6. The clandestine portion of the correspondence chiefly refers to modes of applying paint to the face and to means of getting articles of dress different from other patients.' Mary was seen to encourage the behaviour by giving in to the demands and obtaining articles for her sister. Over the course of the time Christiana was in Broadmoor, Mary bought her many small articles, the most interesting being a piece of false hair concealed in a cushion. Mary could hardly deny that she was doing these things without realising the consequences since she was actively involved in the deceit. In the end, Dr Orange wrote to Mary and informed her she must stop. Mary agreed, but still sometimes faltered under the pressure Christiana imposed upon her.

Meanwhile, Christiana was practising her clandestine correspondence in other ways:

1874 July 2. Has recently been found to have been endeavouring to set on foot a clandestine correspondence with the chaplain of Sussex County Prison...

1875 April 27. Removed from one room to another and room searched when numerous articles were found secreted. Also a letter addressed to an attendant. Her love of deception is quite a mania.

July 30. She deceives for the pure love of deception and with no sufficient motive.

Christiana also took pleasure in manipulating and upsetting her fellow inmates, especially those who were most vulnerable. This shows a truly nasty side of her character:

1876 July 8th. While in ward 3 her delight and amusement seemed to be in practising the art of ingeniously tormenting several of the more irritable patients so that she could always complain of their language to her whilst it was difficult to bring any overt act home to herself.

Aside from her compulsive need for deception, there is little in Christiana's notes to indicate a truly deranged individual. She was spiteful and nasty, and wanted to distance herself from the other patients by looking better than them. However, it would be difficult to argue on this evidence alone that she was insane. Even in 1883, Dr Orange had to remark, 'Goes on without excitement and free from actively insane indications.' It took Christiana five years to settle into life in Broadmoor and to accept that she was not going to leave, after which her notes referred to her as a settled and quiet patient. Christiana had at long last given in. She still placed great stock in her appearance and her vanity became more ridiculous the older she became, but otherwise she was one of the easier inmates to deal with.

In 1897, Christiana contracted influenza. She recovered well, but three years later was struck down again with a prolonged attack that left her unwell for over four months. By 1901, her sight in one eye was failing due to a cataract and she was constantly struggling with indigestion and constipation. The latter may have been due to the rather bland diet patients ate or general old age. The sight loss slowly continued and she gradually became more and more feeble. In 1906, she was unable to walk far without assistance and was transferred to the infirmary. Christiana was deluded about her state of health and continued to indulge her vanity, remarking to another inmate who visited her, '...I think I am improving. I hope I shall be better in a fortnight. If so, I shall astonish them. I shall get up and dance. I was a Venus before and I shall be a Venus again!' Christiana Edmunds died 19 September 1907. She was seventy-eight.

CHAPTER EIGHTEEN

Life after Murder

Christiana's freedom and effectively her middle-class life ended in January 1872 after she was found guilty of murder. But what of the other individuals that made her story? Victims often become forgotten in the annals of crime. Unlike the perpetrator of the crime, they vanish from the official records and submerge into the hubbub of ordinary life. Quite easily, the victims and heroes of Christiana's story could be seen as background characters, yet the impact of her crime was far reaching in their lives and, in many respects, shaped their futures.

For Inspector William Gibbs, the solving of the mysterious Brighton poisoning case was a feather in his policing cap and helped pave the way to his promotion within the local force. By 1881, Gibbs was Superintendent of Police and living at Rose Hill Torr, a progression from humble Belgrave Street. His wife, Emily, proudly called herself the 'Superintendent's Wife'. However, wages were never excessive in the police force and Gibbs found it prudent to take in a boarder: a young clerk. Gibbs retired from the police force at the turn of the nineteenth century. He had moved with Emily to Preston a few years previously and there they remained until his death in the winter of 1904, aged seventy-three. William left his effects, the sizeable sum of £867, 5s, 10d, to his widowed daughter-in-law Sarah Gibbs, expecting her to maintain Emily until her death. In fact, his wife lived for another two years, finally passing in 1906 aged seventy-nine.

What became of the family of Christiana's only murder victim Sidney Barker? Albert and Leticia Barker returned to London after the death of their son, but the following year was haunted by Christiana's trial. That she had sent those insistent letters to Albert was a bitter pill to swallow, but the family remained stoical throughout. Unfortunately, it would do little for Leticia's health. Family life for the Barkers would never be the same and the family had to feel a touch cursed by the chain of events that now overtook them. Leticia would have no more children and concentrated instead on her only daughter Florence. Albert threw himself into his work as a silversmith, expanding the business by designing larger and grander pieces and moving into producing furniture such as cabinets and writing tables with his own unique inlays of silver.

In 1881, a decade after the incidents in Brighton, Charles Miller, Sidney's uncle, died aged only twenty-eight. Initial thoughts might suggest this was a direct consequence of his poisoning by strychnine as the drug could cause lasting long-term damage to the body, particularly the liver and kidneys. However, his death certificate lists cause of death as 'pulmonary consumption' – tuberculosis – and stated he had been suffering from the condition for three years. Seven years later in 1888, Leticia would follow him to the grave aged only forty-four.

Albert now lived alone with his young daughter Florence. His work was still his great distraction in life and his business was at least finding success. He now called himself a manufacturer as well as a silversmith and could afford to employ a cook and maid to take care of his house. Florence's life was on the whole far more lonely. She had no siblings and no mother to keep her company. She drifted through her days paying visits to neighbours and friends and mulling away the time in ladylike pursuits. One of the girls she visited and was friendly with was Lucy Jane, a young woman just two years junior to Florence. It was probably through their acquaintance that Albert met Lucy and was attracted to the young and vivacious girl. Albert was lonely, his work could not entirely distract him from his personal life and he missed having a wife as his companion. Still, it must have been a shock to Florence when her father married Lucy Jane in 1892 – a woman younger than his own daughter!

Once again, fate overtook the Barkers. Florence died in 1898 aged only twenty-nine. She had managed to outlive her uncle by barely a year. Albert was devastated, the last of his biological family were dead and, despite having a young wife, it seemed unlikely he would have further children. But he was not one to let demons haunt him and decided in 1901 to pay a return visit to Brighton, the place where Albert's life had changed forever.

Brighton had faded slightly from the Victorian high-class tourist scene by the early twentieth century: it was now a hotbed for day-trippers and holidaying factory workers. After thirty years, Brighton's image as a luxury resort where the rich and famous spent their winter season had evaporated, leaving behind a typical seaside holiday town that we can still recognise today. The Royal Pavilion had come close to being demolished and now stood as an awkward monument to better times. The elite had sold their Brighton townhouses and property developers found their buildings in danger of standing empty for the long term. In a few more years, the Great War would come and Brighton would suffer considerable damage from German bombardments. The Victorian town would either be destroyed or demolished in place of blocky and bland new-builds.

Albert and Lucy stayed at the Fairfax Hotel, German Place. The temptation was to explore the old haunts that had been the scene of so much heartache thirty years before, but perhaps fortunately, much of that past had gone, including Maynards. Brighton was entering a new era and the Victorian period was being swept aside. In the same way Albert was moving forward. In the same year as his return trip to Brighton, he registered his very own silver-mark [A.B]. Albert's little silversmith business was now Albert Barker Ltd with its headquarters at 5 New Bond Street, London.

Albert's business life was thriving. By 1911, he was living in the luxurious 27 Richmond Mansion, Earls Court, and was the entitled 'Chairman of Albert Barker Ltd'. His company was now at its peak and Albert could retire from the main running, handing it over to his various nephews and live contentedly with Lucy. The last years of Albert's life were his finest. His mansion was expansive and beautiful. The business was bustling and now included his extended family, giving them a security they could never before have imagined. From his humble beginnings as the son of a bookseller, Albert had risen high. The only sadness was that his children were not there to see it. Albert died in 1933 aged eighty-eight. He left a considerable fortune, £30,269, 14s, 6d, to Frank Barker, his company director and Henry Geoffrey Elwes, solicitor. A further £27,211, 7s, 9d was later granted to Percy Barker, listed as a dealer. Lucy was still alive (she would survive until 1949), but as a woman of 'independent means' who Albert had probably already provided for before his death, she was not mentioned in the will.

Albert Barker Ltd did not last long after Albert's death. He was not only its driving force, but its main designer and with his death the business faded away. The many products he produced are highly collectible to this day and the Victoria and Albert Museum has in its collection an engraved silver cigarette case in the form of a stamped addressed envelope, showing how clever and quirky Albert's designs were. In many respects, Albert had created his own legacy, though few who buy his exquisite silverware today would ever suspect its maker was one of the first people to suffer at the hands of the notorious Brighton poisoner.

After the trial of Christiana Edmunds, the Boys family returned to their regular lives. For them it had been nothing more than a nasty incident. The children, Emily and Gertrude, had recovered well and there was no reason not to continue life as normal. Elizabeth was not the healthiest of women. Her condition, though far from life-threatening, required her to employ a nurse. Though records do not tell us the exact nature of her sickness, it was something that made her weak or infirm. For most of her life, Mary, Elizabeth's older sister, took care of her. In 1883, Jacob Boys, who had been the centre of attraction for Christiana due to his unfortunate surname, died aged eighty-seven. He left £20,730, 15s, 3d to his family. A year later, Mary died. Elizabeth continued to live at 59 Grand Parade until the end of her days, employing various nurses to take care of her. Neither of her daughters married and Gertrude Mary died in 1907 aged forty-two. Elizabeth, despite her infirmities, proved remarkably long-lived and lasted to almost see the conclusion of the Great War, dying in early 1918 aged ninety-three. Emily inherited most of her father's wealth, including the portion that had belonged to Gertrude and was able to live quite satisfactorily for the rest of her days. She was fifty-five when her mother died and it seems Elizabeth was the one who tied them to Grand Parade as Emily moved the short distance to Hove shortly after the death. She died there in 1934 aged seventy-one, leaving behind over £20,000.

The Beards' existence after 1871 was far more complicated. Emily Beard had lost faith in her husband after the revelations produced by Christiana Edmunds. She was no longer content to remain at home while her husband vanished on his lengthy trips to London or other places, supposedly to do with his work. After the trial, Emily travelled wherever her husband went and never let him out of her sight. In 1881, Emily was with her husband in Lancashire while he acted as a medical inspector for the local government board. Her eldest son Hugh Spencer (not at home at the time of the crimes of Christiana) was training to become a reverend while her son Arthur was an apprentice at an engine works in Leeds. 64 Grand Parade appears to have been sold. There is a suggestion in the records that the Beards' financial fortunes were not as strong as they once were. After the commotion Christiana caused, it would have been difficult for Charles to maintain his private practice while scandal surrounded him.

In 1891, Emily and Charles returned to Brighton, but residing in a lodging house in German Place (ten years later, Albert Barker would be staying in the same road). Charles was no longer a medical inspector, but while listed as a medical practitioner it does not appear that he was working. It seems the scandal of twenty years before still clung to him. Eventually, he went to London, Emily in tow, and returned to practice as a physician. He took a house in Hammersmith and lived there with Emily and two of his children, Arthur who was now a civil engineer and his unmarried daughter Edith. Emily had grown infirm. She was now seventy-three and had to have a sick nurse employed to take care of her.

Life now takes an interesting twist in the story of Charles Beard. Between 1901 and 1911, Charles deteriorated rapidly. He went from a practicing physician to being declared insane and sent to the Holloway Sanatorium for the middle-class insane. It seems his condition was acute or else his family had less sympathy for him than Emily. While Charles was in an asylum, Emily, who had been declared 'feeble-minded' since 1907, resided with her son Hugh Spencer. Hugh was now a clerk in Holy Orders living at St Matthews Vicarage, London. He had married late in life to a woman (Octavia Eleanor Somerset) who was fifteen years his senior. He employed a sick nurse for his mother and took care of her until the end of her days. Charles remained at Holloway Sanatorium until his death in 1916.

For the Edmunds, nothing would ever be the same. Ann Christiana now only had three surviving children: William who was working at a lunatic asylum in Africa, Christiana who was in Broadmoor and Mary. Mary married the Reverend Edward Benjamin Foreman in 1856 and had four daughters (Agnes, Ethel, Mary and Mabel) before the events of 1871. In 1873, the same year Mary was first in trouble for sending her sister false hair, Ann Christiana gave birth to a boy and named him Sidney. It is tempting to speculate that this was in memorial to the little boy her sister had killed. Ann Christiana took rooms at 39 York Road, Hove, after her eldest daughter's conviction. She had enough income to maintain herself there as a lodger for ten years before moving to 31 York Road where she remained the rest of her days. She lived out of two rooms in the household of John and Mary Pinder. Listed in the census return of 1891, alongside her is Mary Jane Steven, described as a lady's companion and it seems certain she was living with Ann for company. Ann was now, after all, in her nineties.

Ann died in 1893 and left £141 to her daughter Mary. As the only surviving sane child of William Edmunds, Mary was the last keeper of her sister's story. But these days, Christiana was less and less thought about. Mary was busy watching her family thrive and was determined to keep her sister's dark history a secret, especially as her daughter Agnes had married Richard Freeborn. Agnes' husband was tutor secretary to HRH Princess Mary and her mother had no intention of ruining her daughter's prospects by letting it slip that her aunt was an insane murderess. Mary did not have to worry long as the burden of her secret was taken away from her when she died in 1898. She left £2,147 to her daughter Ethel who had made a less prosperous marriage than Agnes to a farmer.

However, if the family hoped Christiana's crimes would be forgotten with her death in 1907, they would be mistaken. Christiana's case appears in numerous books, both factual 'true crime' recollections and in fictional works. Her name remained a byword for a crazed female poisoner. In

1970, a play was written about her story and performed on television for LWT. Ann Christiana was cast as an accomplice to murder by keeping her daughter confined to the house while she maintained a 'fluttering respectability'.[113] The premise of the play was that Ann was working with Dr Beard in an attempt to keep her daughter confined to mask from the world her madness while Christiana (played by Anna Massey) was equally determined to escape. In this version, Christiana was the typical lunatic – rolling eyes, screams and frenzies – a far cry from the real Christiana the bulk of this volume has described. This was the way the Brighton poisoner was remembered, even if the truth was remarkably different.

What would be a modern interpretation of Christiana's crimes? Christiana had a clear motivation for her crime and her methods were both logical and carefully calculated. She knew her goal and took steps to both cover her tracks and lead investigators astray. Similar cases have surfaced in modern times, including the famous Stella Nickel case. Stella murdered her husband with cyanide and then tried to throw suspicion off herself by lacing painkillers with the poison which she then replaced on shop shelves. She claimed one other victim before the tampering was discovered and eventually traced back to her. Stella was found guilty of the tampering and thus the murders in 1988 and was sentenced to serve ninety years.

It seems likely from the example of this case that had Christiana been tried in a modern court she would not have been deemed insane. In fact, there is little evidence to suggest she was any different from most criminals who commit or attempt murder, but are not certifiable insane. If anything, she may have a dubious case for being claimed a psychopath as she showed such disregard for others, but then again many criminals show just such tendencies so it is hardly a case for insanity. Perhaps Christiana was not crazy or deranged, but a woman with ambitions and a natural tendency for deceit. As even today it is challenging for the legal system to judge a person insane or not, we should not offer a distinct answer on a woman who can no longer be interviewed or examined.

At the end of the day, Christiana set out to harm and murder for her own personal benefit and self-gratification. Should we feel sympathy for her as a scorned lover? Or should we regret she escaped the noose? Maybe even both. At least one thing is certain, she put Brighton back on the map for all the wrong reasons.

Bibliography

Babington, Anthony, *The English Bastille: A History of Newgate Gaol and Prison Conditions in Britain 1188-1902* (Macdonald and Company, 1971)

Bailey, Victor (editor), *Policing and Punishment in Nineteenth Century Britain* (Croom Helm Ltd, 1981)

Braddon, Mary Elizabeth, *The Doctor's Wife* (Oxford World Classics, 2008)

Carter, Robert Brudenell, *On the Pathology and Treatment of Hysteria* (John Churchill, 1853)

Chesterton, G. K. *The Victorian Age in Literature* (Oxford University Press, 1966)

Crow, Duncan, *The Victorian Woman* (George Allen & Unwin Ltd, 1971)

Dale, Antony, *The History and Architecture of Brighton* (S. R. Publishers, 1950)

Diamond, Michael, *Victorian Sensation or the Spectacular, the Shocking and the Scandalous in Nineteenth-Century Britain* (Anthem Press, 2003)

Drysdale, George, *The Elements of Social Science or Physical, Sexual and Natural Religion* (E. Truelove, 1861)

Eigen, J. P., *Witnessing Insanity: Madness and Mad-Doctors in the English Court* (Yale University Press, 1995)

Foucoult, Michel, *Madness and Civilisation: A History of Insanity in the Age of Reason* (Routledge, 1999)

Fruton, Joseph Stewart, *Methods and Styles in the Development of Chemistry* (American Philosophical Society, 1912)

Gamber, Wendy, *The Female Economy: The Millinery and Dressmaking Trades, 1860-1930* (University of Illinois Press, 1997)

Guernsey, Henry Newell, *The Application of the Principles of Homeopathy to Obstetrics* (F. E. Boericke, 1867)

Hawkins, Sir Henry, *The Reminiscences of Sir Henry Hawkins (Baron Brampton)*, Edited by Richard Harris K. C. (Edward Arnold, 1904)

Hayhurst, Alan, *More Lancashire Murders* (The History Press, 2011)

Hibbert, Christopher, *The Illustrated London News: Social History of Victorian Britain* (Angus and Robertson, 1975)

Hughes, Winifred, *The Maniac in the Cellar: Sensation Novels of the 1860s* (Princeton University Press, 1980)

Kay, Alan, *Margate: Town and City Series* (Frith, 2006)

Kidd, William, *The Picturesque Pocket Companion to Margate, Ramsgate and Broadstairs & The Parts Adjacent* (London, 1831)

Knelman, Judith, *Twisting in the Wind* (Toronto, 1998)

Lock, Joan, *Scotland Yard Casebook: The Making of the CID 1865-1935* (Robert Hale, 1993)

Maines, Rachel, *The Technology of Orgasm* (Johns Hopkins University Press, 1999)

McLevy, James, *The Casebook of a Victorian Detective* (reprint) (Canongate Publishing, 1975)

Musgrave, Clifford, *Life in Brighton* (Faber and Faber, 1970)

O'Neill, Gilda, *The Good Old Days: Crime, Murder and Mayhem in Victorian London* (Viking, 2006)

Robinson, Ronald and Gallagher, John, with Denny, Alice, *Africa and the Victorians: The Official Mind of Imperialism* (Macmillan, 1961)

Pakes, Francis and Pakes, Suzanne, *Criminal Psychology* (Willan Publishing, 2009)

Porter, Roy and Wright, David, *The Confinement of the Insane: International Perspectives 1800-1965* (Cambridge University Press, 2003)

Priest, R. G. and Steinert, J., *Insanity: A Study of Major Psychiatric Disorders* (MacDonald and Evans Ltd, 1977)

Scull, Andrew T. *Museums of Madness: The Social Organisation of Insanity in 19th Century England* (Allen Lane, 1979)

Warren, Ira, *The Household Physician; For the use of Families, Planters, Seamen and Travellers, being a Brief Description in Plain Language of all the Disease of Men, Women and Children, with the Newest and Most Approved Methods of Curing Them* (Higgins, Bradley, and Dayton, Boston, 1859)

Whorton, James C., *The Arsenic Century: How Victorian Britain was poisoned at Home, Work and Play* (Oxford University Press, 2010)

Other sources

http://www.oldpolicecellsmuseum.org.uk/page_id__418_path__
op77p204p183p.aspx

http://www.boysandmaughan.co.uk/cms/section/aboutus.html

Barbour, Llewellyn P., *Pelvic Massage* (Journal of the American Medical Association, 1899)

Berrow's Worcester Journal

Blackburn Standard, 1865, *The Lunatic Murderers of Great Britain*

Bloom, Homer C., *A Clinical Study in Pelvic Massage* (Journal of the American Medical Association, 1898)

Brighton and Hove Gazette, 1796

Circular Walks, The Blean, Explore Kent

Derby Mercury, The Anomalies of Justice 1872

The Lancaster Gazette and General Advertiser for Lancashire, Westmorland, Yorkshire &c 1865

Kentish Gazette

Lee, Anthony, *The Sad Tale of the Margate Architect and the Brighton Poisoner*

Leeds Mercury, The Watson and Edmunds Cases 1872

Liverpool Mercury

London and Provincial Medical Directory and General Medical Register (John Churchill, 1860)

Manchester Times, Extraordinary Attempts at Poisoning in Brighton 1871

Mnookin, Jennifer L. *Scripting Expertise: The History of Handwriting Identification Evidence and the Judicial Construction of Reliability* (University of Virginia School of Law, Public Law and Legal Theory Research papers)

Morning Chronicle

Morning Post, The

Nordhoff, Sofie A., *Kinetic Therapies in Gynaecology or Thure Brandt's System* (Journal of the American Medical Association, 1895)

North Wales Chronicle

Ron, Maria, *Explaining the Unexplained: Understanding Hysteria* (Brain: A Journal of Neurology, 2001)

Sheffield and Rotherham Independent, The Alleged Wholesale Poisoning at Brighton 1871

Times Digital Archives, The

Westerschulte, F. H., *Pelvic Massage* (Journal of the American Medical Association, 1899)

Endnotes

Chapter One – The Accidental Murder

1. *The Times*, 8 September 1871, 'The Alleged Poisoning at Brighton'.
2. Ibid.
3. Ibid.
4. Ibid.
5. Letheby was a well-regarded medical expert. Usually written as 'chymist' in the papers.
6. The nineteenth century is littered with such examples as vendors regularly 'doctored' their products to increase profits.
7. Poor water quality was a leading cause of cholera in London. Pumps were inspected to see if they contained the harmful bacteria, a job that fell to Letheby and was underwritten by the water companies. In 1867, he was almost the only expert to state that poor water was not to blame for the cholera outbreak in East London.
8. *Poison: A Social History*, Joel Levy.
9. Letters to the Editor, *The Times*, 12 June 1856.
10. *The Times*, 8 September 1871, 'The Alleged Poisoning at Brighton'.
11. *The Times*, 17 January 1872, 'Central Criminal Court, The Brighton Poisonings Jan 16'.

Chapter Two – The Poisoned Parcel

12. In 1871, a census error occurs erroneously listing Mary Ann as a 'domestic nurse'. In fact, this title belonged to Amelia Mills on the next line down as the court records prove when she was called as

a witness and described as a nurse to Mrs Boys. Amelia has been mistakenly listed as a cook, the actual role of Matilda Hope on the next line down. These errors continue through the list of servants for the Boys family.

13. *The Times*, 1 September 1871, 'The Alleged Poisoning at Brighton'.

Chapter Three – Poor Mr Maynard

14. *The Times*, 9 September 1871, 'The Alleged Poisoning at Brighton'.
15. Ibid.
16. *The Times*, 9 September 1871, 'The Alleged Poisoning at Brighton'.
17. Cadbury's had only recently introduced their creams with fruit-flavoured centres after a visit to a Dutch chocolate factory around 1866. At that period, the courts carefully defined English creams, which would almost exclusively be Cadbury's, from French creams. In the 1870s, Cadbury's new chocolates, the first truly palatable English 'eating' chocolate, would come to dominate the market and break the monopoly French creams had previously had. Even without the strychnine incident in 1871, Mr Ware's business was in danger of being undermined by the arrival of a superior quality English product.
18. *The Times*, 9 September 1871, 'The Alleged Poisoning at Brighton'.
19. Ibid.
20. Summarised from *The Manchester Times*, 'Extraordinary Attempts to Poison at Brighton'.
21. Also reported as 'John Walker'.
22. *The Manchester Times*, 'Extraordinary Attempts to Poison at Brighton'.

Chapter Four – Inspector Gibbs becomes Curious

23. Musgrave, Clifford, *Life in Brighton* (Faber and Faber, 1970).
24. In 1911, the population had managed to creep up to 131,237.
25. Musgrave, Clifford, *Life in Brighton* (Faber and Faber, 1970).
26. Austen, Jane, *Pride and Prejudice* (Whitehall, 1813).
27. *Brighton and Hove Gazette*, 17 October 1796.
28. Dialogue adapted from witness testimony, *The Times*, 8 September 1871, 'Alleged Poisoning at Brighton'.
29. Newspaper accounts disagree as whether the chemist's name was Glaisyer or Glaisher, as the former appears in *The Times* and the

latter in provincial papers reporting the story as second-hand. It has been assumed Glaisyer is the correct spelling.

30. Gamber, Wendy, *The Female Economy: The Millinery and Dressmaking Trades, 1860-1930* (University of Illinois Press, 1997).
31. Musgrave, Clifford, *Life in Brighton* (Faber and Faber, 1970).

Chapter Five – Could it be a Coincidence?

32. *Morning Chronicle*, 10 February 1820, 'Adulteration of Food and Drink'.
33. *Morning Chronicle*, 30 March 1839, 'Adulteration of Food'.
34. *Liverpool Mercury*, 12 July 1844. 'Frightful Adulteration of Human Food – Death in the Loaf'.
35. *Berrow's Worcester Journal*, 14 December 1848, 'Accidental Poisoning'.
36. *The Morning Post*, 9 January 1849, 'Accidental Case of Poisoning'.
37. *North Wales Chronicle*, 15 February 1848, 'The recent case of accidental poisoning at Anglesey'.

Chapter Six – The Chemist's Art

38. This is not the noted W. H. Smith who founded a newsagent and bookselling chain
39. *Hampshire Advertiser and Salisbury Guardian*, 22 March 1856, 'The Poisoning by Strychnia at Leeds'.
40. *The Times*, 13 June 1856, 'The Detection of Strychnine'.

Chapter Seven – Poison is a Woman's Weapon

41. Knelman, Judith, *Twisting in the Wind* (Toronto, 1998).
42. McLevy, James, *The Casebook of a Victorian Detective* (reprint) (Canongate Publishing, 1975)

Chapter Eight – The Secret Love Affair

43. The last will and testament of William Izard of Brighton, coal merchant, 1 September 1817.

Chapter Nine – The Missing Motive

44. Old Police Cells Museum, Brighton. History by Jo Blake: http://www.oldpolicecellsmuseum.org.uk/page_id__418_path__op77p204p183p.aspx

45. The alms houses were named in memory of Mrs Marriot's friends Dorothea and Philadelphia Percy and were later added to by Reverend Wagner. They are now referred to as the Percy and Wagner Alms Houses. They became listed buildings in 1971.

46. Lee, Anthony, *The Sad Tale of the Margate Architect and the Brighton Poisoner.*

47. Ibid.

48. Boys and Maugham History: http://www.boysandmaughan.co.uk.

Chapter Ten – The Arrest

49. *Daily News*, 16 January 1872.

50. Ibid.

51. Kidd, William, *The Picturesque Pocket Companion to Margate, Ramsgate and Broadstairs & The Parts Adjacent* (London, 1831).

52. *Kentish Gazette*, 24 May 1825.

53. Kidd, William, *The Picturesque Pocket Companion to Margate, Ramsgate and Broadstairs & The Parts Adjacent* (London, 1831).

54. Notebook held at East Kent Archive Office R/U19/131.

55. Kidd, William, *The Picturesque Pocket Companion to Margate, Ramsgate and Broadstairs & The Parts Adjacent* (London, 1831).

56. *Kentish Chronicle*, 18 August 1829.

57. Circular Walks, The Blean, Explore Kent.

58. *The Times*, 31 August 1839.

59. Crow, Duncan, *The Victorian Woman* (George Allen & Unwin Ltd, 1971).

60. Ibid.

Chapter Eleven – Prosecuting Poison

61. *The Times*, 1 September 1871, 'The Alleged Poisoning at Brighton'.

62. William Hepworth Dixon (1821-1879) came to London in 1846 and began writing articles on social and prison reform for the *Daily News*. He was the author of several books including *John Howard and the Prison World of Europe* (1850).

63. Babington, Anthony, *The English Bastille: A History of Newgate Gaol and Prison Conditions in Britain 1188-1902* (Macdonald and Company, 1971).

64. Ibid.

65. *The Times*, 1 January 1872. 'The Brighton Poisoning Case'.

66. *The Times*, 16 January 1872.

67. *The Solicitor's Journal and Reporter*, 3 September 1859.

68. Mr Schweitzer was an analytical chemist who worked at the German Spa in Queen's Park where various mineral waters were manufactured for visitors to drink. He appeared frequently in medical and scientific journals with his experiments on artificial digestion and the local sea water. *The Encyclopaedia of Brighton* (Tim Carder, 1990) states that by the 1850s, the spa's popularity had waned so greatly that it was closed and the building used to manufacture bottled waters for sale across the country. Mr Schweitzer would have worked analysing and approving the processes for each batch, but clearly had enough spare time on his hands to conduct outside experiments.

69. *The Times*, 16 January 1872.

70. Ibid.

Chapter Twelve – Experts on Trial

71. *The Times*, 1 September 1871, 'The Alleged Poisoning at Brighton'.

72. Netherclift's name was regularly misspelled appearing as Nethercliffe in the newspapers of 1871-72. His preferred spelling was Netherclift and this is the variation used in this text.

73. Hawkins, Sir Henry, *The Reminiscences of Sir Henry Hawkins (Baron Brampton)*, Edited by Richard Harris K. C. (Edward Arnold, 1904).

74. 1881 census.

75. There was a third Nethercliffe, but his relationship to Frederick and Joseph is not obvious, though some family connection is likely. He was employed as a lithographist and facimilist at the British Museum and was regularly engaged in work detecting forgeries for the Bank of England. His name appears in a forged will case and as an expert witness on faked signatures in the 1850s. This is not Joseph Netherclift who was residing at a different address to that given for Joseph Nethercliffe and never indicated he worked for the British Museum. This third Joseph (who also spelt his name Netherclift) died in Fulham in 1896 aged eighty. He was two years

older than Frederick (who died 1892 aged seventy-four) and it is highly probably he was his brother.

76. The Royal Medical Benevolent College was founded in 1853 and funded itself by offering a liberal education to 100 sons of 'duly qualified medical men'. To educate a boy at the college cost twenty-five pounds a year. It was rapidly found that this was not enough to provide accommodation for the 100 pensioners and widows the college hoped to help, so the limitations on who could send their sons to the school were swiftly removed. The Royal Medical Benevolent College is now Epsom College in Surrey.

77. *On the Detection of Strychnine* (1856), *Process for obtaining Strychnine from organs and tissues of the body* (1856), *Tests for Strychnine* (1856), *On Poisoning by Strychnia* (1857) and *The Case of Thomas Smethurst* (1859).

78. *The Times*, 8 September 1871.

79. *The Times*, 9 September 1871.

Chapter Thirteen – A Plea for Insanity

80. Braddon, Elizabeth Mary, *Lady Audley's Secret* (1862).

81. *Oxford Dictionary of National Biography*.

82. 'The origin of insanity as a special verdict: the trail for treason of James Hadfield (1800)', R. Moran. *Law and Society Review*, 1985.

83. Eigen, J. P., *Witnessing Insanity: Madness and Mad-Doctors in the English Court* (Yale University Press, 1995).

84. Modern theories suggest Daniel MacNaghten was a political activist who had been paid to assassinate the Prime Minister. During the two years prior to the murder, MacNaghten had travelled widely in Britain and France and had accumulated the hefty sum of £750 that was found on him at the time of the murder. As a wood-turner, such a sum of money would have been hard to save, unless he had other sources of income. And that he was carrying it at the time of the murder suggests he was planning an immediate escape with his savings. MacNaghten was clearly involved in radical politics and his reader's tickets from the Mechanics Institution in Glasgow (a lending library) shows that his reading matter would have familiarised him with the symptoms of insanity. Strong evidence now indicates MacNaghten was feigning madness.

85. In America, twenty-four states were still using the MacNaghten rules at the end of the twentieth century.

86. Bailey, Victor (editor), *Policing and Punishment in Nineteenth Century Britain* (Croom Helm Ltd, 1981).
87. Howard Association.
88. Bailey, Victor (editor), *Policing and Punishment in Nineteenth Century Britain* (Croom Helm Ltd, 1981).

Chapter Fourteen – Family of Lunatics

89. *Oxford Dictionary of National Biography*.
90. *The Times*, 17 January 1872.
91. Ibid.
92. Ballantine had asked the question whether Edmunds was suffering from delirium tremens (severe alcohol withdrawal), a term still used today. He was trying to make a case against hereditary insanity by proving William's symptoms were induced by heavy drinking.
93. *Canterbury Journal*, 3 September 1842.
94. There are a long list of alcohol withdrawal symptoms and some contradict each other. Patients may suffer problems staying awake rather than insomnia, for instance.
95. Ron, Maria, *Explaining the Unexplained: Understanding Hysteria* (Brain: A Journal of Neurology, 2001).

Chapter Fifteen – A Pregnant Verdict

96. *The Times*, 18 January 1872.
97. Broadmoor Hospital case notes for Christiana Edmunds, Berkshire Record Office.
98. Bailey, Victor (editor), *Policing and Punishment in Nineteenth Century Britain* (Croom Helm Ltd, 1981).
99. Report of Governor Hansbrow, 2 March 1846.
100. Saunders, Janet, *Magistrates and Madmen: Segregating the Criminally Insane in Late Nineteenth Century Warwickshire* (1981).

Chapter Sixteen – The Victorian Sex Sensation

101. From *The Lancet*, reprinted in the *Leeds Mercury* under 'The Watson and Edmunds Cases'.
102. *Derby Mercury*, 'The Anomalies of Justice – The Cases of Mr Watson and Miss Edmunds'.

103. Hughes, Winifred, *The Maniac in the Cellar: Sensations Novels of the 1860s* (Princetown University Press, 1980).

104. Braddon, Mary Elizabeth, *The Doctor's Wife* (Oxford World Classics, 2008).

105. A collection of around sixty ancient Greek medical treatises associated with the famous physician Hippocrates and his teachings, hence its name. However, the works are of different ages and different authors. The work was first translated in English in 1597, though the first complete version was not produced in English until 1849.

106. Warren, Ira, *The Household Physician; For the use of Families, Planters, Seamen and Travellers, being a Brief Description in Plain Language of all the Disease of Men, Women and Children, with the Newest and Most Approved Methods of Curing Them* (Higgins, Bradley, and Dayton, Boston, 1859).

107. Guernsey, Henry Newell, *The Application of the Principles and Practices of Homeopathy to Obstetrics, and the Disorders Peculiar to Women and Young Children, Henry Newell Guernsey* (1867).

108. Journal of the American Medical Association, Kinetic Therapies in Gynaecology, 1895.

Chapter Seventeen – Insane, but still Alive

109. *Blackburn Standard*, 18 January 1865.

110. *The Lancaster Gazette and General Advertiser for Lancashire, Westmorland, Yorkshire &c* 21 January 1865.

111. Ibid.

112. Broadmoor Hospital Case Notes for Christiana Edmunds, Berkshire Record Office.

113. *The Times*, 23 February 1970, 'A Horrid Case'.

Index